All her preconceived notions about this man had been suddenly upended.

She had seen him as self-assured, hard-edged, arrogantly masculine. Now her own sense of fairness required that she regard him on different terms. She could see in his eyes that the threat of her rejection bothered him.

"What did you have in mind?" Angel asked.

Matt raked long fingers through his unruly hair and smiled ruefully. "I'm committed to baseball practice with Patrick's team. That could be amusing, if you'd like to watch."

Patrick would be with them. Angel wondered if that was a maneuver to win her trust. If so, it was an effective one. Matt would hardly be likely to come on to her with his big-eyed son to witness the seduction.

A hundred reasons why she should say no came to Angel's mind. But in the end, all the rational arguments for not going couldn't outweigh the single reason why she would. She wanted to.

Dear Reader,

We've got a terrific lineup of books to start off the
New Year. I hope you'll enjoy each and every one.
Start things off with our newest Intimate Moments Extra,
Kathryn Jensen's *Time and Again*. This book is time travel
with a twist—but you'll have to read it to see what I mean.
One thing I can promise you: you won't regret the time
you spend turning these pages.

Next up, Marie Ferrarella's cross-line miniseries,
The Baby of the Month Club, comes to Intimate Moments
with *Happy New Year—Baby!* Of course, this time we're
talking *babies* of the month, because Nicole Logan is
having twins—and it's up to Dennis Lincoln to prove
that a family of four is better than a family of three.
Sharon Sala's *When You Call My Name* brings back
Wyatt Hatfield from her last book, *The Miracle Man*. This
time, Wyatt's looking for a miracle of his own, both to
save his life and heal his heart. Beverly Barton continues
her miniseries, The Protectors, with *Guarding Jeannie,*
Sam Dundee's story. Alexandra Sellers gives the ever-
popular secret-baby plot line a whirl in *Roughneck,*
and I know you'll want to come along for the ride.
Finally, welcome new author Kate Hathaway, whose
His Wedding Ring will earn a spot on your keeper shelf.

Until next month—happy reading!

Yours,

Leslie J. Wainger
Senior Editor and Editorial Coordinator

Please address questions and book requests to:
Silhouette Reader Service
U.S.: 3010 Walden Ave., P.O. Box 1325, Buffalo, NY 14269
Canadian: P.O. Box 609, Fort Erie, Ont. L2A 5X3

HIS WEDDING RING

KATE HATHAWAY

Published by Silhouette Books

America's Publisher of Contemporary Romance

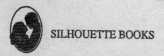

SILHOUETTE BOOKS

ISBN 0-373-07690-8

HIS WEDDING RING

Printed in U.S.A.

KATE HATHAWAY

was born in Chicago and raised in California. She always wanted to write and, harboring that desire, obtained a degree in English literature. Reality intruded—the need to make a living!—and she spent a number of years as a registered nurse, working and teaching in the operating room. During that time she developed a deep appreciation for the courage, humor and selflessness people show at times of great crisis. The lessons gleaned from those years are the ones she most hopes to express in her writing.

Kate makes her home in Baltimore, Maryland, with her husband, John, a mathematician—yes, opposites do attract. She provides the flights of fancy in his life, while he keeps her solidly based. According to the oldest of their three children, "together they make up one pretty complete person." That's the best definition of a successful marriage Kate's ever heard.

For Jackie

Chapter 1

Angelina Martino was accustomed to second glances. She had learned to ignore the assessing male gazes that drifted leisurely over her face and form. So it was with almost casual indifference that she became aware of the steady green gaze leveled in her direction from across the busy emergency room.

Not that she could totally ignore the commotion arising from that corner of the room. She stole another quick glance past the curtain she had partially drawn around her E.R. cubicle. What appeared to be a gunshot victim had been rapidly wheeled in by paramedics and a team had immediately assembled around the man. Tony Levering, from Anesthesia, had already intubated and Gary Chapman, E.R. Physician in charge, looked to be inserting a central line. Annie Mays, one of the staff nurses, rattled by with the red metal crash cart, positioning it alongside the stretcher.

Angelina assessed the situation with an experienced eye. The activity only looked chaotic. In reality, every move was carefully choreographed. The E.R. personnel were well-prepared for just such circumstances. Blocking out both the distracting noise and the disturbing scrutiny she sensed upon her, she focused her attention on the small bundle of false bravado and incipient panic huddled on the stretcher in front of her.

Brian Joseph Crutcher, eight years old, she read from the history and physical on his chart. He had been doing wheelies off the curb on his new birthday bike when the rear wheel had wedged in a grating over a storm drain, sending him headfirst over the handlebars. His parents had wisely included a helmet with his bike, so Brian's injuries were limited to an arm fractured in two places and various minor contusions and abrasions. Brian, however, would not be doing wheelies for some time.

One facet of Angelina's position as nurse liaison for the critical care units at Sherman General Hospital in suburban Pittsburgh was to ease the transition for patients who would be going directly from the emergency room into surgery. At the moment that meant trying to ignore the rest of the bustle around her and helping this thoroughly scared little boy understand what to expect. Angelina could hear snatches of the orthopedic surgeon's conversation with Brian's equally frightened parents a few feet away as she weighed what to say.

"Hi, Brian," she began gently. "My name is Angelina, but my friends call me Angel. That arm hurts, doesn't it?"

Huge brown eyes filled with tears he was determined not to shed as he nodded his agreement. Seeing them, Angel felt the familiar tug of loss, still sharp after all these years. "It'll hurt a lot less after Dr. Hibbs puts a cast on it," she said, "but you'll have to go to sleep for that. It would hurt too much to do it while you're awake."

"Won't..." The word came out as a croak. Brian swallowed and tried again. "Won't it wake me up if it hurts a lot?"

Angel ran a hand through the thick, brown curls that spilled over his forehead, feeling the clammy perspiration that told of his discomfort and fear. "Dr. James, the anesthesiologist, will be giving you some medicine to make you sleep, Brian. You won't wake up until everything is all over, I promise."

"Will the medicine he gives me taste bad?" Brian's expression said exactly what he thought about having something else to worry about.

Giving a wry smile, Angel answered him. "Dr. James is a woman, Brian. She has two boys just about your age, so she understands all about the things that might bother you. And you won't be drinking the medicine she gives you. She'll have to put a needle in your good arm to give it to you. It'll hurt just a little bit for a second, kind of like a mosquito bite, and then nothing will hurt you at all. When you wake up, you'll be in the recovery room, and your mom and dad will be with you." This information seemed to mollify the little boy somewhat.

"When will I be able to go home?" Brian asked. A crucial question. At an age when a boy could feel pangs of homesickness during an overnight at a friend's house, though he'd eat snails before admitting it, a night spent in the alien environment of a hospital was beyond contemplation.

Reaching for Brian's uninjured hand, Angel softly rubbed her thumb over his knuckles. That he allowed this indignity was a measure of his apprehension. "You may be here a couple of days. But it won't be as bad as you think," she reassured him. "You'll be on a floor with other kids your age. You can have snacks whenever you're hungry. There're loads of games to play, and they even show a movie in the lounge every afternoon. Best of all, your mom or dad can stay with you all night."

Apparently that won him over. Something like relief was chasing the anxiety from his eyes.

Angel tucked the chart under the mattress at the head of the stretcher, rested her forearms on the raised side rail, and gazed at Brian steadily. "Any more questions?" she asked. "Are you ready for surgery now?"

"I guess I'm ready," he replied hesitantly. "I can't think of anything else." Angel reached over again to place an encouraging hand softly against his cheek, and he blurted, "I like your name. You look like an angel." She had heard similar words countless times before from older members of his sex, but none of them had been rewarded with the dazzling smile she gave him.

Across the room, Detective Lieutenant Matthew Flanagan wondered what the little guy had said to be blessed with that smile. Responding to a patrolman's report of a possible drug-related shooting, Matt found himself stymied at present in obtaining any information while the doctors and nurses worked over the victim.

Matt hated hospitals. He associated them with searing loss and psychological wounds still not nearly healed. The very proficiency of the professionals working around him conjured up feelings of helplessness, fear and inadequacy, feelings that were anathema to a man whose very life depended on his wits, courage and competence. Giving the medical personnel a wide berth, Matt's gaze scanned the rest of the busy E.R. It was then that his attention had been drawn to the attractive woman talking softly with the small form on the stretcher.

As a police officer, Matt's keenly developed observational skills were essential to the performance of his job, but he was seldom able to make use of them with such relish. Even the shapelessness of the standard hospital-issue scrub suit could not disguise the enticing curves of the young nurse's willowy form. The simple V neckline, which could only be described as modest, directed attention to the lush curve of her breasts. The loose shirt was neatly tucked into equally loose-fitting scrub pants, which were tied in front by a drawstring. The strong gentian blue of the uniform, death to a sallow or ruddy complexion, complemented her fair skin and accentuated the lambent blue of her eyes. Those eyes, large and lustrous, were the most striking feature in the flawless oval of her face.

Matt was willing to bet his detective's shield that those same eyes had taken note of his perusal, but they gave no indication of it. Her face, he granted, was every bit as lovely as her figure, but it was disquieting in its perfection. He could find no fault with the small, straight nose, the full pink lips, high cheekbones, and wide, smooth brow, but it might have been a beautiful mask. It gave no hint of the personality behind it. If this angel had strong emotions of any kind, her tranquil expression kept its secrets. Given his line of work, it was the kind of face Matt had learned to distrust. At this disquieting thought, he saw her smile.

Until the smile that transformed her face, Matt had paid scant attention to the object of her care. Taking a closer look, he realized with a start that he knew the boy. Brian Crutcher and his own son, Patrick, were in different third-grade classrooms at St. Michael's grade school, but they played on the same baseball team. Brian's father was the team coach, and Matt had agreed to help out when he could. Practice had started only the week before. Matt mumbled instructions to the patrolman nearby and strode toward the boy on the stretcher.

From the corner of her eye Angel saw the tall stranger make his move. Immediately her defenses went up, enclosing her in a protective cocoon of haughty indifference. That she was attractive to men was simply a fact of her life. Certainly, she didn't invite that interest. Her looks were both a blessing and a curse, and she did little to enhance them. If the truth be told, her job was her life. It provided her with both a sense of self-worth and the only real excitement she found in an otherwise quiet and rather dull existence. Her rapid rise in the nursing administration ranks gave testimony to her intelligence and skill as well as her selfless dedication. She was amply rewarded financially, but, more important to her, she gained the approbation and respect of her colleagues. Her past relationships with men, on the other hand, had left her with only pain, self-loathing, and regret, but none of these feelings were reflected in the icy disdain with which she awaited the approaching man.

"Hi, I'm Matt Flanagan," he began.

If his easy smile was meant to disarm her, she was having none of it. "I'm very busy, Mr. Flanagan," she said coolly. "If you need information, I'm sure someone at the desk can help you." She turned her attention back to Brian.

"Actually, I—" Again he was interrupted, this time by the man behind her, Brian's father.

"Matt! Good to see you," he said, his hand stretching past Angel to grasp that of the other man in a firm shake. "What brings you here?"

"Another dustup on the streets of our fair city, I'm afraid," Matt answered, an edginess creeping into his voice. With an effort, he banished it. "How about you, Harry? What's happened to ol' Brian here?"

"He took a tumble off his new bike," Harry said, ruffling his son's hair. "He's going into surgery now to get a cast put on that arm. I'm afraid we're going to be out our shortstop for the season."

Matt felt a tug of sympathy as he took in the boy's downcast expression. "I'll be needing a lot of help coaching third base, Brian. What d'ya say?"

"Sure, Mr. Flanagan. I know the signals real good." He gave a weak smile that said he'd try to make the best of a bad situation.

"Good for you, Brian. That's the spirit." Matt turned his eyes to the quiet, dark-haired woman standing next to Harry Crutcher. "I don't believe I've met your mom."

"Sorry, Matt. This is my wife, Sylvia." Harry made the introductions as Angel stood quietly by, uncomfortably aware that she had been, at the very least, uncivil to Matthew Flanagan in assuming his approach implied an interest in her. She felt like a chastened schoolgirl who had spoken out of turn. But, as his gaze drifted back to her, the mischievous gleam in his eyes confirmed her suspicion that she had not been entirely wrong.

"I'm sorry to have bothered you Ms...?" His eyes narrowed as he read the plastic name badge pinned to her shirt.

"Martino," she completed for him, thinking he didn't sound sorry at all. She was gratified to see his puzzled eyes fly back to hers.

His bemused gaze traveled over her face, taking in the fair skin and delicate features. Though her eyes were fringed with thick, dark lashes, the few silky strands that escaped the pale bouffant cap she wore to contain her hair in the operating room were the color of moonbeams.

"Not all Italians are tiny and dark, Mr. Flanagan," she said with a smug grin, pleased to have caught him off balance.

Angel made the most of his momentary discomfort to make her own appraisal and sensed that this was a man who was not often off balance. His looks assured him an advantage where women were concerned, at any rate. Even with her height, she reached only a little past his shoulder. The conservative cut of his dark gray suit would have served to make a less striking man indistinguishable from the great gray hordes of bankers and accountants. On him, it only emphasized the blatant masculinity of his lean, well-muscled body. He wore his suit coat unbuttoned, revealing a flat abdomen, no doubt rock-hard, and a narrow waist. Angel noted the taut pull of the jacket covering the spread of his broad shoulders. The crisp, white collar of his shirt, buttoned above a precisely knotted tie, circled the strong neck of a natural athlete. Slowly, Angel's eyes rose to his face.

She had to admit, albeit grudgingly, that he was nice to look at. He had the face of an altar boy, seemingly open and forthright, but with a hint of devilment, not above filching nickels for candy from the collection basket in payment for services rendered. He was tanned, especially for this time of year, as if work or pleasure had him often out-of-doors. Thick, dark hair, which showed a tendency to curl, tumbled over his forehead. His face seemed to be composed entirely of angles and planes; broad, high cheekbones and a straight, high-bridged nose. Except for his mouth. That feature was wide and sensuous, with deep creases at the outside corners, suggesting that it curved easily and often into a smile. Looking at his mouth, Angel felt an unfamiliar but not unpleasant warmth spread deep inside. He was smiling now, his amusement clearly reflected in his unguarded green eyes. She sensed his good humor was at her expense; having regained his own composure, he relished the fact that hers was rapidly slipping away.

"Excuse me, Lieutenant."

Matt's eyes broke their hold on Angel's and turned to the uniformed patrolman who had quietly approached.

"The doctor would like a word with you."

Making his excuses to the Crutchers and with an abrupt nod to Angel, Matt followed the patrolman to the curtained alcove where the stretcher waited. Angel noted the green-flagged chart, which indicated another patient bound directly for the operating room, and realized with some annoyance that she had not felt the last of Matt Flanagan's disturbing presence. She continued to watch the lieutenant as, conversing with the E.R. physician, he casually held his jacket open, resting his hands on his hips. Her eyes registered two images with equal parts of surprise and dismay: the handgun held in a black leather holster clipped to his belt, and the wide, gold band on his third finger, left hand.

With a mental shake, Angel turned her attention, once again, to her duties. Ray Hibbs, the orthopedic surgeon, was making a final pre-op note on Brian's chart.

"Everything all set, Angel?" he asked.

"We're all ready in O.R. 7," she answered. "The permits have been signed for surgery and anesthesia, the lab work is complete, and X ray is available when we need them."

"I'll see you inside, then." He headed for the automatic sliding doors that led to the operating room suite.

"I'll be taking Brian into the O.R. now," Angel explained gently to his parents. "Dr. Hibbs will be out to talk to you as soon as he finishes, and you'll be able to see Brian in Recovery. There's a waiting room around the corner to the right," she directed them, "and coffee and juice are available if you would like some."

She saw the tears gathering in Mrs. Crutcher's eyes and the clenched jaw of her husband's face as he struggled to retain control of his emotions. This was always the most difficult point for parents as they gave over the well-being of their child to the care of strangers. Every time it brought forth the never forgotten pain of Angel's own loss, and her sympathy welled up anew. She watched as they kissed their son and noted that he didn't even object as he blinked back his own tears. With a final comforting smile, Angel unlocked the brake of the stretcher and began to wheel it away. This time she was totally unaware of the green eyes that watched with interest as her trim figure disappeared behind the sliding doors.

"Hope you aren't getting any ideas about our ice princess," Dr. Gary Chapman warned as he noted the direction of the police lieutenant's gaze. "Angel's a damn good nurse, but her work is her life. She doesn't have time for men.

Don't take it personally if she blows you off. She may look like every red-blooded male's fantasy, but it'd take a crowbar to get her legs apart."

Accustomed as he was to the casual vulgarity of the squad room, Matt was, nevertheless, repulsed by the offhanded coarseness of this remark. If it was any example of the behavior Angel contended with from men, it went a long way toward explaining her antagonistic attitude toward them. He turned his attention back to the doctor, his expression hard. He'd met this kind before. Gary Chapman looked the epitome of the playboy physician. Suave and darkly handsome, his snug scrubs emphasized the taut musculature of his compact body. He exuded confidence and seductive charm. No doubt his position as a trauma physician gave him access to, and authority over, large numbers of pretty young women who yearned to bask in the glow of his power and prestige. If Chapman's use of this power didn't amount to outright sexual harassment, Matt suspected he was not above applying the more subtle advantages it gave him with women. Ignoring the tasteless remark, Matt schooled his features to conceal the instinctive dislike he felt for the man and steered the conversation back to the shooting victim.

"When will we be able to question him?" he asked, indicating the still figure connected to tubes and monitors.

"I'm afraid that won't be possible for quite some time," Dr. Chapman answered. "He's got a collapsed lung as well as a bullet wound to the liver. And he's lost a lot of blood. We won't know what other damage has been done until we get him to surgery. We'll be taking him in any minute, now. I'll be honest with you. I'm not sure he's going to make it." He spoke with the assurance of one whose orders are followed without question. Matt was willing to concede his medical expertise but chafed at the delay in getting the answers he needed. If this patient died, two years of steady, diligent police work could be lost with nothing to show for it. Rubbing the back of his neck in frustration, he searched his mind for a plan of action.

"I'll want a police guard with him constantly," he snapped. "That includes the O.R. I want that bullet as soon as it's out. It should be handled as little as possible and then only with fingers. No metal instruments that might scratch it. I want any markings on it to be undamaged for Ballistics. I want access to that room limited to people who absolutely have to be there. Is that understood?'' His staccato commands were punctuated by an index finger jabbing toward the physician's chest. Matt, too, was used to giving orders that were obeyed without question.

''I won't be doing the surgery myself,'' Dr. Chapman explained. ''I only see the patient here in the E.R. One of our trauma surgeons will take over in the O.R.'' He sounded relieved to be able to hand the hot-tempered lieutenant over to someone else. ''I'm sure our liaison nurse can help you with any arrangements you need to make.''

''And who would this liaison person be?'' Matt asked, releasing his breath with a hiss and wondering how many more people he'd have to deal with before he got the cooperation he wanted.

''That would be Ms. Martino,'' the physician answered, his expression telling just how much cooperation Matt could expect from that quarter.

''Naturally,'' Matt growled. He strode to the E.R. desk to page the elusive Ms. Martino.

Angel had barely replaced the phone in its cradle when the sharp rapping on her office door told her Lieutenant Flanagan had arrived. She had little time to compose herself for what she sensed would be a confrontation. Calling for him to come in, she reached up to pull the scrub cap from her head, massaging her forehead where the tight elastic binding had contributed to her already full-blown headache.

Matt entered, shutting the door behind him. Again, in spite of himself, he was struck by her beauty. The thick, pale tresses, which had been coiled in a neat topknot, were now straggling down in silky waves against her slender neck, giving her a fragile, deceptively vulnerable look.

Angel rose and moved around to the front of her gray metal desk, speaking before Matt had a chance to air his demands. ''I've relayed your requests to the operating team, and I assure you every effort will be made to cooperate fully." His dark eyebrows rose, expressing his skepticism at her words. "However..." The belligerent set of his mouth told her he had expected this qualification. "Our policies do not allow for a policeman to be in the operating room." She stood rigidly, braced for his angry rebuttal. It didn't come.

He assumed a relaxed stance, his back resting against the closed office door, and eyed her with a bemused expression. "Why not? He's seen blood before," he challenged.

Angel's hands gripped the edge of the desk behind her as she searched her mind for the words that would make this man see reason. "I've heard fourth-year medical students make that claim and have to be carried from the room," she said calmly. "I can't permit my nurses to be distracted by a queasy patrolman. They need to concentrate fully on the patient and the surgery. Besides, with all the equipment and personnel we use, there's nowhere he could stand where he wouldn't be in the way. I can assure—"

"How many doors?" Matt interrupted, cutting off her further assurance of cooperation.

"Pardon me?" Angel answered, disturbed by his insolent manner.

"How many doors are there into the operating room? How many ways to get in and out?"

"Each O.R. has two doorways," Angel explained. "One from the outer corridor and one that leads to the sterile supply area."

"That means two patrolmen," Matt said. "Nothing and no one goes in or out of the room without being checked out by one of them."

Angel recognized the futility of further argument. "All right," she conceded, "but the one posted in the sterile area will have to change into scrub clothes."

"I don't care if he's buck naked," Matt concurred, "as long as he keeps his gun. Just show him where to change." The smile he gave her didn't reach his eyes. "And, Ms. Martino," he added, stepping away from the door and trapping Angel between her desk and his own hard body, "make sure nothing happens to that bullet."

Angel refused to be cowed. Stiffening, she replied, "Shooting victims are not routine at this hospital, I grant you, Lieutenant. But we have them occasionally. We know how to handle evidence. I can assure..."

Matt almost laughed at that. Only the sparks that flared in her wide blue eyes stopped him. "I don't need any more of your assurances, Ms. Martino. You just take care of your job and let me take care of mine. I'm going back to my office, but I expect to be notified as soon as the surgery is over. I want this man alive. It's important that we find out what he knows."

He loomed so close to her that she could feel his heat. His words, his manner, were meant to unnerve her, and they did, but she fought to maintain a brave front, refusing to bow to his arrogance. Her own anger lent force to her words.

"This man may be nothing but a sleazy drug dealer to you, Lieutenant, but, whatever he's done, he's a seriously injured patient to us, and we'll do everything we can to save his life."

Matt's eyes narrowed at her words, his expression hardening. "See that you do," he said. "I'll be back." With that threat, he left the office, slamming the door behind him.

When Angel's beeper summoned her to Operating Room 3 ninety minutes later, she sensed the news was not going to be good. Still, even the errand she had run to the room earlier hadn't prepared her for the upheaval she found there. Jay Burdick, the fourth-year surgical resident, and one of the policemen were engaged in a shouting match, complete with wild gestures and threats of bodily harm. The patient was already out of the room, his stretcher, flanked by a medical cadre tending tubes and machines, was being wheeled at a breakneck pace toward the recovery room. Dr. George Albert, the anesthesiologist, pushed the stretcher while breathing the patient through a ventilator bag. That meant, apparently, that the victim still lived.

As she stepped into the operating room, Angel saw something out of a war zone. The huge cell-saver had been set up to capture the patient's own blood and transfuse it back to him. Judging from the empty plastic blood bags in the room, he had needed other blood, as well. Instruments, surgical sponges, and dressings were scattered haphazardly throughout the room, but the anesthesiologist's cart at the head of the operating table seemed to be the epicenter of the confusion. Syringes, tubing, rubber gloves and crumpled packaging covered every available surface and overflowed onto the floor.

Angel's mind had barely registered the chaos when the policeman, apparently sensing fresh meat, turned away from Burdick and lumbered threateningly toward her. He was young, Angel thought, certainly younger than her own twenty-seven years, but with an inflated sense of his own importance. His eyes bulged in his florid face as he descended on her.

"Listen here, you," he shouted. "I thought it was understood that no one was to leave the room without my okay. I'd like to haul the lot of those bastards in for obstruction and contempt."

Angel suppressed the sharp retort that would have come naturally, took a deep breath, and sought a more diplomatic response.

"I'm very sorry, Officer," she said. "I'm sure they didn't mean to overstep your authority, but these people are so used to acting automatically when a life is in the balance that they just didn't consider the trouble this would cause for you." Not that they would have done anything differently if they had, she thought, but there was no point in saying that and riling him further. Her deference to his authority seemed to soothe him somewhat. "Perhaps," she continued, "it would be better for you to go to the recovery room. You can question everyone involved there. I believe your partner's already gone," she added with a meaningful glance toward the other door.

A quick survey of the immediate area told him she was right. Fearful of being accused of further dereliction of duty, he muttered a few more words of complaint and hurried stiffly off down the corridor.

Angel stifled a smile at the ludicrous sight he made and turned her attention to the mess in the operating room. She donned rubber gloves and began to pick up the debris, disposing of it in the large plastic bags kept in each O.R. for that purpose. She was quickly joined by two nursing assistants who began gathering the soiled linen and mopping the floor. Angel, leaving the less hazardous work to them, started cleaning off the anesthesia work cart, plunging the used syringes through the hole in the top of the red plastic container used for disposing of needles and scalpel blades. She turned at the whoosh made as the corridor door opened and saw that Carla Briggs, the circulating nurse, had returned, looking troubled.

"Is the patient not doing well, Carla?" she asked, voicing the most obvious reason for the nurse's concern.

"He expired, Angel," Carla said. She used the common hospital euphemism. Confronting death every day, the doctors and nurses still found it difficult to utter its simple name when it prevailed. "I think he was gone before we left the O.R., but they wanted to pronounce him in Recovery."

Angel nodded silently. It was a common practice, though one she had misgivings about. When it was obvious that their efforts were hopeless and the patient would not survive, the surgeons and anesthesiologist scrambled to finish the procedure and get to the recovery room before death was confirmed. A death in the O.R. itself meant nothing could be touched until the county coroner gave the go-ahead. Depending on how busy he was and what questions he wanted answered, that could put the operating room out of commission for hours, possibly even days if foul play were suspected. Angel knew in this busy O.R. suite that could wreak havoc with the surgical schedule. A death in the recovery room, on the other hand, tied up only the stretcher the patient was on and one small, curtained cubicle. As callous as that seemed, she realized it had to be a consideration.

"Are you okay, Carla? Could you use a break?" Angel knew that nurses, like anyone else, differed in their reactions to death. Some needed a little time apart to collect themselves, while others preferred to keep busy.

"Thanks, Angel, but I'd rather finish up my charting here. Do we have another case posted for this room?"

"There's a thoracotomy being moved here from Room 6 right away. Another team has been assigned to it, though.

You'll be able to leave as soon as you've finished here. That is, if the police don't need you for anything further.''

"I'll check before I leave." Carla gathered up her paperwork and was rummaging through the solution bottles and specimen cups on the writing table. "Did you take the specimen cup with the bullet in it, Angel?" she asked, growing alarm evident in the rising pitch of her voice. "I thought I left it right here."

Angel felt a cold hand close around her stomach and squeeze. "No, I haven't seen it," she said, immediately concerned. "And nothing has gone out of this room since I've been here." She hurried over to where Carla was now frantically searching through bottles and containers.

"We had just gotten the bullet out when the guy really started to go bad, Angel, and everything got pretty confusing. But I had the cup labeled ahead of time, and I'm sure I put it right here," Carla declared, slamming her hand down on the countertop. "That cop is going to stroke out when he hears about this.''

Angel was inclined to agree with that assessment, and the aspirins she had taken were proving no match for the pounding in her head. Nevertheless, she tried to reassure her nurse.

"Don't get so upset, Carla." She placed her hands gently on the ones Carla was now wringing in front of her. "If it was here, it'll turn up. There's no reason why it wouldn't," she added with more optimism than she felt. "I'll have Terry and James go through the linen and trash before it leaves the room. You go ahead and get out of here. It's been a long day."

"Thanks, Angel. Nothing like this has ever happened to me before. I guess losing that patient bothered me more than I realized. I'd better leave before I screw something else up." She sighed, her shoulders slumping. "I'll just drop these papers off at the front desk on my way out," Carla added as she headed for the door.

Angel nodded and turned to give further instructions to the nursing assistants when the pager attached to her waistband again went off, signaling a call for her. With a few final words to Terry and James, she went to the wall phone and dialed the number that had flashed on her beeper. The message came as no surprise. Lieutenant Matthew Flanagan had been informed of the shooting victim's death and was waiting for her in her office.

Chapter 2

As she entered her office, Angel guessed the lieutenant's manner was meant to intimidate her. It succeeded admirably. He was slouched in *her* chair behind *her* desk, hands clasped nonchalantly behind his head, the ankle of one long leg resting across the knee of the other. He had slung his suit coat over the back of a chair alongside the desk. In shirt-sleeves, with his collar unbuttoned, tie loosened, and sleeves rolled up to reveal tautly muscled forearms, Matthew Flanagan appeared very much at ease. He made no effort to rise when she entered; nevertheless, he managed to convey the impression that it was her behavior that was subject to reproach.

"Come in, Ms. Martino, and have a seat." He gestured with an elbow toward the chair that held his jacket. His voice was flat and expressionless. His face, partly shadowed by the late afternoon sunlight coming through the window behind him, gave no hint of his mood.

Her irritation at his behavior notwithstanding, Angel felt little would be gained by challenging him. She seated herself stiffly in the chair he had indicated.

"As you know, Lieutenant, despite all of our efforts, we lost the patient." The words that spilled from her sounded stilted and pompous, betraying her nervousness. He made no response, only a narrowing of his eyes gave any indication that he had heard her. "He really was in very bad shape when he got here. We did all that we could," she added lamely, her voice faltering. "I'm sorry."

"I'm sure you are, Ms. Martino." His words were bland and noncommittal, but Angel heard the hard edge of sarcasm behind them, felt the heated currents that flowed from his body. He was seething. "I want that room quarantined until our investigation is complete," he demanded.

"I'm afraid that's impossible," she replied hesitantly. "We've already begun another procedure there." The situation had caught her off guard. She expected trouble but not over this issue. "We didn't receive any instructions to the contrary from the officers who were posted there," she added defensively.

Angel flinched at the obscenity that served as his reply. "Another screwup!" He straightened abruptly in the chair, planting both feet flat on the floor. Elbows resting on the desk, he pressed a fist against his mouth and scowled.

Irritably, he snatched a pencil from the mug that held them and jabbed it repeatedly into the blotter until the lead broke. He swore again under his breath, then tossed it aside. Angel felt a twinge of sympathy for the patrolmen who "screwed up," but it didn't help much to realize she wasn't the sole cause of the lieutenant's ill temper. She was the only one here to bear the brunt of it.

"I don't understand why the operating room would be pertinent to your investigation, anyway, Lieutenant. No one there had anything to do with the shooting," Angel began. "As for the loss of the bullet—"

"What about the bullet?" His words cut sharply into her remarks.

So he didn't know about that. Well, he had to be told sometime. She just wished she didn't have to be the one to give him the news. "I—it seems it was misplaced during all the commotion at the end. I'm afraid it's often the case that when people are trying to be most conscientious, things seem to go wrong.''

He was on his feet now and pacing, restless animal energy barely contained in his tall, lithe body. Although his hands were shoved casually into his pants' pockets, the bunching of the muscles in his arms gave evidence that they were clenched into fists.

Angel's irritation with his domineering manner had reached its limit. Throwing caution to the wind she said caustically, ''I find your great concern for a sleazy drug dealer most commendable, Lieutenant Flanagan. One would think—''

He moved toward her then, looming over her, his powerful hands clutching the arms of her chair. With his face only inches from her own she could clearly see the rage flaring in the hard green eyes, the clenching of the muscles in his jaw as he spoke.

''Don't get snotty with me, Angel,'' he breathed, his fury barely suppressed. ''That 'sleazy drug dealer' was a cop. ''He'd spent two years undercover trying to crack this case. He leaves a wife with three kids under eight years old. What kind of a life do you think they'll have on a policeman's pension?''

Matt was close enough to feel the soft breath expelled with her gasp. He watched the luminous eyes widen with shock and dismay and felt the undercurrent of an emotion he vaguely identified as relief. He was certain his information had come as a surprise to her. In a more controlled tone he went on. ''We have reason to believe that someone at this hospital is involved in the case he was investigating. Furthermore, we believe he was very close to an identification and probably could have given us a name, if he'd been able to talk to us before surgery.''

''But surely,'' she began, her voice barely a whisper, ''you can't believe anyone here was involved in his death? He was shot on the street! He was nearly dead when he got here.'' The rising agitation in her voice gave evidence of the troubled nature of her thoughts.

''Maybe so,'' he responded. ''But the paramedics who first treated him seemed to think he had a chance.'' He released his breath on a sigh, holding her gaze with his own. "He was shot on the street, Angel, but he was murdered here. The fact that the scene of the crime has been compromised just makes our job that much harder."

"You mean, the operating room." It was not a question. She no longer fought the import of his words.

"Yes." He released his grip on her chair and rested a hip on the desk behind him. His stance was relaxed, but his eyes were alert and watchful. "I mean the operating room, the emergency room, and anyone who came in contact with Marty."

She lifted her chin and gazed pensively out the window where late afternoon was giving way to a languid twilight. "Marty," she whispered. "We never knew his name."

"Someone did, Angel," Matt said with conviction. "Someone here wanted him dead."

"And we're all suspects," she finished for him. She closed her eyes, pressed her fingers to her brow and rubbed the frown lines that had gathered between her eyes.

Absentmindedly, she reached up to remove the cap confining her hair. The elastic band that had anchored the coils on top of her head had given way completely and her hair tumbled in a shimmering cascade over her neck and shoulders. She pushed the wayward strands behind her ears in a guileless gesture.

Even in the face of his anger and suspicion, Matt was struck by her artless sensuality and felt the heavy pull of desire. At another time, in another place, he would have welcomed the sensation, but not here, not now, and not with this woman.

Angel, her eyes wary and distressed, turned her gaze to his once again. "How can I be of help, Lieutenant?" she asked.

He eyed her speculatively, his arms crossed in front of his chest, wondering just how far her efforts at cooperation would extend this time. "There's nothing to be gained in looking for physical evidence at this point. Anything in the O.R. or emergency room would have been thoroughly obliterated by now. The medical examiner will do the autopsy, of course, but I don't think he'll find anything conclusive. We'll have to start with the personnel. Look for motive and opportunity," he said, almost to himself. "I'll need the employment files of anyone who had any contact with this case, doctors, nurses, lab techs, anyone. Can you get those for me?"

"You realize, of course," Angel interjected quickly, "that would involve a breach of confidentiality."

"And *you* realize," Matt countered, "that this is a homicide investigation. Now, I can waste my time going down to the county court for a warrant to make you hand the records over, but I can't say that'll sweeten my mood any. Or you can give them to me now without any hassle. Either way, I'll get the records." He eyed her thoughtfully for a moment and then added, "Unless, of course, you don't have the authority to do that. Then let me talk to someone who does."

That got the response he anticipated. Her chin came up sharply, and she gave him a mutinous look. "I have the authority," she snapped. "I can compile a list of the names you'll need from the operating room and emergency room notes. How soon would you like these records, Lieutenant?"

"I'd like them now, Angel. I'll wait here."

It had taken some time for Angel to assemble the list of names and collect the necessary files from the personnel office. By the time she had handed them over to the insufferable lieutenant, received his receipt for them, and escorted him from her office, full darkness had fallen. Vaguely aware that she hadn't eaten since the Danish and coffee that had been her breakfast, Angel decided to stop for a sandwich at the Italian carryout near her apartment. She glanced at the list of pink phone messages her secretary had accumulated for her during the day, but saw nothing that demanded her immediate attention. Donning cap and mask once more, she entered the operating room suite to check with the evening staff before leaving for the day.

Angel stepped into an entirely different milieu from that which existed in the same rooms during the day. All the cases had been finished and no emergencies had been added, so the staff was engaged in cleaning up and preparing for the next onslaught. The cleaning crew was washing down walls, floors and equipment, while technical personnel were restocking shelves and drawers with the wherewithal of surgical procedures: dressings, syringes, catheters, sutures. The workroom was abuzz with the washing, sorting, wrapping and sterilizing of instruments for the next day's schedule, which, although a Saturday, was already filled until four in the afternoon. Angel found Harriet Irwin, the evening charge nurse, in the anesthesia workroom ordering pharmacy supplies.

"You still here, Angel? I thought you left hours ago. It's been a helluva day, huh?"

"You can say that again, Harriet," Angel answered. She liked this nurse a lot. A middle-aged woman with grown children, Harriet didn't mind working the evening shift, a spot that was notoriously hard to fill full-time. She had been with the hospital for years and remained unruffled by the internal politics and power plays that went on in any large organization. She was secure in her position simply because she was very good at what she did. She took no guff from anyone, and janitors and doctors alike had learned to be wary of her sharp mind and equally sharp tongue. Angel had always found her advice sound and her assessments of people and situations on the money. She filled her in now on the day's events, providing verification and fact where there had been only rumor and speculation.

"So this Flanagan fella seems to think it's an inside job?" Harriet murmured, a frown clouding her plain, broad face.

"I don't know what evidence his opinion is based on, but he seems certain of it," Angel replied. "He must have good reasons for his suspicions. He doesn't seem like the kind of person who's wrong too often," she added, a vision of the handsome, arrogant detective filling her mind. She rubbed at the frown lines between her brows as if that would rub out his image.

Harriet watched her friend's characteristic gesture, her quick brown eyes troubled and sympathetic. "Gave you a hard time, did he?" she asked commiseratively. "Don't let the bastard grind you down." Noting her companion's tired eyes and listless expression, she added, "You need a break from this place, Angel. Take some time off... get away for a while."

"Maybe I will when this investigation is over," Angel answered with a wan smile. The prospect of a vacation did not cheer her. It meant empty, aimless hours to fill and no one to share them with.

As if reading her thoughts, Harriet commented, "You need to find a good man, Angel. God knows the pickings around here are pretty slim. They're either married or not worth the trouble. I don't suppose this lieutenant would be a candidate?" She eyed her colleague searchingly. Although Angel's exasperation with the man had been clear, there had been an underlying trace of something else.

Angel's smile broadened at that remark. "Not likely, Harriet," she said with a soft laugh. "He's one of the married ones. Thanks for your concern, though," she added, seeing her friend's disappointed look. "I'll be leaving in a few minutes if you don't need me for anything. Keep your eyes and ears open, and let me know if you come across anything suspicious."

"I'll do that. Now you go on and get out of here. And try to stay away from this place until Monday."

With a quick hug for the older woman, Angel turned and headed for the locker room where she would change into her street clothes. Her route took her past O.R. 3 and on impulse she pushed open the door and went inside.

The room had been cleared of the debris from the last procedure but was still awaiting the final cleaning of the day. Angel's eyes roamed over the squat operating table, cold and stark, its shiny black padding stripped of its linen coverings. A man had been murdered there today. She felt chilled and knew it was more than just the cool temperature of the room. Overwhelming sadness engulfed her. She envisioned the faces of her colleagues. Who might have been behind this horror? They all had their own peculiar human flaws. With her own past, who was she to judge? But who among them hid a much darker secret?

Making an effort to shake off her gloomy thoughts, Angel picked up a faint hissing sound coming from near the head of the table. She realized the suction to the anesthesia machine was still turned on and, walking around the table, she reached up to disengage it from the connecting tube hanging from the ceiling. It was almost out of her reach, and she stumbled backward, bumping into the anesthesia cart, when the connection gave. Her elbow hit the red sharps container, knocking it to the tile floor with a resounding crash. The rigid plastic shattered, scattering used needles, syringes and blades over the floor. Annoyed at her clumsiness, Angel pulled on gloves and stooped to clean up the mess. She froze as her eye caught a shape that didn't belong there. Gingerly she picked up the small plastic specimen container, still bearing the John Doe label, lid still in place. It was empty, of course.

She glanced at the wall clock. It would be fruitless to try to reach the lieutenant at his headquarters at this time. Fingers trembling and thoughts in a tumult, she placed the container in a small plastic bag to take home with her. She quickly finished cleaning up the mess on the floor and hurried to the locker room to change.

Angel was grateful for the snugly lined trench coat she wrapped tightly around herself. The early spring weather was changeable, and, though the day had been fairly warm, a stiff breeze had brought cooler temperatures for the evening hours. The wind whipped at her coat as she turned up the collar and, waving to the garage attendant seated in his booth, made her way to her car. The automobile, a sleek, silver gray BMW, was the one real luxury she permitted herself. She turned her key in the lock that shut off its alarm and slid into the driver's seat, feeling a familiar thrill of pride. Although her childhood could not be described as deprived, materially at any rate, her memories of those early years were uniformly bleak. What clothing and playthings she had had were given grudgingly and out of a sense of duty. She had lived with constant reminders that her life was an unsought and ill-appreciated burden, and could not recall a single instance of spontaneous affection. Was it any wonder, then, that the rejected child sought love or its impostors elsewhere and with any means at her disposal? Blossoming into a beauty as a teenager, she had discovered a potent means to gain attention and realized too late that she was bound for disillusionment and disaster.

As she guided her car onto the thoroughfare, Angel reflected on the course her life had taken. Blessed by nature with both a youthful resilience and a willful obstinacy, she had refused to surrender her future to the failings and limitations of her past. Through discipline and hard work she had achieved the goals she had set for herself. She could now afford to look after her own needs and wants, and, though her tastes were not extravagant, her possessions bore the mark of quality. She had built a wall of fine things to keep the scared, lonely, neglected little girl staring from the window of her past at bay. Only recently had she come to consider the cost.

Over the years during which she had pursued her single-minded course to better herself, Angel had not regretted the barrenness of her personal life. Close relationships would mean entanglements and questions for which she had no desire to provide the answers. Now, with her objectives achieved and her reputation established, she was becoming ever more aware that the future that stretched out in front of her seemed every bit as bleak as her past. She foresaw year after year of duty, diligence, and discipline; many colleagues, neighbors, and acquaintances, but few close friends; many pats on the back, but no embraces. She had made for herself a life free of shame and disgrace, but one also bereft of warmth and passion.

The problem was, she saw no way out of her predicament. In her heart she could not accept that the people she knew might understand and forgive her past. Told so often as a child that she was worthless, she had internalized this feeling until it was the way she saw herself. Her only defense was to keep the door to the past tightly closed in hopes that the accusations and insinuations she dreaded would never break through. She kept the past and all who might try to discover it at a safe distance. And so, to those who would get closer, she was remote, unapproachable, the "ice princess."

The brief stop at the carry-out provided a distraction from Angel's dreary thoughts and, arriving home, she attributed her somber mood to weariness and a feeling of unease at the day's events. She entered the thickly carpeted living room of her spacious condo, kicked off her shoes and switched on the flowered porcelain lamp on the end table next to the couch. She leaned her head back, stretching her neck and rotating her shoulders to relax her tight muscles and release some of the kinks. Her home was her haven, the one place she could drop her defenses along with her professional attire and feel as comfortable in her own personality as in her old chenille bathrobe.

She placed her handbag and carryout dinner on the table in the breakfast area, and went to her bedroom to change into that comfy old robe, taking little notice of her familiar surroundings. The rooms were furnished traditionally in dark, gleaming cherrywood. The soft blue, cream and rose of the carpeting and upholstered pieces were feminine without being fussy. Still, the rooms gave little hint of the personality that inhabited them. They would have made suitable pictures for a glossy home magazine or an advertisement for an elegant hotel suite. Only the framed pieces decorating the walls throughout the apartment gave a suggestion of the owner's temperament and interests. Angel expressed her love of color and harmony in needlework. Her samplers and floral pieces gave evidence of both her talent and her life-style, needlework often being a pastime for a person who spends much time quietly alone.

Returning to the breakfast area, Angel ate her solitary meal listlessly, her mind preoccupied with the day's happenings. After cleaning up the few dishes she had used, she rummaged through her handbag searching for her pager. She pulled out the specimen container in its clear plastic bag and was once more uncertain about what to do. It occurred to her that any delay in reporting her find might appear suspicious. She wondered if she would be able to reach Lieutenant Flanagan at home and decided to try.

She punched the numbers of the precinct station on the phone in her kitchen and was told by the officer on desk duty that the lieutenant had left for the day.

"I was afraid that might be the case," Angel said. "Would it be possible for me to get in touch with him at home?"

Angel detected the wary hesitation in the officer's voice. "We're not allowed to give out the phone numbers or addresses of law enforcement officers to civilians, ma'am," he answered. "Can you tell me what this is about? Maybe I can help you."

Angel felt strangely reluctant to discuss her finding with anyone else. Her mind raced to find a plausible explanation for her call. "I'm a nurse at Sherman General," she began, deciding a general description of the situation was in order. "I have some information concerning an incident that occurred there today."

Obviously that "incident" was something the desk officer knew to be a homicide—that of a fellow police officer, no less. Alert now, and anxious to talk, the officer responded, "If it's not convenient for you to come to the station now, ma'am, I can send a man out to take your statement. I just need your name and address."

Angel did not relish the idea of explaining to a stranger why she had brought evidence in a murder investigation home with her. Not that the temperamental detective was likely to be very understanding, but better the devil you know, than the devil you don't know. At least he was the devil she knew.

"I really would prefer to talk to Lieutenant Flanagan," she said hesitantly. "Perhaps he'll be available tomorrow?" She knew it was Saturday, but she also knew that cops, like nurses, worked irregular hours.

The officer exhaled deeply. "Tell you what, ma'am," he said in a conciliatory tone. "Give me your name and phone number, and I'll give Lieutenant Flanagan a call. He can get back to you tonight if—"

"That would be fine," Angel interrupted. "I plan to be home all evening." After giving the officer the required information, she hung up.

To keep herself occupied while waiting for the lieutenant to return her call, Angel fixed herself a cup of tea. She had just sat down at the table with her tea and the evening newspaper, emblazoned with headlines of the events at the hospital, when the phone rang. Taking a deep, calming breath, she reached for the receiver and answered in what she hoped was a normal tone of voice.

"This is Matt Flanagan," he said, as if she weren't already only too familiar with his disturbing voice. "I understand you have some information you think might help us out." His tone was noncommittal, neither accusatory nor conciliatory, neither friend nor foe. Angel couldn't for the life of her recall why she had thought talking to him would be preferable to talking to a stranger.

"Not information, exactly, Lieutenant," she answered cautiously. "Just before I left the hospital this evening, I found the specimen cup that had contained the missing bullet. I brought it home with me," she added in a rush, hoping an explanation of her behavior would not be required.

"I take it the operative word here is *had,* right? You didn't happen to locate the bullet and bring that home with you?"

Angel gritted her teeth. In her personal life and in her work, she was accustomed to feeling competent and in control. From her first encounter with this man she had been made to feel foolish and inept. This present circumstance was certainly no exception.

"No, I didn't," she answered lamely. "I'm sorry," she added, despising the note of submissiveness in her voice.

There was deadly silence over the phone as he pondered this for a time. "It would be hard for me to see you tonight," he replied at last. "And I don't think there's any real need to, anyway. Tomorrow morning will be soon enough. You're not planning on leaving town, are you, Ms. Martino?" he asked insolently.

"Of course not. Tomorrow morning will be fine. I can give you my address." Her answers were short and curt. She wanted only to end this conversation.

"I have your address, Angel," he said, and she remembered the files she had given him, her own included. "A very nice address it is, too. I didn't realize nurses could live so well."

She didn't care for the snide implications she heard in his voice. "I live within my means," she answered evenly. "Do I need a lawyer, Lieutenant Flanagan?"

"I don't know, Angel. Do you?"

He hung up, leaving her to face a long night of apprehension and dread.

Chapter 3

It had rained during the night, but the morning brought with it a perfect spring day. The sky was high and bright and bluebell clear. Angel stood at the French doors in her living room sipping coffee and gazing on the splendor of the morning. The jonquils and early tulips in the raised flower bed alongside her small brick terrace were straining their bright heads to the sun, much like eager young children in a classroom shooting up their hands to be called upon. A little beyond, down a gently sloping lawn, a wooded stream meandered through the common ground in the condominium complex. Angel could see a small group of youngsters absorbed with some find at the water's edge. She smiled softly as she watched them, but her eyes held an expression of unutterable sadness.

She was shaken from her reverie by the ringing of the doorbell, and, setting her mug on the kitchen counter, she went to answer the door in the small foyer. Out of habit Angel peeked through the security peephole in the door. Expecting her viewing range to be filled with broad shoulders and a ruggedly handsome face, she was startled to see . . . no one. Before her surprise could translate into any activity, a small, sturdy hand shot into her view, the fingers wriggling at eye level in front of her. Convinced now that this was one of the kids from a neighboring condo come to seek the professional advice of "the nurse" about some minor hurt, Angel opened the door, a bemused smile on her face.

"Hi, I'm Patrick." He smiled shyly up at her, his snaggle-toothed grin typical of a child whose teeth are still coming and going. She figured him to be about eight or nine, though somewhat small for his age. He wore the clothing universal to little boys—scruffy jeans, T-shirt, denim jacket, and sneakers. His thick black hair, shiny and board straight, and olive complexion hinted at Mediterranean ancestry. But his most striking feature was his eyes. Doe-brown, huge, and thickly fringed with soft black lashes, they gave him a sensitive, almost vulnerable appearance. No doubt he took some teasing about them now, and he hadn't yet learned what an advantage they could be with susceptible females, but he would. He would. Beautiful eyes or not, Angel didn't recognize the urchin.

"Patrick?" She looked at him inquiringly. "Do you live around here?"

"I'm Patrick Flanagan," he explained with another half smile. "I came with my dad." He gave a little shrug and added, "He's around the side, checking out your other door." With a dip of his head he indicated the direction his father had gone, as if this bizarre behavior were an everyday occurrence.

No sooner were the words out of his mouth than Angel heard a vigorous rattling at her French doors. Hustling the youngster inside, she marched off to confront his father. He was jiggering the bolt on the door, prying at it with some small instrument she couldn't identify.

"What do you think you're doing, Lieutenant Flanagan?" she asked, raising her voice to carry through the multipaned glass.

"They put the same damn locks on all these places," he muttered disgustedly in way of an answer.

"The security was one of the main features that attracted me to this complex, Lieutenant. I was assured that these locks were state-of-the-art. *Not* the type you could slip open with a credit card!''

"Yeah, you're right about that. You don't need a credit card, but just about anything long, skinny, and rigid enough will do." As if to underline his words, the door swung open, and he stepped into her living room, thrusting what she now recognized as a small jackknife into his pocket. She would have liked to further expound on the invincibility of her locks, but faced with such incontrovertible evidence to the contrary, she remained silent.

"Would you care to show me how you did that?" she asked feebly when she had regained some semblance of composure.

"And be accused of corrupting the innocent? Not a chance," he answered with a devilish grin.

His smile was devastating, Angel noticed, her composure slipping even more. It spread across his face, crinkling up the corners of his eyes and lending him a boyish charm. *Like a Boy Scout,* Angel thought. Unbidden, the qualities of a good Scout ran singsong through her mind: trustworthy, loyal, helpful, friendly, courteous, kind, obedient, cheerful, thrifty, brave, clean, and reverent. Well, okay, she'd give him clean, and she wouldn't quibble about brave, but she wouldn't trade her bandage scissors for the rest of his virtues.

She broke the hold of his penetrating gaze and surveyed the damage to her door. The lock clicked pathetically and ineffectually, but would not catch.

"Thank you very much for your concern," she said, twisting the knob, her voice laced with sarcasm. "But now I have no lock at all."

"Which is essentially what you had before," he answered, his voice equally sarcastic. "Only now you know it." In a friendlier tone he continued, "I can get a decent lock for the door this afternoon and put it in tomorrow. That leaves only tonight to worry about."

"Well, I'm sure piling pots and pans in front of it will give me plenty of time to escape." She wondered at his apparent interest in her life.

Matt bent down, mumbled something to his son and handed him his car keys. As the boy darted out through the open door, he straightened and smiled again. "I think we can manage something better than pots and pans. You live alone?" He stepped further into the living room and eyed the roomy, comfortable space.

"Yes, I do." *Not that it's any of your business* was left unspoken but clearly implied in both her tone and manner.

"You've been lucky, then." He nodded toward her now useless door. "A young woman, living alone, with a ground-floor entry backing up to a secluded area. The crooks are a hell of a lot better than I am at jimmying those locks. They can do it twice as fast with half the noise. You're a sitting duck," he stated flatly.

Despite her indignation Angel could see the reasonable-ness of what he said. "I really do appreciate your concern, Lieutenant..."

"Matt."

"Matt..." she repeated, her tone softened. "I guess I was too quick to accept the builder's claims about security. I should have investigated further."

Their attention was captured by the return of Patrick loping across the terrace and bursting through the door, a pair of handcuffs dangling from his fingers.

Handcuffs?

Angel's initial thought was that they must be for her, and shock washed over her like a pail of cold water. She watched in stunned silence as Matt took the handcuffs from his son and, closing the French doors, slipped one of the manacles over each of the doorknobs. Racheted down to their small-est diameter, they could not be slipped over the knobs. Nei-ther could the doors be opened more than a few inches, insufficient to permit entry of even the smallest body.

Grinning over his shoulder at Angel, Matt was distracted by her wide-eyed, dumbfounded expression. He turned, took his keys from his son and, removing one from the ring, strode over to where she stood, still gaping at his handi-work.

"That ought to keep the riffraff out—at least until we can come up with a more permanent solution." He cradled her small cool hand in his own larger one and pressed the key into her palm. "This is in case *you* need to get out."

"Thank you," Angel mumbled dazedly, her eyes going from his to the makeshift lock and back again. "But suppose you need them?"

"I have more." He laughed. "Besides, I can't remember the last time I used them."

Certain that she looked every bit as foolish as she felt, Angel was grateful for a sudden distraction from Patrick.

"Dad," he piped up, his face pressed against one of the panes in the door. "Can I go down by the stream?"

Matt walked over to stand behind his son. He placed his hands on the boy's shoulders and squinted at the children still absorbed in their activity at the edge of the water.

"Do you know any of those kids, Angel?" he asked.

Angel moved to his side, her gaze following the path of his. "I know all of them, actually," she answered, smiling wryly. "I'm the only nurse in this building. Mothers get to know that." She narrowed her eyes to more accurately gauge their activity. "They're catching tadpoles, would be my guess."

"Sounds safe enough." Matt gave Patrick's shoulders a squeeze. "You can go down there, but don't run off."

"Thanks, Dad." Not waiting for any further exhortations, Patrick headed for the foyer door and seconds later they heard it slam.

Angel was the first to break the uneasy silence that followed Patrick's departure. "Would you care for some coffee, Matt? It's fresh."

"I could use a cup. Thanks." He followed as she led the way into her small kitchen with its cheerful breakfast area. Matt pulled a ladder-back chair away from the heavy pedestal table of scrubbed pine that was centered in front of a large bow window. He shrugged out of his tan windbreaker, draped it over the slats of the chair, turned the chair around and straddled it. Resting his chin on his folded arms, he settled into the pleasurable task of watching Angel as she busied herself getting the coffee.

Matt had yet to get a handle on her. As his gaze took in her appearance, he noted once again her efforts to make the least of her assets and the utter failure of the result. Her thick, shoulder-length hair was swept back from her face and fastened at the nape with a wide clip, but nothing could disguise its healthy luster. She wore little, if any, makeup as far as he could tell—maybe a dash of pink to those full, soft lips. Matt wasn't sure if the lush lashes surrounding her blue eyes were naturally that dark or if she enhanced them, but he'd be willing to bet her creamy skin, its color heightened from the warmth of his steady scrutiny, was the way God had made it. She was dressed in a white knit T-shirt, long sleeves pushed up to her elbows and the tiny buttons at the front neckline partly undone. Her breasts were properly confined, he noticed with some disappointment, by a modest white bra, its lines faintly visible through the soft cotton of her shirt, but nothing could completely conceal their firm thrust. Her pale blue jeans, belted at the waist and loose-fitting, softly skimmed over the swell of her buttocks. Her only jewelry was the pair of small pearl earrings adorning the delicate lobes of her ears. Her fingers, Matt observed, were ringless, even out of uniform.

Appreciating the view afforded him as Angel stretched to reach another mug from the cupboard above the stove, Matt reflected on what he knew or could surmise about the lady. That she was bright, ambitious, and hardworking was self-evident. No one got to where she was at her age without those attributes or some very powerful connections—connections that seemed to be singularly lacking in her résumé. Beyond the bare essentials of her professional education and work history, she appeared to be a woman without a past. She had been at Sherman General for five years and in her current position for about nine months. Her file listed no relatives and no one to notify in the event of an emergency. Even her hospital-provided group life insurance policy named the hospital itself as sole beneficiary. Matt's experience told him this was a pattern consistent with a person who had something to hide. Then there was that fancy car in her parking area and the elegance of her furnishings. They didn't jibe with what he suspected her legitimate income to be. Tearing his eyes from his study of her, he mused that there was too much about her that didn't appear on the level. He wanted her to be, he admitted. She was touching him in ways a woman hadn't in a long time.

Angel had been conscious of his scrutiny and, out of the corner of her eye, she noted the instant he turned his attention elsewhere. She made her assessment of him as she worked. He was dressed casually, much like his son, in jeans, T-shirt—his emblazoned with the logo of the local classical music station—and sneakers. Nevertheless, Angel was headily aware that a man, not a boy, filled these clothes. His soft, worn jeans were faded at the pressure points. They were bleached almost white over the long muscles of his thighs. The orange T-shirt hugged his chest, its short sleeves revealing the bunched muscles of his shoulders and upper arms. The color emphasized the healthy bronze of his skin and the piercing green of his eyes. He has nice eyes, she mused silently. She well remembered the cold fury they could hold, but right now they weighed his surroundings with an almost gentle regard. The dark waves of hair spilling over his forehead were even more disheveled than the day before, seeming to have had the attention of fingers rather than a comb or brush. At this thought Angel's eyes dropped to the strong hands draped over the chair back and the wide gold band gleaming on one of them. Not caring to speculate on whose fingers might be responsible for the unkempt condition of his hair, Angel shoved her wayward thoughts aside.

She placed the mugs and spoons on the table and poured the steaming coffee from the automatic coffeemaker. Replacing the coffeepot on its element and setting the control to keep it warm, she returned to the table with a small tray containing sugar, cream, and a plate of Pepperidge Farm cookies.

"Oh, jeez, Patrick's favorite." Matt grinned, displaying deep laugh lines in his tanned cheeks as he reached for some. "These won't last long if he sees 'em."

"That's okay," Angel responded with a smile. "They're my favorites, too. I'd be better off without the temptation."

Taking a sip of her coffee, she set her mug on the table.

"I'll get that container I told you about," she said, turning to go into her bedroom.

She returned less than a minute later with her handbag and, taking the small plastic container from it, she handed it to Matt.

"It would be useless to check it for fingerprints," she said, still standing tensely next to the table. "Any number of people would have handled it, most of them wearing gloves. With the precautions we all take now for hepatitis and AIDS, that wouldn't even arouse suspicion."

Matt turned the container slowly in his hands and nodded his agreement. "I need to ask you some questions, Angel," he replied, glancing up at her. He noticed her anxious expression and a wry smile curled his lips. "My mood's improved a little since yesterday. Why don't you have a seat? I won't bite."

Provoked at being made to feel like an interloper in her own home, Angel pulled the only other chair away from the table and sat down. Inadvertently her knee bumped Matt's and she jerked it quickly away, her whole body stiffening.

Matt caught her overreaction and gave her a puzzled glance, but said nothing.

Fingers trembling, Angel took another sip of her coffee. She willed herself to relax and returned Matt's stare with her own level gaze. "What would you like to know?"

"Where exactly did you find this thing, Angel?" He set the container on the table, tapping it absently.

"It was in the sharps bucket. I was doing some straightening up in the operating room and I knocked the bucket to the floor. That came spilling out, along with everything..."

"What's a 'sharps bucket'?" he asked, his eyes narrowing.

Angel thought a few moments, a frown marring her brow. "It's not a bucket, really. It's more like a big, red, plastic jug with a wide mouth. We have one in each operating room and in various places throughout the department. Used needles, syringes, knife blades are put in them to protect the staff from injury. They're easily identifiable and used only for that purpose."

"So whoever put it there could feel reasonably sure that it wouldn't be discovered until the 'bucket' was emptied," Matt mused half to himself. "How often is that?"

"Oh, they're never emptied," Angel answered quickly. "There would be too much risk involved. When they become full, they're sealed and disposed of with the rest of the hospital's hazardous waste."

"In other words, if it hadn't been for your accident, chances are this little container would never have been found?" Matt rubbed his thumb over his lower lip, his eyes fixed thoughtfully on the wall behind her.

Angel's eyes were riveted to the sensual curve of that lip, her stomach doing unfamiliar cartwheels inside her. "That's right," she answered, forcing her eyes to his.

He met her troubled gaze. "You understand this blows any possibility that this thing was misplaced accidentally, don't you, Angel? Whoever put it there did it deliberately, knowing full well it would never be found. In the confusion, it would be easy enough to conceal something as small as a bullet, but this would have been more of a problem."

"Yes, I know," she answered softly. During the long hours of the night she had come to grips with the implications of this find. One of her co-workers, possibly someone she knew well and trusted, was deeply involved in the policeman's death. She'd already guessed the direction Matt's next question would take.

"So, what can you tell me about the people you work with? Any unusual behavior? Anything that might arouse your suspicion?"

Angel watched as he burrowed into the pocket of his jacket, pulling out a pen and a small spiral notepad. He laid the pad on the table and flipped through it until he found what he was looking for. She glanced at the bold markings on the paper, but they were upside down to her line of vision, and even after years of deciphering doctors' handwriting, she couldn't make out his scrawl.

Angel raised her eyes and caught him studying her, his cool, remote expression again in place. So this is going to be an official interrogation, she thought. "Some people would say the behavior of most of the people I work with is unusual, Matt. That doesn't make them murderers." She gave a little shrug, unaware of the rippling effect it had on the soft T-shirt clinging to her breasts.

Matt wasn't. He shifted in the chair as he felt his groin tighten and swell. It had been too damn long since that particular need had been eased, and this woman was the embodiment of temptation, but he was the investigating officer in a homicide, and she was a material witness at best, a suspect at worst. That she was igniting sparks that hadn't fired in too long a time was just something else he would have to deal with. He frowned at the list in front of him, stabbing at one of the names with his pen.

"What about Chapman?" he asked abruptly.

"Gary?" Her eyebrows rose in surprise she couldn't conceal.

"'Gary'?" he mimicked. His dark brows rose in imitation of hers. "Are you chummy with him?"

"Not especially." That shrug again. Again he shifted.

Her eyes focused on him in concern. "Are you uncomfortable, Matt? We could move into..."

"I'm fine," he answered flatly. It had been years since his body's response to a woman had caused him embarrassment, but he didn't trust himself to stand up now. He was grateful for the shield the chair back and his jacket provided.

Her frown lifting, Angel thought about his question.

"Some of the older physicians and nurses still stand on ceremony," she offered by way of explanation. "Most everyone else is on a first-name basis, though. It just seems more natural considering the tensions we work under. What makes you suspect Gary?"

He's got a dirty mouth, and I don't like the way he looks at you, came immediately to mind but hardly seemed an appropriate response. "I'll ask the questions, Angel" didn't appear likely to get him on her good side, either, but it kept the conversation in safe territory, so he used it. "He's married, isn't he?"

"Yes, he's married," she admitted reluctantly. "And yes, he has quite a female following, but that doesn't mean he's a drug dealer or a murderer. Basically, I think Gary is harmless."

"Is that right?" His eyes watched her over the rim of his mug.

Sensing his animosity, Angel sipped at her coffee while considering her response. She set her mug on the table and absently traced its rim with her fingertip as she replied.

"Gary was a poor kid and had to work hard to get where he is. He didn't have much time for fun in school. Besides, he was small and brainy. Kind of a nerd, I suppose. Not exactly the type to set teenage female hearts aflutter. I think he suffered his share of rejection." Her eyes turned to his, her gaze level and direct. "I don't suppose that's an experience you're familiar with, is it?"

Although a grudging one, it was the first overt sign she had given that she found him attractive, and Matt felt a rush of pleasure. His eyes darkened as they held hers.

"We were talking about Gary," he said, but the harshness was gone from his voice.

Angel rested her chin in her hand. "I can't say I condone his behavior," she continued, "but it's understandable in a way. Now that he has the money and prestige to attract any woman he wants, he's gone a little crazy. The rumor is he has a very understanding wife. He married while still in med school and she's a career woman in her own right. Kind of a take-charge type. She does her thing and he does his. I know she's out of town a lot. That may be part of the reason he strays."

Unable to comprehend a marriage where mutual infidelity was considered acceptable behavior, Matt could only nod incredulously. "Have you met this paragon of wifely tolerance?"

Angel's lips parted in an impish smile and playful laughter bubbled from her throat. "I've never actually met her, but I've talked to her on the phone when she's called to leave messages for him. She's a bit older than he is, I understand, and her voice is, well, kind of mannish. I picture her in tweed suits and sensible shoes. But, apparently, they're happy with each other. At least, there's no talk of any trouble, and, believe me, there would be. Really, Matt—" that laughter again "—I can't picture Gary with any deep, dark secrets. His flaws are all pretty up-front."

"No indication of drugs?" he persisted.

Her mood sobered immediately. Releasing her breath on a long sigh, she answered, "I'd be lying to you if I said I never heard talk of an occasional joint at parties. Some of the staff have had problems with alcohol, too. We have policies in place to test anyone who seems impaired while on duty. Anyone who tests positive is offered assistance through a treatment program. A refusal or a second positive test results in dismissal. We're responsible for people's lives and—"

"Have there been any of those recently?" Matt interrupted. "Any dismissals for drug use?"

Angel wrestled with her answer for a few moments before replying. "We let one of the nurse anesthetists go several months ago. She would sign narcotics out to patients, but when her charts were reviewed we discovered only a fraction of the drugs were used. Apparently she was taking the rest. Our evening staff caught the discrepancies, but her dismissal was handled by the anesthesia department."

Angel hesitated a moment and then went on. "I don't want to tell you your job, Matt, but that's the kind of problem you'll find in a hospital. There just isn't the access to drugs in large amounts, and there are too many controls. You might find the occasional person supporting a personal habit, but not a full-scale drug operation."

"We've never suspected the access to drugs was through the hospital," Matt answered. "And the person we're after isn't necessarily a user—the kingpins usually aren't—though he may be supporting someone else's habit. The hospital just provides a respectable cover." He eyed Angel closely, aware of her inner turmoil but unable to make out the cause of her distress. "Is there anything you're not telling me?" he probed gently.

She hesitated a moment and then shook her head. "No," she answered firmly. "There's no one I suspect of being involved in this. I'm sure if you dig, you'll find some messy personal lives. Even Dr. Albert is rumored to have something going with one of the switchboard operators. We all work irregular hours under a high degree of stress. That can take its toll on a happy family life." An eyebrow arched meaningfully as she went on. "I understand it's much the same in police work, Lieutenant."

"Are we back to 'Lieutenant' again, Angel?" Matt murmured. He eyed her thoughtfully. "There wasn't much in your file."

Angel's chin came up defensively and he caught the flare of defiance in her eyes. "There isn't much to know," she answered, a challenge in her voice. "I have no family. That may be unusual, but not unheard of, and it's the truth. My work is my life. Anyone who knows me can tell you that."

"Several people have, as a matter of fact," he answered. He closed his notepad and slipped it and the pen back into his jacket pocket. "The question is, why would a bright, beautiful young woman choose to lead such a narrow life?" He watched as her aloofness surrounded her like a shield, but one that was no match for his sharply honed skill for reading human behavior. Whatever she was hiding, it wasn't drugs and it wasn't murder. He was certain of it.

"My reasons are personal. Surely that's not a crime."

"No, but it's a damn shame."

Matt rose and stretched. Angel, rising to her feet, also, felt the walls of her kitchen close in around her as she watched the slow extension of his lithe body. He made no move to approach her, but she felt almost overwhelmed by his virile presence. She crossed her arms in front of her chest, hugging herself in the age-old gesture of self-protection.

Matt slipped his arms into the sleeves of his jacket, his eyes never leaving hers. "Thanks for the coffee."

"You're welcome." Angel shook herself from her unabashed absorption with his body. "Let me wrap the rest of those cookies up for Patrick."

Glad for the diversion, Angel got a sandwich bag from the cupboard by the sink, scooped up a handful of cookies and secured the package with a twist tie. When she turned to hand the cookies to Matt, she noticed he was examining the lush, green houseplants she had growing in terra-cotta pots on the wide sill of the bow window.

"You must have the right touch," he said, fingering the luxuriant purple leaves of a wandering jew. "All of our plants are dying," he murmured half to himself.

Angel sensed the implied criticism in his voice and again wondered about the state of his marriage. Trying to strike a lighter note, she replied, "I'm just careful to choose plants that thrive on neglect. They get watered once a week, no more, no less, and if they don't like the light from this window, out they go. I can be ruthless when it comes to plants."

Matt smiled but made no response. He took the cookies from Angel, shoved them into his jacket pocket, and strode through her living room as she followed close behind. When they passed her French doors, he gestured toward them. "I can come by tomorrow morning to fix that lock." He stopped abruptly and turned to face her, seeming at a loss for words. He slipped his hands into the back pockets of his jeans and stood with legs spread in a manner both boyishly casual and blatantly masculine. "Maybe you'd like to do something afterward," he suggested.

It took a few moments for his words to register. When they did, a rising flush of anger and surprise stained Angel's cheeks. "B-b-but you're married!" she stammered.

Angel glimpsed the fleeting expressions that crossed Matt's face—surprise, embarrassment, chagrin. He rubbed a hand over the back of his neck. "I'm widowed," he said quietly. "My wife died a little over a year ago." He pulled his left hand from his jeans pocket and looked at it sheepishly. "I've had this ring on for so many years, I haven't been able to get it off. Most of the time I forget that it's there."

Angel was momentarily speechless at this unexpected revelation. All her preconceived notions about this man had been suddenly upended. She had seen him as self-assured, hard-edged, arrogantly masculine. Now her own sense of fairness required that she regard him on different terms. She could read in his face the vulnerability his loss had left. With that understanding came the realization that his apparent discomfort with the role he was forced to play was very real. He was as unaccustomed to the dating scene as she was, and if rejection was an unfamiliar experience for him, she could see in his eyes that the threat of it caused him a noticeable unease.

"What did you have in mind for tomorrow?" she asked, her sympathy for him not overriding her natural caution.

Matt raked long fingers through his unruly hair and smiled ruefully. "Nothing special, I'm afraid. I'm committed to baseball practice with Patrick's team. That could be amusing if you'd like to watch. We could have a picnic lunch along the river. It's right next to the field where they practice." He shoved his hands back into his jeans pockets and stood facing her in his former stance, waiting for her response.

Patrick would be with them. Angel wondered if that was a maneuver to win her trust. If so, it was an effective one. Matt would hardly be likely to come on to her with his big-eyed son in tow to witness the seduction.

"I go to church on Sunday mornings, Matt." It wasn't an outright rejection, but it left both of them with some bargaining room.

"So do we," he answered. His smile spread across his face and mischief lit his eyes. "We'll pick you up for the nine-thirty service at St. Michael's. You can come back here and change into something more comfortable while I work on that lock. Thanks again for the coffee, Angel." He gave her a quick nod. "See you tomorrow."

Before she could form a reply, he had turned and was out her door. A hundred reasons why she should not risk a relationship with him came instantly to mind, but she made no attempt to call him back. Instead she went to stand by her now very secure French doors and observed as Matt walked into her line of vision on the slope leading to the stream. Cupping his hands around his mouth, he shouted and then waved for his son to join him. Angel watched as the boy scampered eagerly up the grassy knoll to his father's side and ducked under the strong arm that reached out to encircle his shoulders. She still had time to back out of the plans for tomorrow but made no effort to do so. In the end, all of the rational arguments for not going did not outweigh the single reason why she would. She wanted to.

Chapter 4

She had never been to church with a man. That inane observation floated unbidden into Angel's mind and niggled at her consciousness as she stood in front of her bedroom mirror assessing her reflection and wondering if she should change her clothes for the third time. Perplexed, Angel searched the corners of her memory for a single instance with which to contradict that bald assertion. She could find none. Her father, who had not lingered around long enough to make her acquaintance, had by all accounts not been a church-going man. Her maternal grandfather had died before she was born, sparing himself, as her grandmother had been fond of telling her, the pain and humiliation her presence would surely have caused him. Information concerning her paternal grandfather was, naturally, even more elusive than that of her father. Angel sincerely doubted they had ever shared the confines of any house of God. Her mother, an only child, had died in a car crash, after a night of drinking and partying, when Angel was only six months old. The brevity of her life ensured, her continued sexual promiscuity notwithstanding, that no brothers accompanied the little Angelina to Sunday services. Uncles and

cousins were also singularly lacking in Angel's history. She
had, in fact, no memory of any living male relative. She had
never formed close bonds of any sort with men or boys
during her childhood years. Then had come adolescence;
but those relationships, though certainly intimate, had never
been either emotionally close or long lasting. The young
men had made all sorts of suggestions about activities Angel might like to try, but not one of them had ever suggested she might like to go to church. No, Angel concluded,
she had never been to church with a man.

Perhaps, she reasoned, that accounted for the fluttering
in her stomach and the dampness of her palms. She rubbed
her palms against the skirt of her ice blue knit dress and
dismissed that thought out of hand. No amount of ration-
alization could convince her that the company of any of the
other men she knew would have this effect.

The jangle of her doorbell ruled out any further costume
changes. Slipping into the white knit cardigan, striped to
match the blue of her dress, she slid on a pair of low-heeled
pumps, made a final check of the hair she had left flowing
loosely to her shoulders, and went to answer the door.

Angel's automatic check of the peephole brought a win-
some smile to her lips. She watched as Matt, chin lifted, ran
an index finger between his tanned neck and the crisp white
collar of his shirt—a typically male gesture of discomfort.
Evidently the handsome detective was no more relaxed than
she was.

Angel's smile struck Matt speechless as she opened the
door. A night spent wrestling with himself over the wisdom
of any kind of involvement with a principal in a homicide
investigation had left him feeling irritable and restive. Aside
from being patently against departmental regulations, his
behavior could be dangerous and foolhardy. He'd ap-
peased his conscience with the lame excuse that he might
learn something. Her smile effectively quashed all the
doubts.

"Hi." He grinned. "You're all ready, I see."

"Yes. I'll just get my handbag." She left Matt standing
at the open door and returned moments later, slinging the
strap of her white leather bag over her shoulder.

They walked through the vestibule of Angel's condo and out glass double doors into brilliant sunshine. Angel was intensely aware of Matt's hand, gentle on her arm, guiding her toward the deep maroon minivan parked alongside her own car.

"We've only got one car, now," Matt remarked, opening the passenger door, "so it made sense to have one that could do everything."

"It's very nice," Angel answered, wishing she could relax. Also freshly washed, she strongly suspected as she climbed into the charcoal gray upholstered seat. There was no trace of the recent rain on the gleaming exterior paint or windows. The interior, she noted, also showed signs of recent attention. Remnants of the packaging from various fast-food meals had been gathered into a plastic grocery bag on the floor next to Patrick's seat.

Patrick, strapped into the seat behind the driver's, gave her another of his shy grins by way of a greeting. He had spruced up for the occasion, in a white open-necked shirt, dark brown cardigan sweater, and khaki pants. Even his hair had been tamed, slicked back from his forehead in a small pompadour. He looked about as comfortable as most little boys would in similar circumstances.

As Matt opened the door on the driver's side and climbed into his seat, Angel slid a glance at him. Again she wondered at his motivation. He appeared awkward and ill-at-ease, but obviously making an effort to be congenial. He ran a hand through the thick waves of his hair, and Angel's stiff smile became more natural. If his shaggy mane had been tamed earlier, there was no evidence of it now. Disheveldment appeared to be his natural state.

Conversation on the way to the church centered on the innocuous, and the service eliminated the need for conversation at all. Afterward Matt suggested a local pancake house for breakfast, seconded enthusiastically by Patrick, and Angel readily agreed. By the time they headed back to Angel's condominium, they had traded enough of the trivia of their lives to feel a comfortable companionship. Angel appreciated the wisdom of including Patrick. In his presence she found both Matt's masculinity and his authority less threatening.

When they arrived at the condo, Matt pulled a metal toolbox from the back of the van. He removed his jacket, rolled up his shirtsleeves, and set to changing her lock. Leaving Patrick to rummage through the toolbox for his father's requests, Angel went to her bedroom to change.

She didn't take long, but by the time she returned, Matt had already finished and was cleaning up. He had sent Patrick out to the van with the toolbox and was washing his hands at her kitchen sink. His head came up as she walked into the room.

She had dressed simply, in slim white jeans and a pale blue chambray shirt with the shirttails tied at her waist. Her hair was pulled back into a thick French braid fastened with an elastic band. A few tendrils escaping around her brow softened the severe effect. Matt's gaze never left hers as he reached for a towel to dry his hands, and she read his approval in his eyes.

"You're pretty secure now, Angel. Most crooks would figure it's more trouble than it's worth to bust that lock. They'll look for easier pickings." He replaced the towel on its hook and drew nearer.

"How can I thank you?"

The moment the words were out of her mouth, Angel regretted them. They sounded like an invitation, one Matt was quick to accept.

He lifted her chin, rubbing his thumb softly over her full lower lip. Of their own volition, her lips parted and he gently pressed his thumb into the warm, moist inner recess, softly stroking. A reckless need surged through him. His pulse hammering, he slid his free arm around her back to pull her close as his rigid body pressed her unyieldingly against the countertop behind her. He lowered his head to cover her open mouth with his own.

The fear in her eyes stopped him. That and the small fisted hands pushing firmly against his chest. He felt her swallow tightly against the backs of his fingers resting on her throat. Her breathing was rapid and shallow. With her whole body strained against his, he could sense the faint trembling that coursed through her. Her "Don't touch me" couldn't have been clearer if she'd sprouted quills.

Puzzled, he released her slowly. Reluctance he could appreciate, and even outright hostility would be understandable, but *fear* was a response he couldn't comprehend. He wondered what past experiences had triggered this response and whether she would ever trust him enough to tell him.

"No thanks is necessary," he answered finally. "We'd better get going if we're going to make that practice."

Patrick's chatter filled the uneasy silence on the way to the ballpark. His enthusiasm was contagious, and the mood had lifted considerably by the time they pulled into the gravel parking lot adjoining the baseball diamond. Matt again went to the back of the minivan, this time pulling a duffel bag from its roomy interior. As he and Patrick headed off to change in the locker room of the adjacent recreation center, Angel found a seat among mothers and friends in the bleachers along the third base line.

A few minutes later Matt approached to leave the duffel bag in Angel's keeping. He introduced Angel to some of the women and strode off to confer with the other coaches and begin practice. The women glanced at Angel idly, until one of them engaged her in conversation.

"Have you known Matt long?" the woman Matt had called Janet asked.

"Not long at all. We've only just met."

"We were kind of wondering," Janet replied. "Matt only moved here since his wife died. To be near his sister and her family, I think. She helps him out with Patrick, him working irregular hours and all," she went on pleasantly. "We've been trying to fix him up with sisters and girlfriends, but I can't say he's shown much enthusiasm." She eyed Angel assessingly. "I can see where he might make an exception for you, though."

Angel smiled and murmured a modest reply. Her eyes scanned the baseball diamond, spying Patrick at shortstop and Matt standing near third base. Her attention riveted on Matt's muscular frame. He had his back to her, and she could look her fill without fear of detection. He was dressed

simply in a black T-shirt and faded jeans that were molded
to his powerful physique. His broad shoulders pulled the
stretchy fabric tight as he raised his hands to rest them on his
hips. The swell of the muscles in his upper arms was boldly
defined with every movement he made. Angel's eyes drifted
down to his narrow waist and the taut curve of his buttocks
revealed by the soft denim that clung like a second skin. She
felt that warmth she had begun to associate with thoughts
of him flooding through her belly and settling very low.
Angel gave herself over to a sensual pleasure she had never
permitted herself before—the leisurely scrutiny of a male
body for the sheer enjoyment of it.

"Angel?"

Slowly Angel drifted from her reverie, becoming aware
that Janet was trying to get her attention, probably not for
the first time.

"Would you like a soda, Angel? We've got a cooler full."

Angel accepted the cold, droplet-covered can graciously
and took a long swallow, trying to cover her embarrassment at being caught gaping.

"Isn't Matt a hunk?" Janet laughed, oblivious to Angel's discomfort. "He makes my nostrils flare, I'll tell you.
Not that I'm not crazy about Howie, understand, but he
could stand to lose the paunch. He's over there behind home
plate, the one with the red hair, or what's left of it." She
pointed to a tall man in his mid-thirties who, indeed, carried a considerable spare tire above his belt.

Angel was grateful for Janet's good-natured banter and
quickly regained her aplomb. "Is the redheaded boy at bat
your son?" she asked.

"How'd you guess?" Janet replied with a grin. "They're
kind of playing round robin right now," she explained.
"Trying to figure out batting order and what positions the
boys play best. My Jason's got his heart set on pitcher, but
so does just about every other kid out there. The men will
have their hands full trying to prevent hurt feelings."

Angel gave her full attention to the activity on the field
then, matching boys to some of the other mothers around
her. She watched Patrick closely. With his small size, he
wasn't much of a threat at bat, taking a roundhouse swing

at each pitch and seldom connecting. When he did hit the ball, he usually popped up to the infield. He was fast, though, and could be trouble when he'd get on base. His arm was pretty accurate, too, and he knew where to make the play when he got the ball. He'd make a decent infielder. Angel was struck by Matt's patience with him and the other boys. He spurred Patrick on with words of encouragement, and Angel was touched that a man who was such a natural athlete could be so accepting of a son who was not.

The time passed quickly and before she knew it the bleachers were emptying out and Patrick and Matt were heading her way. Patrick was in earnest conversation with his father, apparently dejected over his poor showing at bat.

"I don't know, Patrick. Maybe we can stay a little longer," Angel heard Matt say as they approached. "We'll have to see how Angel feels about it."

"Feels about what?" she asked. She rose and grabbed the duffel bag that had been at her feet.

"Patrick would like a little more batting practice. I think he'd do fine if he'd just concentrate on getting on base instead of swinging for the fence every time. But we'll leave it up to you. If you're hungry, we'll practice another time."

Matt's hand brushed hers as he took the bag from her, and Angel felt the tingle all the way up her arm. If Matt's response was the same, his expression didn't give it away, although a certain quirking of his lips gave a hint of awareness.

"That breakfast was bigger than I'm used to and, besides, I had some munchies here. I can wait." Her response was carefully nonchalant.

"Ah, but can you catch?" Matt asked with a grin.

"As long as it's underhand and there's a backstop behind me, I think I can manage." Angel laughed. "But it's been awhile."

"Let's put you to work, then," Matt answered as Patrick raced off to the now empty diamond.

The duffel bag provided Angel with a mitt, which was only a little too small, and a mask, which she balked at. She crouched down behind Patrick and held the mitt to make what she hoped was an appropriate target for Matt. She

found his lobs fairly easy to catch and managed to get the
ball back to him accurately most of the time.

After a little while she needed to catch less and less often, as Patrick found his rhythm and pounded the ball first
along one baseline and then the other. Matt shouted encouragement, reminding him to use his eye and let the bad
ones go by, but Patrick was in his glory. He knew he was
fast, and, if he could get on base, he could score. He'd never
be a power hitter, but there was a place for him all the same.

Angel's mind drifted to her own childhood and what it
had lacked. She had never known this camaraderie with a
parent, this gift of self and time. Still, she was grateful to be
able to share as an adult what she had missed as a youngster.

She was shaken from her thoughts as Patrick connected
solidly with the ball, sending it inches over Matt's glove as
he leapt up to catch it. That stretch hiked up his shirt and
slid his jeans downward, leaving a broad expanse of taut
male abdomen bared to Angel's gaze. She glimpsed coarse,
dark hair swirling around his navel, thinning into a line as
it arrowed down into his jeans, and her mouth went dry. Her
distraction proved to be short-lived, however, as Patrick,
waving his cap in the air, launched himself at her in a frenzy
of exhilaration.

Matt chased the ball down near the edge of the wooded
slope leading to the river. As he picked up the ball and
turned back toward the diamond, he was astonished to see
his shy, mild-mannered son hurtling himself at the cool,
dignified "ice princess." His easy lope quickened to a trot
when he saw Angel teetering under the weight of the excited boy. Patrick's legs were clasped tightly around her
waist and he thumped her back exuberantly with his cap.
Matt watched, his heart in his throat, as Angel stumbled
backward, landing on her backside in the dirt behind home
plate.

Rushing up, Matt pulled his son off the supine woman,
who was shouting, "I knew you could do it, Patrick," in
between gales of laughter. He watched in amazement as she
pulled herself up on one elbow and wiped her streaming eyes
on the sleeve of her shirt. That shirt had lost a button near

the top and had a rip in one of the shoulder seams. Angel's braid had come loose and most of her hair was hanging heavily over one ear. The high color on her cheeks was streaked with the dirt she had smudged on her sleeve and transferred unwittingly to her face when she'd wiped her eyes. Matt had never in his life seen a more beautiful woman.

"Are you still in one piece?" he joked. He reached out a hand to pull her to her feet.

"I think so. I won't be sure till I stand." Still weak with laughter, Angel grasped Matt's hand and hauled herself up. Taking stock of the damage to her appearance brought on new paroxysms of laughter. Friday night's rain had insured that the dirt Angel had picked up could not easily be dusted off. She had grimy splotches on each sleeve where her elbows had hit the dirt and a large, heart-shaped smear on the bottom of her white jeans.

"That was a great hit, Patrick," she said, giving his shoulder a playful squeeze, "but I think practice is over for me. I'm going to the field house to make whatever repairs I can, and then I'm ready for lunch."

"That sounds good," Matt answered. "I'll get the cooler out of the van, and we'll meet you outside the field house." He watched as she picked up her purse and ambled off. Splattered with dirt and with a stain the size of the catcher's mitt covering her lovely bottom, she stole his breath.

Matt found Angel's allure even more captivating when she rejoined them a few minutes later. She had washed her face and hands, removing the most obvious grime, but her eyes still sparkled with laughter. Her hair was pulled back into a simple ponytail that swayed as she walked. His attention was drawn, however, to the adjustments she had made in her clothing. To cover the large splotch of dirt on her jeans, she had removed her torn shirt and tied it by its sleeves around her waist. Underneath her shirt she had worn, obviously in lieu of a bra, a white knit camisole top embroidered around the scooped neckline with pale flowers. It was completely opaque and perfectly appropriate as an article of clothing; Matt had seen similar ones worn in this manner numerous times before. They had never affected him like this. It didn't help his comfort level any that a light breeze was pressing the clingy top more fully against her and causing her nipples to stiffen.

Matt forced his eyes to meet hers and read the uncertainty there. He could well imagine the argument she had had with herself, faced with the choice of appearing sloppy or provocative. It was a no-win situation, although he didn't count himself the loser. He was half tempted to offer her the white shirt he had worn to church that morning and stashed in the duffel bag when he had changed his clothes. His gallantry didn't extend that far, though, and besides, he'd left the bag back in the van.

"Are you ready to eat?" Angel asked warily. The gleam in his eyes caused her to rue her choice of words. He was looking at her like she was dessert.

"I'm starved," he replied with a devilish grin. "Patrick's already down by the river." He hitched the stadium blanket he carried higher up under his arm and picked up the cooler. Angel followed his lead to a grassy area not far from the river's edge. As she helped Matt spread the blanket, she spotted Patrick, shoes and socks off and jeans rolled up to his knees, ankle-deep in the water and absorbed with some small creature there. He came running up when Matt called to him and wiped his feet on a corner of the blanket.

"Boy, that water's cold, Dad! My feet are froze."

"Frozen," Matt corrected absentmindedly. "Here you go. One peanut butter and jelly for you," he added, handing the sandwich to Patrick and shaking his head bemusedly as the youngster began to stuff his face.

Angel sincerely hoped there was something besides one peanut butter and jelly for her. Guiltily she thought she should have offered to contribute to the picnic lunch, but her hopes were raised when Matt pulled some sandwiches, wrapped in white paper with familiar red lettering on it, from the cooler.

"Cream cheese and lox on bagels!" she exclaimed, her eyes lighting up as she unwrapped the sandwich he handed her. "Are these from Bailey's?"

"Mmm-hmm," he mumbled around a bite of his own sandwich. He swallowed, and added, "I'm a passable cook when I have to be, but with just the two of us, we've gotten to be real familiar with the carryouts.''

"I know what you mean. I can't remember the last time I had two meals in a row with company," Angel responded, a note of wistfulness in her voice.

"What would you like to drink, Angel?" Matt asked, dipping into the cooler once again. "We've got soda, water, and beer."

"A soda will be fine, thanks, Matt."

He slid her a telling glance, letting her know her abstemiousness had not gone unnoticed, as he handed her the can. Taking a soda for himself, he sat cross-legged, eating and watching as his son, finished with his own sandwich, was rummaging in the cooler for whatever else it had to offer.

Patrick pulled out plastic containers of grapes and cookies, setting them on the blanket within comfortable reach of everyone. He continued to eat his fill with the easy unselfconsciousness of childhood. After a short time the quiet between the grown-ups appeared to capture his attention, and he looked around him for something to break the uneasy silence. His eyes came to rest on Angel. "That's a real pretty undershirt you got on, Angel," he observed cheerfully.

Swiftly Angel slid her knees up snugly against her chest and wrapped her arms around them, her color rapidly deepening to a cherry red. Matt had been caught in midswallow and took a long swig of his soda to stifle the fit of coughing that had erupted from him. Patrick's gaze drifted uncertainly from Angel to Matt and back again. "Can I go look for salamanders, Dad?" he asked when his father was able to breathe again.

"Go ahead. Just stay where I can see you," Matt answered. "And don't bring any over here to show Angel," he added, noting that Angel's bright pink coloring was taking on a greenish cast at the mention of crawly creatures.

On the heels of Patrick's departure, Angel's hands went to the knotted sleeves at her waist, struggling to undo them to cover herself with the shirt. Matt's hand on her wrist stayed her.

"You're fine, Angel. You don't need to do that." She looked at him doubtfully, her embarrassment almost palpable.

"He's just a little boy, Angel," Matt continued, gently stroking her arm. "He doesn't know camisole from camouflage. He didn't mean anything, really. You're fine."

Slowly Angel's hands relaxed, but she kept her knees raised and rested her chin on them as she clasped her arms loosely around her legs.

Matt stretched himself out on his back beside her, resting his head on his arms. With his eyes almost closed, he had a view of Angel's profile and, beyond her, Patrick romping in the shallow river water. The scene was tranquil, almost idyllic, but he could sense the agitation that churned in the woman.

"So tell me about yourself, Angel."

She shifted her gaze slightly, but her eyes sought Patrick instead of him, and a soft smile touched her lips. "What would you like to know?" she asked warily.

"Have you ever been married?"

"No."

So much for scintillating conversation. Clearly that was a topic she didn't care to pursue.

"I don't know much about you, actually," Angel remarked, resting the side of her head on her knees as she faced him. "How long were you married?"

"Eleven years."

"Happily?"

"Yeah," he said without hesitation. "Happily. Rosie and I had known each other since we were fourteen years old, freshmen at Our Lady of Mercy High School. Neither of us ever really dated anyone else. We got married as soon as I finished college. It was as long as I could wait." *Where the hell had that come from,* he wondered. The next thing he'd be telling her was that he'd never slept with any woman but his wife. He held out a faint hope that she hadn't caught the implication of his words.

"You mean, you were a virgin when you got married?"

So much for faint hope. He let out a long breath between his teeth. "Jeez. Yeah, I guess I was." He ran a hand over his face. Damn if he couldn't feel himself reddening. "Hell, it's not that I didn't try," he explained. "I made the usual attempts. It's just that by the time she loved me enough to let me, I loved her enough not to push." He shrugged. "Waiting was important to her, and she was important to me." He sent Angel a scathing look. "If you tell me you think it's 'sweet,' you're gonna walk home."

Angel thought it was more than sweet. She was shaken. He was so unlike any man in her experience. But she'd spare him her blandishments. What he had told her only served to underscore their differences. Her past was like a chasm between them, an abyss. What could he possibly want with her? Her thoughts translated into a question that was more blunt than she intended. "Why are you interested in me?"

Matt didn't seem offended by her candor. He studied her thoughtfully before replying. "You intrigue me," he answered finally. "Every time I see you, I find a side of you I didn't suspect was there." He shifted his gaze to Patrick, who was overturning rocks to find what wiggly treasures they concealed. "Ever since Rosie died, I haven't found a woman who could interest me. I've been numb." His eyes moved back to hers. "When I'm with you, I don't feel numb."

"How did Rosie die?" Angel asked, hesitant to explore what he did feel.

He raised himself to rest on his elbows, his eyes focused in the past. "She was pregnant," he said quietly. "Only a few months along. She hadn't had any problems with Patrick, and we never suspected anything was wrong. We were on vacation, a little cabin out on Lake Catherine. Real rustic, you know? No phone. She started to bleed. I drove like a bat out of hell to get into town, and they sent a helicopter to get her to the medical center, but it wasn't in time." In his mind he saw her again. So pale . . . so much blood. He had driven desperately, while Patrick sat solemn and round-eyed in the back seat, counting on his father to make things all right. But he had failed.

With an effort, Matt brought himself back to the present. Pushing himself up, he sat cross-legged, resting his elbows on his knees. He turned his gaze to Angel once again.

"They said the baby was located someplace where it didn't have room to grow."

Angel nodded her head. "A tubal pregnancy."

"That's not the word they used."

"Ectopic?"

"Yeah, that's it."

"That's just a pregnancy that occurs somewhere other than the uterus, Matt. One of the tubes is the most common place. Often the bleeding and sudden pain are the only symptoms that anything is wrong. There's no way you could have known. Don't blame yourself."

Matt sighed heavily. "Ever since we had Patrick," he continued, "we tried to prepare ourselves for the event that one of us would have to raise Patrick alone. Given my line of work, we just always assumed it would be her. Life's strange." He turned and gave her a quick smile. "And I still don't know anything about you," he said.

Returning his smile, Angel suddenly felt cold, wet splatters on her bare arms and face. She looked around and realized that the sky had grown overcast, the wind had picked up, and a spring squall was upon them. Matt yelled for Patrick and began stuffing the remains of their picnic back in the cooler while Angel folded the blanket. Patrick grabbed his shoes and socks and took off like a shot across the open space toward the minivan. Matt took Angel's hand and followed Patrick at a rapid clip. Still, they were pelted by heavy raindrops all the way, and by the time they reached the van, they were soaked. Panting and doubled over with laughter, Angel helped Matt stuff the equipment into the back of the van as Patrick climbed in.

Matt tried to shelter Angel from the downpour as they moved around to the passenger door. When he reached to open the door, his body pressed hers against the van. Looking down, he saw that her wet camisole had become less opaque and even more clingy. The fabric was molded to her generous breasts, and her nipples, stiffened from the chill air, were plainly outlined. Enthralled, Matt watched a fat droplet of rain trace a slow meandering pathway down Angel's throat and over the soft swell of a breast. It disappeared into the valley between them. He felt a wild urge to follow the droplet with his tongue, and he was powerless to control his body's inevitable response. With his body welded intimately against hers, his arousal became immediately apparent. Her gasp brought his gaze to her face.

The laughter was gone from her eyes, replaced with an awakened sensuality and awareness. Her breath came in soft pants, her head lolled against the side of the van and raindrops glistened on her parted lips. Matt reached to encircle her and his arms brushed her chill, damp skin. He glanced down, his eyes taking in the gooseflesh on her bare arms as he felt the shiver that coursed through her. The contact brought him back to their circumstances.

"You're cold," he said, rubbing his hands along her arms. "Let's get this shirt on you." His hands reached down to untie the knot at her waist.

"I'll get your car seat all dirty," she warned.

"Don't worry about it." He laughed, his warm fingers grazing her breasts as he pulled the shirt closed over them. "That's why they're gray." Reluctantly he let her go. "Just get in and warm up." He held the door open for her as she climbed in.

The ride back to Angel's condo was quiet, the adults wrestling with their private thoughts. Even Patrick was subdued. He waited in the van while Angel and Matt made a dash for her building.

Matt stood with Angel outside her door while she dug through her purse for her key. She felt strangely ill at ease, aware that these post-date niceties were something most girls mastered by the time they were sixteen. She never had.

"I had a lovely time, Matt." She knew her smile was artificial. She couldn't help it. He took her key from her and inserted it into the lock, letting the rest of the keys dangle there.

"So did I." He rested a forearm on the wall behind her head, looming over her. "Lovely." He repeated her word, his gaze drifting lazily over her face and form, leaving the distinct impression he was not referring only to the day. "Do you think we could do it without the chaperon next time?" he asked, a teasing note in his voice.

"Matt, I don't . . ."

"How about Friday? We could go for a pizza. Does that sound safe enough? I'll have you home early, I promise."

"Matt, we..."

He lifted her chin, tilting her face toward his, searching her eyes. He read acquiescence there, and he lowered his mouth to hers.

His kiss was warm, firm, but undemanding, and over too soon. She had never in her life known a kiss like this, one that waited for her response and left her wanting more. Her hands crept up on his chest and she felt the solid throb of his heart against her palms through the warm, damp fabric of his shirt. Matt raised his head, gauging her response, his eyes dark and heavy lidded.

"Matt, we shouldn't," she whispered.

"But we will," he murmured, and she knew he referred to more than a kiss. His mouth descended on hers again, and both were keenly aware that her lips were the first to part. His tongue probed gently into her yielding softness, tasting the sweetness she offered. She welcomed his thrusts with a sigh, her fingers clenching into his shirt, straining to get closer. Matt slid his hands under her shirt, his fingers lightly stroking over her rib cage up to the soft swell at the sides of her breasts. Angel melted against him as his thumbs played lightly over her nipples, coaxing them into tense little buds. She tore her mouth from his, desperate for breath, and burrowed her face into his chest, filling her head with his clean male scent.

Sensing her turmoil, Matt's hands became soothing, moving to her back and caressing gently. He brought one hand from under her shirt to lift her chin and placed a soft kiss on her tender mouth. His forehead pressed to hers, he rubbed her puffy bottom lip with his thumb.

"Friday," he muttered. "I'm off early. I'll pick you up at work." Then he was gone.

Still dazed, Angel entered her apartment. Oblivious to her surroundings, she passed through the living room and dining area, going directly into her bedroom. She pushed her sneakers off alongside the bed, and once again became aware of her damp clothes and general grubbiness. She slid her shirt down her arms as she headed toward the bathroom to shower, passing the mirror above her dresser on the way. Her reflection brought her to a halt. The woman who stared back at her appeared sensual, voluptuous, wanton. Her wet hair hung heavy and loose, plastered in places against her neck. Her shirt had fallen halfway down her arms and her breasts thrust forward, the nipples taut and clearly outlined. She was flushed from the heat of desire, her color deepening even as she watched. Her mouth was swollen and moist, the tender skin around it reddened from the abrasive stubble of a male beard. Angel shook an arm free from her shirt and raised a hand to cover that traitorous mouth, while her lambent eyes filled with revulsion and disgust.

She pulled off her shirt and pressed it against the mirror, attempting to block out the loathsome image, but she couldn't shut out the vile words screaming from her past.

You little slut. You whore! You're just like your mother.

She dropped the shirt and stumbled to her knees at the foot of her bed, covering her ears with her hands. Still the accusations came.

You're worthless. You're a tramp. You'll never be any good.

In the end, the hateful epithets were only stilled by the louder sound of her own harsh sobs.

Matt stared at his computer, the blinking cursor nagging at him like a disapproving scold. He had sat there for hours, loading the data from the files he had gotten from Angel, arranging and rearranging, waiting for some clue, some inconsistency, some telltale hint to leap out at him.

Nothing. *Nada.* Zero, zip, zilch. He leaned back in the chair and stretched, crackling the stiffness out of his neck. Resting his head in his hand, he rubbed his tired eyes. At a muffled sound behind him, he turned.

"Hey, sport. What are you doing up?" He slid an arm around Patrick's waist and pulled him onto his lap in an embrace that would never be permitted in public, in the light of day.

"I had to go to the bathroom, Dad." Patrick blinked sleepily at the computer screen. "When are you going to bed?"

"Soon. Are you feeling all right?" He pressed his face to his son's smooth cheek, decided the warmth there was natural after being roused from sleep, and buried his nose in the thick, clean-smelling hair above Patrick's forehead. "No bad dreams?"

"Nah." He yawned widely. "I just came to see what you were doing." He settled himself more comfortably, leaning his head back against his father's solid shoulder.

Matt savored these moments with his son. They had always been close, but had grown more so since his wife's death. It had been Patrick's desperate need of him that had gotten him through those first hellish weeks. Together they had muddled through, learning the tasks that had always been done for them, withholding criticism of those jobs imperfectly done, being there, one for the other. Sometimes, when the loss felt especially keen, they would hold each other through the long, dark hours of the night, filling their arms, though an emptiness still remained.

Patrick stirred and struggled to climb off Matt's lap. He let him go, gazing at him with understandable pride. The boy had suffered the greatest loss a child could endure, but he had seemed to come through it all right.

"I'm gonna go back to bed, Dad."

"Okay. I'll be up in a few minutes."

Rubbing his eyes, Patrick shuffled off toward the door of the den. At the opening he turned. "Dad?"

Matt trained his attention on Patrick, waiting for his words.

"I like Angel, Dad, a lot."

Matt watched his son pad quietly down the darkened hallway toward the stairs. "So do I, Patrick," he whispered. "So do I."

Angel. He pressed a key to reactivate the darkened computer screen, tapping the cursor until it reached her name.

His chin resting on his clasped hands, he stared, willing a solution to the mystery that was Angel.

He had been honest when he told her she intrigued him, but not entirely so. She roused him, disturbed him, excited him. In the past year there had been opportunities for involvement with other women, but no inclination. Now he found himself seeking, pursuing each next step with a woman who was clearly reluctant to let him get close. He was honest enough with himself to admit he was letting her affect his judgment, but he wouldn't let his interest in her jeopardize this investigation. He didn't really believe she was a willing participant in crime, yet she could be vulnerable to blackmail. His instincts told him she was hiding something, and a cop ignored his instincts at his own peril.

Matt considered his options. By rights he should report what he knew and open her record to a thorough investigation. Whatever she was trying so desperately to hide would be flashing across computer screens just like this one throughout the precinct. He flinched at that.

He would free-lance. Every successful cop had his informer, his "weasel."

Matt's was Trevor. He was a petty crook, involved in some small-time bookmaking and check kiting schemes; nothing violent, and nothing involving kids. Matt turned a blind eye to his activities occasionally, and Trevor provided Matt with some much-needed and hard-to-come-by information, sometimes. Trevor was a vast wellspring of local and not-so-local scuttlebutt. He mingled easily with the riffraff, but his snooty British accent gave him entrée to a higher level of losers and deadbeats. Matt didn't know how he acquired his information, and he was pretty sure he didn't want to know, but that he was a valuable source was undeniable. If there was any dirt to be unearthed about Angel, Trevor would dig it up.

He glanced at the wall clock above the desk. Almost two. At least he could be reasonably sure Trevor would be home.

Reaching for the phone, he punched the numbers he had committed to memory.

Chapter 5

Angel spent a week in turmoil. She was distracted at work and knew her distraction was readily apparent to her co-workers. There had been several insipid remarks about spring fever and lovesickness that she ignored but had been unable to shake. She had been determined from the start to break her date with Matt, but he hadn't tried to get in touch with her, and she found herself in an awkward position. She could name without hesitation the after-shave he wore, feel the texture of his tongue in her mouth, and describe to a hair the swirling pattern on his belly, but she still didn't know his phone number. She wasn't about to go through that little routine with the desk officer again, either. Somehow she felt their relationship had progressed beyond that.

So, here it was Friday and she had done nothing about the situation. Matt was expecting to pick her up at the end of the day, and she was still determined not to go with him.

Short of slinking away like a lily-livered coward, though, she didn't see any way to avoid meeting him. As the day wore on, the lily-livered coward route was looking mighty attractive.

She checked the day-at-a-glance calendar on her desk.

Carla Briggs was due in her office in fifteen minutes. Carla needed major moral support over the statement she had signed for the police concerning the missing bullet. Angel sighed and straightened her back. If nothing else, this should prove diverting.

"Matthew?"

"Trevor!" Matt glanced quickly around the area surrounding his desk. It was unusual for Trevor to call him at work. They both preferred to keep their contacts discreet.

"I've got some information on the woman you asked me to investigate. You sounded anxious, or I wouldn't have bothered you at work. Is this a bad time?"

"No, no. Let's hear what you've got."

"As you suspected, the lady has quite a history. In her present capacity, I can see why she'd want to cover it up."

Matt felt a sinking sensation in the pit of his stomach. "Go on," he said.

"Well, to be brief, her mother died when she was an infant. No father anywhere around. She was raised by her grandmother, who, by all accounts, kept her on a very short tether. Along came adolescence and apparently the leash broke. Anyway, our Angel went wild, more than a bit. Very popular with the young men, she was. Football players, especially. The whole team from the sounds of it. They still get this look in their eyes when one mentions her name. Very accommodating young lady. She had a specialty. Would you like to hear what it was?"

"No," Matt answered tightly, "I wouldn't."

Trevor hesitated a moment before continuing. "Well. Right. She was sixteen when she got caught. Found herself in the family way. She named a father, but he got half a dozen of his cronies to swear it could have been any one of them. Little Angel was left hanging out to dry. Granny was no help. Went bonkers from all appearances. Anyway, the baby was put up for adoption. Those records are sealed, by the by. I'll need more time if you want any of that information."

"That won't be necessary."

"I say, Matthew. You don't sound too pleased about any of this. I thought this was one of your routine little jobs. Are you involved with this girl?"

"You're telling me what I need to know, Trevor. Is there anything else?"

"Not much. The baby's birth seemed to convert the girl. One of the older nurses at the hospital where she had the baby took her under her wing. Angel stayed with her while she went through nursing school. The woman's dead now, died of cancer several years back."

"When did the grandmother die?"

"Oh, Gran's not dead. She's in a nursing home in Milton. That's where Angel's from originally. Angel pays for her care, and she visits once a year to check on her, but there's no love lost there."

"Any chance of blackmail?"

"Not likely, I wouldn't think. Granny's batty. Doesn't recognize a soul. Runs on and on about the evil that men do. That hasn't changed much, I suppose."

"No, I suppose not. Have you got anything else more recent?"

"No. Apparently Angel's been a model of rectitude since she straightened out. Couldn't find so much as a traffic ticket. Her finances check out. With that high-powered job she has, I'll wager she makes more than you do. I stayed away from the people she works with, though, just as you wished."

"What about where she lives?"

"I used the usual scam. Said she was applying for an insurance policy. I was checking out any risky behavior. She doesn't have any."

"Thanks, Trevor. You've been a big help."

"Somehow that's not the impression I get, Matthew. Anything else I can do for you?"

"Not now, Trevor. Thanks, again. I'll be in touch."

Matt replaced the receiver in its cradle, oblivious to the commotion signaling the change of shifts in the busy squad room. He stared sightlessly past the low partition that separated his "office" from the desks of the other detectives. He tried to visualize a younger Angel, just coming into womanhood, fresh and new and lovely. He pictured that loveliness coarsened and defiled in obscene couplings with raunchy, impatient, overeager louts, and was sickened by what he imagined.

Matt checked his watch. Another couple hours at least before he could pick Angel up. In all honesty, he was more than a little surprised that she hadn't tried to back out.

He'd made damn sure he didn't give her an opportunity. Still, this new information was going to make things tense. He knew he'd have to broach it with her, if only to make sure no one was putting the screws to her. He cast about for a way to defuse the situation and reached again for the phone.

"Keep your chin up, Carla. This is bound to blow over eventually." Angel passed the nurse another tissue from the container on the corner of her desk. "And it isn't just you. Everyone here has been on edge all week, having the police in and out with their questions and probing."

Carla blotted her eyes, blew her nose, sniffed, and pocketed the tissue. "I know, Angel," she said in a calmer voice. "I just feel responsible about that bullet, but misplacing it is one thing. I never imagined someone would take it deliberately. It really gives me the creeps to think that someone around here is involved."

Angel saw Carla's shudder and felt an answering frisson of fear. "I know," she said softly. "We just have to leave the investigation to the police and hope whoever did this is caught soon." She hoped her words conveyed more confidence than she felt. A week of sensing hostile eyes upon her as she worked and turning to find no one, or only persons that she trusted, had left her nerves jangled.

Her thoughts were interrupted by a sharp rap on her door. Judy Neale, the unit secretary, poked her head around the edge of the door, a look of pure delight on her round, good-natured face. "This is for you, Angel," she said, bubbling with excitement. She entered the office bearing a long, rectangular white box in her arms. "You've been holding out

on us." As Judy set the box on the desk in front of Angel,
Carla craned her neck to get a glimpse.

"Oo-oh, from Barron's," she exclaimed. "Open it up and
see who it's from!"

Angel could easily guess who it was from. The last thing
she wanted to do was open this box in front of these women,
but she couldn't see any polite way to avoid it. Gingerly she
lifted the lid, prompting further gasps of pleasure. Nestled
in white tissue paper and green ferns lay a dozen long-
stemmed red roses.

"Oh, Angel," Carla breathed, her eyes and mouth
rounded in an expression of disbelief.

"Here's the card," Judy said, reaching down among the
roses and handing it to Angel. "You don't have a vase in
here. I'll look around and see what I can find to put these
in." She bustled out, headed for the utility room.

Angel sat in stunned silence, oblivious to Carla's continued ramblings. Another first, she thought. She had never
received flowers from a man. He had taken her to church.
He had shown her what a kiss was meant to be. And now
this. She, who had thought to experience nothing new with
a man, had been proven very wrong. Gently she caressed a
crimson bud, inhaling its heady scent. Remembering the
card, she glanced down at the message in her hand. *I'll see
you at five. Matt* the note read simply. Well. It seemed that
he would.

Judy returned carrying a plastic jug used to provide water for patients at the bedside. "This is the best I could do,
Angel. I'm afraid we'll have to cut the stems some."

Angel took her bandage scissors from the pocket of the
lab coat she had worn over her civvies and began to trim the
flowers, helping Judy to arrange them in the makeshift vase.

Left to her own devices, Carla could no longer contain her
curiosity and stole a glance at the card Angel had placed on
the desk. "Who's Matt, Angel?" she asked. "Oo-oh, the
lieutenant, the tall, good-looking one with the wedding..." She clapped a hand over her mouth, her eyes widening further at the words she had blurted out.

"He's widowed," Angel responded testily. "Over a year
now."

"So it is him," Judy interjected teasingly. "And you didn't tell us. For shame, Angel."

"This isn't what it seems," Angel said, struggling to maintain her composure. "I've merely been helping him out with the investigation and he's grateful." The bland looks the two women gave Angel told her just how effective her words had been in quashing their suspicions. Not that the roses wafting their intoxicating fragrance around the room added anything to her credibility. "All right, you two," she said, laughing in good-natured defeat. "I've seen him a time or two, but don't go building this into more than it is."

"Well," Judy answered, her face relaxing into its characteristic grin, "it's going on five now. We'd better clear out of here and give you a chance to finish up."

"Thanks for your time, Angel," Carla said, rising from her chair. Patting Angel's hand, she added, "Anytime you get tired of this guy, send him over to me. I'll be real happy to help him with his investigations." The two women left the office giggling, leaving the door open behind them.

Angel sank back in her chair and sighed ruefully. Despite having a skeleton crew on for the coming weekend, she didn't doubt that by Monday every person in the department would be aware of her budding relationship with Matt. Carla and Judy were sweet, hardworking, and loyal. Circumspect they were not. For once, she would be glad to be somewhere else for the next couple of days.

Clearing off her desk, she prepared to leave for the day. She flicked the intercom switch to let the front desk personnel know she was leaving. Judy's voice came back over the line. "Have a good time tonight, Angel. Your date's on his way around to your office now." As if to make good her words, Matt emerged from the hallway through the still open office door. Judy continued in a voice that could etch glass, "Watch out for his 'nightstick.'"

Only the flickering amusement in Matt's green eyes gave any indication that he had heard Judy's remark. Angel chose to ignore it completely. She rose and smiled a weak greeting to Matt as she slipped off her lab coat and hung it on the hook on the back of her door. Moving alongside her,

Matt pushed the door shut, gently pulled her into his arms, and covered her mouth in a soft kiss.

"That's better," he murmured, lifting his head. He cocked an eye toward her desk. "I see the roses got here before I did."

"Yes," Angel answered. She turned her head to look at them and rested her cheek against his chest. "They're beautiful." The steady beat of his heart was a metronome that calmed her own agitated rhythm. Lifting her head, she smiled up at him. "They've caused quite a stir around here. We're going to be the second major topic of conversation for a while."

Her words seemed to cause a change in Matt. He straightened, moved away from Angel, and rubbed a hand across his forehead. "Are you about ready to leave?" he asked abruptly, turning back to face her.

"Yes. Just let me get my handbag." She rounded her desk and retrieved her purse from its bottom drawer. As she slipped the strap over her shoulder, she shoved the drawer closed with her foot. Matt watched her thoughtfully.

"Don't you keep anything locked around here?" he asked.

Angel glanced at him, surprised. "Not usually, no.

"Well, just the file cabinet. I keep confidential evaluations in there."

"And where do you keep the key?"

"Where I keep my other keys. In my purse." She was beginning to be irritated by the criticism in his tone.

"Which is in your unlocked desk, in your unlocked office," he finished.

Angel let out a huff of exasperation. "Matt, we don't have any problem with stealing. I'm not always in the department, and I'm seldom in my office. There are schedules and forms in here that people need access to."

"Angel, wake up!" he growled, his temper and voice both barely under control. "You have a problem with murder here. You have a problem with drugs. This guy can come and go here at will, no questions asked. If he has access to your keys, he has access to your car and to your home. And now it's common knowledge that you're seeing me." He turned his back to her and stood, head bent, hands on his hips. "Jeez, I could be putting you at risk."

A chill pierced Angel at his words. "I never considered that, Matt," she said. She stood silently, her eyes moving over the broad shoulders and dark head. How had he come to be so important to her? When had his company become necessary for her happiness? She forced the next words out. "Maybe we shouldn't see each other for now."

He spun and reached for her, pulling her into his arms. His mouth came down on hers in crushing possession. His kiss had none of the gentleness of before, but asserted his claim to her in the most elemental way possible. His tongue seared her lips, demanding an entry and a response she wouldn't deny him. He lifted his head and, holding her gaze with the intensity of his own, uttered the promise his kiss had already sealed. "I'll take care of you. Nothing and nobody is going to hurt you." He pressed a quicker, softer kiss to her lips. "Let's go."

The problem of two cars became immediately apparent when they stepped outside the hospital. Matt's van was in the short-term lot alongside the emergency room entrance, while Angel had parked her car in the massive garage that most of the employees used. Angel insisted on following him in her own vehicle and Matt agreed, unwilling to argue over such a small point knowing what lay ahead. He waited in his van while Angel went to retrieve her car.

In the cool, shadowed stillness of the garage, Angel reached into her purse for her keys. The handbag had two outside pockets on the front. She kept her keys in one, her sunglasses in the other. The pocket for her keys was empty. With her pulse beating a staccato rhythm, she groped in the other pocket. There they were, behind the glasses. Trembling, she opened the car door and slid behind the steering wheel. Matt's words raced through her mind. *If he has access to your keys, he has access to your car and to your home.*

"He's making you a nervous wreck," she muttered to herself. She took a deep, steadying breath. "You put them in the wrong pocket yourself. You've done it before. It's nothing. Get a grip!'' Still, it was several minutes before she could stop shaking and start the car.

The restaurant seemed more a neighborhood bar than anything else, Angel noted as they entered the dim interior. They had to watch their steps as they followed the host past the long, polished mahogany bar to a small dining room toward the back. Most of the lighting was provided by vigil candles sunken into red cut-glass holders that were centered on each table. There was a lot of dark wood in evidence, bare floors, paneled walls, and scarred tables that had never known the refinement of a tablecloth. Fake ferns, hanging in tarnished brass pots at intervals throughout the place, looked like they had been there since the parting of the Red Sea. Angel thought the spot might even be considered trendy, though less from any attempt on its part than the fact that trends had caught up with its peculiar blend of the garish and genteel. Looking around her she noticed the diners were a mix of young professionals, factory and construction workers, and older couples out for a night on the town. They appeared more interested in the quality of the food than the style of the decor. Attire was casual. Angel's oversized peach sweater and tan slacks were fine. Matt, in a suit and tie, was definitely overdressed.

Matt removed his coat and tie before sliding into one side of the red-vinyl booth tucked away in a quiet corner. Rolling up the sleeves of his shirt, he ordered a pitcher of beer from the hovering waiter. He arched a brow at Angel in anticipation of her objection and favored her with a raffish grin when she made none.

''I've never been here before, but the guys in the squad room recommended it highly. Cops know the best places to eat.''

''And here I thought it was nurses.'' Angel laughed.

The waiter returned with their beer and two large mugs.

''What don't you like on your pizza?'' Matt asked as he filled their glasses.

''Anchovies and olives.''

"We'll have a large Chicago-style, with everything but anchovies and olives," Matt told the young man who nodded and left them alone once more.

An uneasy silence arose between them. Angel watched as Matt took a long swallow of his beer. He set his mug down, seemingly engrossed in the interlocking pattern of circles made on the lacquered tabletop by its wet bottom. He took another deep swig and fidgeted with the mug, his eyes darting around the room, lighting on everything, Angel noticed, but her.

"How did..."

"Angel, I..."

They both laughed self-consciously. "Go ahead," Matt said. "What were you going to say?" He wiped a hand across his mouth and shifted on the vinyl bench. Again he seemed uncomfortable meeting her gaze. Angel sank back into the padded seat. This was more than the awkwardness of a first real date. Matt appeared almost painfully uneasy, anguished. He looked...guilty.

"What is it, Matt?" she asked, perplexed.

His eyes flickered to hers again, then down. "I did some checking..." he began.

Angel straightened, suddenly unmistakably aware of the reason for his discomfort. She looked at the long fingers tapping out a nervous rhythm on the table, the troubled eyes averted from hers. "You know," she breathed.

His jaded eyes fastened to her panicked ones, erasing her last doubt. Grabbing her purse, she rose and began to edge from the booth just as the waiter returned with an armload of pizza. His stunned expression flashed across her line of vision as she felt Matt's hand clamp, viselike, around her wrist. Out of the corner of her eye she spied the man who had seated them approaching rapidly.

"Sir, what seems to be the problem here? If the young lady..." His words came to a halt as Matt reached into his hip pocket, pulled out a leather wallet and flipped it open to reveal his detective's shield and police ID.

"No problem," Matt answered calmly. "This is a police matter. I just want to ask the 'young lady' a few questions. We can talk here," he went on, addressing himself to Angel, "or at the station house. Your choice. Either way, we're gonna talk."

Angel slid a glance to her rescuer who was already retreating, his palms raised in supplication and a plea for restraint in his eyes. Their waiter shoved the pizza onto the table and he, too, beat a hasty retreat. Around them the background buzz of conversation had given way to utter silence.

Defeated, Angel wrested her arm from Matt's grip and slumped back down into the booth. You bastard, she mouthed silently, seething.

"You've got the words, Angel, but not the music. I've heard them before. It doesn't change anything. We're gonna talk."

"So talk," she answered sullenly, rubbing her wrist.

Matt raised his eyes heavenward and let out a loud sigh. "Angel, I'm a cop!" he stated. "I had to know. Better men than me have been led straight to hell by a pretty face. I knew you were hiding something. I couldn't take a chance."

"I don't suppose it occurred to you to ask me?" she snapped, her anger keeping desperation at bay.

"I did ask you. More than once. You weren't exactly forthcoming."

It was Angel's turn to avert her eyes. Her innate sense of fairness demanded she concede Matt's point, but she clung to her anger like a drowning man would a life preserver. "This must be a juicy topic of conversation around the squad room. Is it causing problems for you?" she asked icily.

"No, and no." He paused. "I didn't go through regular channels." Matt shifted uneasily as Angel turned puzzled eyes to his. "I had someone outside the department look into your past. A guy I've used before. An informer." At the expression of stunned disbelief on her face, he rushed on. "It won't go any further than him, I swear. I trust him."

Angel struggled to find her voice, hurt, anger and humiliation warring within her. "You hired some goon to investigate me?" she sputtered. "Am I supposed to feel reassured that some lowlife scum knows all about me? Very nice company you keep, Lieutenant Flanagan," she said caustically, adding in a voice full of self-loathing, "I had a specialty. Did he tell you all about that?"

"No! Dammit, Angel, be reasonable," he growled, keeping his voice low with an obvious effort. "I do hang out with scum. It's part of my job. I'm a cop. We don't hobnob with the elite. Trevor's reliable, so I use him. I'd associate with a lot worse if it'd help me find Marty's killer."

The mention of the dead policeman deflated her anger, leaving only the humiliation and hurt. She pressed her hands into tight fists on the table in front of her. "You can't honestly believe I had anything to do with that, can you?" she asked, her voice barely audible.

"I don't think you would willingly hurt anyone, Angel. But you might be blackmailed."

"Oh, Matt," she whispered. He watched her bring her tented hands to cover her mouth, her eyes wide and haunted with pain above them.

"Are you, Angel? Being blackmailed?" he pressed. "Does someone else know about your past?"

"No. No one knows."

Matt released the breath he hadn't realized he was holding and felt a wash of relief flood through him. He believed her. He saw Angel lift her mug to take a drink, but she was shaking so badly, even with two hands she couldn't manage it. He looked away, her agony too painful to watch.

Angel set the mug back down on the table and focused her eyes, unseeing, on it. "I had a son," she said quietly. "I'm sure you're familiar with the circumstances. He's almost eleven, now. A little older than Patrick." At the mention of his son's name, Matt's gaze swung back to her. She bit down hard on her lower lip to still its trembling. He reached across the table and gripped her slender fingers as if to transfer some of his steadiness to her. At his touch she raised her eyes to his. "I don't remember ever loving anyone before him, Matt, but I did love him. And the best I could do for him was give him up." Her fingers tightened around his. "I swore I would never, never be in that situation again."

"Is there any chance that you might find him again?" Matt asked gently.

Angel sighed and took a sip of her beer. This time her
hand was steadier. "I signed a waiver of confidentiality and
listed with the International Soundex Reunion Registry,"
she replied. "If, when he comes of age, he wants to find me,
there'll be nothing standing in his way. But I wish him such
a happy life that he never feels the need," she added softly.

Matt reflected on his years with Patrick and wondered if
he would have been able to make a similar statement. He
remembered her encounters with children and was certain
she was aware of exactly what she had missed. He felt like a
heel digging deeper, but there were still some questions he
needed answers for. "Why did you lie to me about your
grandmother?" he probed gently.

Matt was pleased to see the familiar defiance gather in her
eyes as she answered him. "My grandmother never wanted
me, but her misplaced sense of what was proper wouldn't
allow her to abandon a child. She always told me I'd end up
just like my mother, so, naturally, I did. When I worked up
the courage to tell her I was pregnant, she washed her hands
of me. Said I'd gotten into the mess and I'd have to take care
of things myself." She paused, remembering. "I knew what
she meant, of course, but an abortion was just not possible
for me." She looked at Matt steadily. "She told me I was
dead to her. I never lied to you when I said I had no family."

Matt lifted her hand in both of his, pressed it to his lips,
and waited. Reassured by his calm acceptance, Angel went
on. "I entered a county home for unwed mothers. They still
had those then, and I finished high school there. When I was
in the hospital, I met an older woman, a nurse who worked
the night shift. She helped me see that no one would ever
think I was worth anything unless I first thought so myself."

Matt nodded. "You lived with her while you got your
degree in nursing."

"Yes. In spite of everything, I'd always done well in
school. I was able to get a scholarship and worked part-time,
but she gave me a place to stay. Martha wasn't warm, but
she was kind, and she didn't judge. I'll always be grateful for
the help she gave me."

Angel was surprised at how easily the words came once she started to tell her story. Still the knowledge that he was privy to her shameful behavior stung, and she tore her gaze from his.

As if reading her mind, Matt grasped her chin and forced her eyes back to his. "Angel," he said firmly, "you were raped. You were abused."

Astonished at his words, her eyes widened and her mouth fell open. "How can you say that?" she demanded. "There was never any force. They never did anything I didn't let them do."

"How old were you when this started? Fourteen? There was no way you were old enough to give consent. You were after affection, attention. There's no way you could have known what you were getting into." He took her hand again and would not heed the denial in her eyes. "Was sex something you wanted? Something you sought? Was there any pleasure in it?" The shudder that shook her was more than answer enough.

Matt went on in a softer tone, his callused thumb rubbing gently over her knuckles. "There are cops who think the laws against statutory rape shouldn't be on the books, but I don't happen to be one of them. Those guys were predators, out for what they could get, not caring what kind of damage they might do." He paused. "Not all guys are like that, Angel. Not even at eighteen." She was quiet now, he noted, seeming to digest his words. "If there's any justice," he continued, "they all have daughters now."

That prompted a weak smile, the first bit of humor she'd ever found in the whole sorry mess. She saw an apt irony in the image of them trying to protect their precious daughters from men exactly like themselves. "I'd never considered it that way before," she admitted.

"You would have," Matt asserted, "if it had been somebody else. You just hold yourself to a higher standard." He squeezed her hand gently. "Our pizza's getting cold."

Angel's smile broadened as she watched Matt scoop up a thick slice and struggle with the dangling strands of gooey cheese. Looking from the drippy pizza to his pristine white shirt, he shrugged, picked up a huge, checkered napkin, tucked it into his collar and spread it over his shirtfront. Angel laughed out loud at that and helped herself to a slice of pizza. They munched for a time in companionable silence.

Seeming intent on her meal, Angel eyed Matt covertly, thinking over what he had said. She tried to picture him at eighteen, already in love with the girl he would marry, cherishing her, putting her wishes ahead of his own desires. She wondered when he had joined the police force. He said he had finished college, although that wasn't so unusual these days. She sat back in the booth, sipping her beer and staring openly.

Her scrutiny did not go unnoticed. Sensing her eyes on him, Matt refilled her mug, then his own. The glimmer of a smile in her eyes made him wonder if he had pizza on his chin. He wiped his mouth with his napkin, but that only seemed to deepen her amusement. Finally he tossed the cloth onto the table and met her gaze directly.

"What?" he asked, his own lips quirking into a smile.

"Nothing, really." Angel laughed. "I'm just trying to picture you in a patrolman's uniform." To her surprise, he looked uneasy again.

"I didn't exactly come up through the ranks," he answered. He took a long pull on his beer and cleared his throat. "I was never a patrolman."

Intrigued, Angel leaned forward, crossing her arms and resting her elbows on the table. "Oh, really," she murmured. "Did you have connections?"

Matt mimicked Angel's position across the table from her. "Only indirectly," he answered. "I'm a lawyer." As her eyebrows raised inquiringly, he went on. "After law school I worked for the D.A.'s office in Pittsburgh for a couple of years. I got sick of seeing the sleazes get off on technicalities—irregular arrests, mishandled evidence, that kind of thing." At Angel's nod, he continued. "My undergraduate degree was in criminal justice, so I had a pretty fair understanding of police work. It wasn't much of a stretch. I joined the force with the intention of providing expert advice on the legal aspects surrounding an arrest and the gathering of evidence. When Rosie di . . ." He paused. "When I decided to move here, the department seemed interested in starting something along the same lines. This town's problems with crime are similar, just not to the same degree as the city." He sighed. "I think I've done some good. We're building tighter cases. But I don't have any illusions. It's a finger in the dike, and we need to rebuild the whole dam."

Angel felt a surge of admiration for him. She knew his monetary compensation must be considerably less than he could make as a lawyer. Still, he seemed content with his choice. "It must be very different from what you thought your life would be at this point," she said.

"Well," he answered with a shrug and a disarming smile, "I had to learn how to shoot. Would you like some coffee? I hear this place is famous for its cheesecake."

"Oh, I can't resist that," Angel replied with a smile. "You're learning all my weaknesses."

With an answering grin, Matt motioned for the waiter, who had been avoiding their table like the plague. He took their order, keeping his eyes scrupulously averted from the hands that had joined on the tabletop, the larger masculine one gently stroking.

When the waiter had returned with the coffee and cake and left them alone again, Angel broached the subject that had been on her mind. "Have you got any leads on the murder yet?"

Matt shook his head disgustedly. "Nothing. At least, nothing that makes one person stand out more than any other."

"You haven't come up with a motive?"

"Motive will be easy," Matt replied with a humorless chuckle. "It'll be money or love, love or money. I keep waiting for someone to surprise me, but it won't happen. It's always the same. The drug angle adds a few new twists, but in the end it'll be the same. Love or money."

Angel seemed to reflect on his words for a few moments, rubbing her fingers between her brows. "Do you have a cause of death from the autopsy report?" she asked.

Matt reached for his suit coat and dug in the inside pocket, retrieving his notebook. He frowned, turning the pages rapidly until he found what he wanted. "Cerebral hypoxia." He raised his eyes to hers.

"Mmm," Angel murmured, her lips compressed into a thin line.

"What's that mean?" Matt asked, watching her closely.

"Nothing much, I'm afraid. It's like saying he died of a fever. Cerebral hypoxia just means insufficient oxygen to the brain. It can occur for a number of reasons. Respiratory arrest, drugs, massive blood loss will cause it. It doesn't tell you the underlying cause."

Matt sat with his chin in his hand, his thumb rubbing over his jaw, eyeing her steadily. "What do you suspect?" he probed.

Immediately her defenses came up. "This isn't my area at all, Matt. I really shouldn't speculate . . ."

"I'm asking you to, Angel. Off the record. Something's nagging at you. What is it?"

She dropped her eyes and her resistance. "It was something you said in my office . . . the day all of this happened. About motive and opportunity." She hesitated.

"Go on," Matt said. "What about it?"

"You haven't been able to single out anyone with a motive. Maybe you should look at opportunity."

"What do you mean?"

Angel squirmed, reluctant to continue. She raised her eyes to Matt's and caught him staring intently; alert, wary, every inch the watchful cop. She took a deep breath. "I think you should look at Anesthesia. Not anyone in particular. There were several people involved in this case."

Matt continued to stare, waiting. He wasn't going to make this easy for her. She straightened her shoulders with resolve and went on in a rush. "Anesthesia is responsible for oxygenating the patient. They'd be the first to be aware of problems along those lines. It wouldn't take much to wait just a little too long to act to correct it. Then, too, they're the experts on drugs. They would know what could have a lethal effect and still be metabolized enough to leave little trace."

While she spoke, Matt had turned back several pages in his notebook. He took a pen from his shirt pocket and drew a box around a number of names. "I've got three people associated with Anesthesia listed here. Is that right?"

"Who are they?"

"Faith Nichols."

Angel nodded. "She's a nurse anesthetist. She's been with us about six months. Going through a very messy divorce. She had to go back to work, I understand, in order to support herself."

"So there's money," Matt replied, scrawling a check next to her name. "What about George Albert?"

"He's an anesthesiologist, the M.D. assigned to the case. He's been with the hospital for years. Long before I started. He's very competent as far as I can tell. A little standoffish. I don't know him very well. He's as rich as Croesus. I can't imagine love or money being a motive for him."

Matt grinned at that. "I take it you don't find him personally attractive?"

Angel shrugged. "He's old enough to be my father, for one thing."

"That doesn't mean anything. Didn't you say there were rumors about him having an affair—"

"With one of the switchboard operators," she finished for him. "You have quite a memory." She shrugged again. "There's no accounting for taste, I guess."

Matt laughed, but Angel noticed Dr. Albert also merited a check mark next to his name.

"That leaves Tony Levering," Matt said, tapping his pen next to the last name on his short list.

A frown marred Angel's lovely face. "Tony's a resident in anesthesia. He's got a couple more months to go before he's finished. He has a wife and two little kids. Nice guy. He hasn't developed the 'attitude' yet."

"Speaking of attitude..." Matt remarked, ruffling back a few pages. "Yeah, here it is. Gary Chapman completed a residency in anesthesia, didn't he?"

"Yes," Angel stated flatly, "he did. I don't think anesthesia was glamorous enough for him. Trauma medicine has more cachet."

Matt leaned back in the booth, his grin acknowledging the mild criticism in Angel's comment. "He told me he was

limited to the emergency room, though. He wouldn't have
had anything to do with anesthesia.'' Matt's grin slowly
disappeared as he became aware of the wary hesitation in
Angel's eyes. ''Would he?'' he added.

Angel expelled her breath on a long sigh and toyed with
her coffee cup. ''He came into the room at one point to see
how the man was doing,'' she said finally. ''That's not unusual. The doctors really are concerned about the patients,
despite how it sometimes seems. Anyway, he came in right
around the time the patient really started to go downhill.''

''Was he involved in the care at all?''

''Apparently so.'' She held up a staying hand as Matt
started to speak. ''That's not so unusual, either. Everyone
knows his background. When you're running four units of
blood at a time, and God knows what else, you need all the
hands you can get.''

Angel watched, troubled, as Matt added Chapman's
name to the list he had circled, adorning it with a large
check. ''You don't like Gary much, do you?'' she asked.

''What's to like?'' he replied with a snort, shaking his
head in disdain and pocketing his pen and notebook.

''Isn't it possible your animosity could color your judgment?''

''I'll keep it in mind,'' Matt answered. Mischief lit his
eyes until he became aware of the uncertainty clouding hers.
''What's really bothering you, Angel?''

''I was in there, too... before the policeman died. I was
in that operating room.''

He really was amazing, she thought. She could swear he
hadn't moved a muscle, but it was as if he had put miles between them. His eyes became distant, unreadable.

''What for?'' he asked carefully. ''Your name's not on the
surgical record.''

So he'd checked. She looked down and fidgeted with her
fork, then raised her eyes to his again. ''It was just an errand, really. There's a substance in transfused blood that
keeps it from clotting in the bag. When a patient receives
massive amounts of blood, as this one did, calcium is given
to counteract that effect. I brought the medication into the
room.''

Matt planted a fist against his mouth and eyed her steadily. "How is calcium given?" he asked finally.

"Intravenously."

"Did you give it?"

"No," she answered with a quick shake of her head. "I laid it on the anesthesia cart. I don't know who administered it. It would say in the anesthesia record."

"I'll check."

She returned his gaze with a level one of her own. She knew he would.

He reached across the table and tipped her chin up. "Don't keep secrets, Angel," he warned. Then his expression softened. "Are you ready to blow this place?"

Angel nodded and Matt motioned for the check. As they waited for the waiter to return with change, Matt said, "I'm finished with those files you gave me. I can give them to you now if you want to stop by the house. It's close. Then I'll follow you home." At her look of skepticism he laughed. "No ulterior motives, I swear," he said with his hands raised. "I'm due in at the station at four-thirty tomorrow morning."

"Four-thirty!" she exclaimed, bug-eyed. "What on earth do you have to be there at that time for?"

He put a finger to his lips in mock secrecy. "We've got a big drug bust coming down," he said in a stage whisper. "The captain wants all hands on deck."

"But why four-thirty?"

"Because the drug dealers, like any sensible people, will be home in bed. The better to catch them all, m'dear," he said, wriggling his eyebrows in an exaggerated leer. "Really. I'll give you the files and then see you home."

It was impossible to suspect him of hidden intentions, Angel decided, laughing. "All right," she agreed.

Chapter 6

Matt did live only minutes away from the restaurant, Angel noted, in an older, comfortable neighborhood of large Colonial-style houses on wide, tree-lined streets. His home was a cedar-shingled dwelling, quite large, but inviting and unintimidating. An expansive front porch spread across the whole front of the house like a broad smile while two curtained dormer windows beamed over the low porch roof like a pair of kindly attentive eyes.

Matt waited for Angel under a towering pine on the front lawn as she pulled her car up behind his, the tires crunching on the gravel stone driveway. It was a little past twilight, not quite full dark, but visibility was low and Matt caught her hand to lead her across the grass, tall and luxuriant from the recent spring rains. "Watch out for booby traps," he teased, stooping to pick up a skateboard that had been abandoned at the bottom of the wide porch steps. He leaned it against a wooden crate, overflowing with other accoutrements of young boyhood, on the porch. He unlocked the front door and reached in to flick a switch and flood the entryway with light before ushering her into the house.

Angel felt a wave of welcome engulf her as she entered Matt's home. It was a sturdy older dwelling with gleaming hardwood floors and wide wooden moldings around the doorways and windows. Through an archway leading from the foyer to the living room Angel caught a glimpse of red-brick fireplace, a large copper tub containing firewood on the raised hearth. The room was furnished with cozy upholstered pieces and was comfortably cluttered, but appeared surprisingly neat for two males living alone.

Taking note of her appraisal, Matt remarked, "I have a lady come in once a week to do some general cleaning and straightening up, but," he added with a smug grin, "I handle the cooking and laundry myself. Make yourself comfortable." He gestured toward the living room. "I have to use the phone, and then I'll get those files for you."

"Where's Patrick?" Angel asked, mindful of the absence of a baby-sitter as she walked into the living room and took a chair near the hearth.

"He's spending the night with my sister, Connie," Matt called out to her as he placed his call from the phone in the foyer. "She lives less than a mile from here, but it'll save getting him up in the middle of the night when I have to go in tomorrow."

Hearing Matt respond to someone on the other end of the line, Angel turned her attention to the bookshelves built into an alcove alongside the fireplace. She wasn't surprised by the heavy bias toward volumes on law and criminal justice.

Matt's recreational reading seemed to lean toward nonfiction and the classics, but the smattering of Hardy Boys rubbing shoulders with Thomas Hardy brought a smile to her lips.

Despite her efforts to direct her attention elsewhere, one-sided fragments of the phone conversation drifted Angel's way.

"Yeah. Yeah. I want the tap on his phone started this weekend. Nah, just him. We don't have enough probable cause to do anything with the others. See if you can get the judge to sign the order tomorrow... I know it's Saturday! O'Malley plays golf every Saturday. You'll know where to find him."

Angel smiled at Matt's rising indignation. She didn't find his temper nearly so threatening since she'd gotten to know him better. Since she'd also learned the depth of his sensitivity. Still, she was just as glad his wrath wasn't directed at her.

She rose and went to stand by the front window, trying to put more distance between herself and the conversation in the hallway. She held the sheer curtain aside with one hand and looked out upon the tranquil evening. An elderly couple, out for their daily constitutional, strolled haltingly down the other side of the street, holding hands. A youngster of about twelve peddled his bike slowly in the opposite direction, while a well-fed cocker spaniel, trotting along behind on a leash, did his stout-hearted best to keep up. It was a Norman Rockwell picture of safety and security, a haven for a man who dealt with murder as a matter of course.

Angel's attention was caught momentarily by a flutter of motion at an upstairs window across the street. She narrowed her eyes but couldn't make out anything in the deepening gloom.

Matt's voice rose again, and further snatches of his conversation reached Angel's ears.

"So what if his place is secure? What the hell do those guys think they get paid for? If it was easy, I could send Patrick to do it!" There was a long pause as Matt paced impatiently. "Yeah. Right. Well, let me know either way." Angel heard the receiver slam down. "I've got a message on my machine, Angel. I'll be with you in a sec," Matt called out to her.

The sound of the message being played back was garbled, but it was a woman's voice, and Angel was certain she heard Patrick's name mentioned. In spite of herself, her attention was riveted. She thought she heard a muffled curse as Matt punched the buttons on the phone.

"Yeah, Connie. It's me. What's the problem with Patrick? He's got what? Are you sure? Ben's driving him over here? Jeez, Con, nothing like giving the kid the bum's rush!" Matt gave a heavy sigh. "Yeah, I understand. No, I don't know what I'm gonna do. I'll work something out. Yeah. Bye.''

Angel heard the receiver click, and moments later Matt walked into the room, frustration written all over his face. He leaned dejectedly against one side of the archway and rubbed a hand over the back of his neck. ''Patrick has chicken pox,'' he said.

Angel raised a hand to stifle the smile that arose unbidden at the glum picture he made. She doubted he'd see any humor in his predicament. ''I'm a little surprised he hasn't had them before this,'' she said when she was sure she could do so without laughing.

''Oh, we've had notices before that he's been exposed at school, but he's never come down with them. I guess he just had to wait for the most opportune time,'' he added with a touch of gallows humor. ''Anyway, my brother-in-law is on his way here with Patrick, now. Connie couldn't wait to get him out of the house once she knew I was home. Can't say that I blame her,'' he continued, moving away from the doorway and into the room. ''Her kids are five and two, and neither of them has had chicken pox.''

Angel did laugh at that. ''I'm sorry, Matt,'' she said, clapping a hand over her mouth, while her eyes twinkled. ''It's just that I'm afraid she's closing the barn door after the horses are out. Patrick was contagious for a good twenty-four hours before he showed any symptoms.''

Matt's own eyes gleamed with amusement then. ''You'll forgive me if I don't give Ben that good news when he gets here,'' he said with a chuckle. He sobered quickly, however, when he remembered his own situation. ''I'm in a hell of a fix for tomorrow,'' he muttered, rubbing a hand over his jaw.

''I could help you out, Matt,'' Angel said quietly.

Startled, Matt's eyes flew to hers. ''How do you mean?'' he asked cautiously.

''I could watch Patrick for you,'' she answered with a little shrug. ''I've got the two major qualifications. Number one, I don't have any special plans for tomorrow.''

''And,'' Matt prodded.

''I've had chicken pox.''

Matt laughed, but shook his head. "I couldn't ask..." he began.

"You didn't ask," Angel countered. "I volunteered. Of course, I understand if you would prefer to get someone else."

At first Matt didn't grasp what she meant. As he took in her stricken face, her meaning dawned on him. She thought she wasn't fit to watch his son. Her self-esteem was so fragile, she would see his reluctance to impose on her as a personal rejection. "Angel," he said slowly, "I can't imagine anyone better suited to watch Patrick."

Relieved, Angel smiled at him. "It's settled then. What time would you like me to get here?"

Before Matt had a chance to reply, the doorbell chimed and he left to answer it. Angel heard a few mumbled words of regret and then sounds of a hasty departure. Moments later Matt and Patrick shambled into the room, Matt's hand gently ruffling Patrick's hair. Patrick looked tired and wan, with the characteristic red splotches dotting his face, but he managed a feeble greeting for Angel. He brightened visibly when told that Angel would be looking after him the next day, but turned sulky when ordered right to bed.

"Aw, Dad, can't I watch *Home Alone?* I'm not sleepy and I promise I'll go right to bed as soon as it's over."

Matt sent Angel a look of exasperation over the top of Patrick's head. "Tell you what, Sport," he bargained. "You get ready for bed, and I'll open up the sleeper sofa in the den. You can bunk down in there, and then if you fall asleep, I won't have to wake you up to go to bed."

Angel helped Matt get Patrick situated in the den, spreading sheets on the sleeper sofa, while Matt filled her in on such essentials of child care as the location of the pediatrician's phone number and the peanut butter. With Patrick cozily ensconced, Matt led Angel back to the living room, carrying with him the hospital files she had come for.

"Why don't you stay?" he asked suddenly.

"'Stay'?" Angel repeated blankly.

"Yeah. Like in overnight."

"I couldn't do that!"

"Why not? Angel, you've got to be back here at four in the a. m.," Matt argued reasonably. "Now if it's Old Lady Carruthers you're worried about—" he moved to the front window and peered out into the gathering darkness "—the curtain she peeks from behind is already closed for the night and your car is still in my driveway." He shrugged. "No hope of redeeming yourself in her eyes, I'm afraid. Besides," he said, turning back to her, "she worries about me. I think she'd be tickled."

"Well, I'm not tickled!" Angel retorted.

"Aw, Angel, come on," Matt coaxed. He eased toward her, dumping the folders on the coffee table. "I'd be the first to admit to having designs on you." He took her hands and pulled her toward him. "But not tonight. You've got nothing to worry about. I plan to be in bed in a very short time. Alone."

"I don't know, Matt," she answered, gazing up at him, her eyes narrowed skeptically.

"Look," he went on, "we've got a spare bedroom. I have an extra toothbrush, still in the package it came in, and you can use my deodorant, if you don't mind sharing. It's unscented, so you won't smell like a guy." He laced his fingers with hers, pulling her nearer still.

"I have a toothbrush and deodorant in my purse," Angel said. She bit her lip in indecision. At his raised eyebrows she added quickly, "I never know when I might pull an all-nighter at the hospital. I'd need something to sleep in, though," she went on, her resolve weakening.

"Mmm. I haven't slept in pajamas since I outgrew the kind with feet, and I know you wouldn't care for my first choice." Matt grinned lecherously at her "get real" look. "I'm sure I could come up with something you'd find suitable, though."

Angel gazed at him steadily, mulling over her options. It was getting late, and it did seem ridiculous to drive all the way home only to return at the ungodly hour he had mentioned. Besides, she didn't really think he would try anything against her will. *Ah. Therein lies the catch,* the niggling voice of conscience whispered, but she mentally swatted it away like a troublesome bug. "All right," she said guardedly. "You've convinced me. I'll stay."

"Great!" He gave her hands a quick squeeze. She winced and he was immediately contrite. "I'm sorry, Angel. I didn't mean to hurt you," he said, releasing her hands.

"It was your ring." She rubbed her injured finger. "I just got pinched between that and bone."

Matt looked down at the wide band and gave a heavy sigh. "I tried to get it off again this week," he confessed, "but I wasn't able to. Not even with butter or Vaseline. This finger's been jammed a few times playing baseball since the ring went on," he added. "It's not exactly in pristine condition."

Angel frowned, taking his hand and examining the finger closely. "Have you tried dishwashing liquid?" she asked.

Matt gave her a doubtful look. "Well, these hands are familiar with soapsuds, but I haven't tried the soap straight, no."

"Come with me," Angel said. She gave him a provocative smile.

Bemused, Matt followed her into the adjoining kitchen. He got the dish soap out from the cabinet under the sink, and warily handed her the plastic bottle.

"Have a seat," Angel ordered. She motioned toward one of the captain's chairs situated around the oval kitchen table. Matt slid her an uncertain glance, but obeyed. As Angel approached, he rested his left elbow on the table and spread his thighs, positioning her between them. Angel squeezed a small glob of the dishwashing liquid on her fingertips and, grasping Matt's hand, she gently massaged it on the knuckle above his ring.

While Angel concentrated on her ministrations, Matt became distracted with her nearness. The slow slipping and sliding of her fingers over his evoked fervent images of other body parts slipping and sliding together. Matt inhaled deeply, in a futile attempt to even his breathing, and the tantalizing fragrance of her perfume and the soap filled his head. He dropped his gaze from the erotic back-and-forth motion of her hand and became uncomfortably aware that, in her concentration, Angel was edging ever nearer to the crotch of the V formed by the junction of his thighs. Desperately in need of diversionary tactics before all hell broke loose, Matt tensed his thighs, compressing hers gently between his. Instantly Angel's head came up and she cast him a withering glance. Matt relaxed his thighs and sweat beaded on his forehead as he watched her leg continue its inexorable journey toward his crotch. In a last reckless attempt to stave off the inevitable, Matt thrust his knee into the back of Angel's legs, causing her to totter backward and land with a soft plop on his muscled thigh. This maneuver earned him another scathing look and a huff of displeasure.

"You looked uncomfortable," he croaked, his eyes widening in affronted innocence. "It'll be easier sitting down."

She pointedly ignored his remark, but remained seated as she turned her attention back to his offending finger. Matt turned his to her soft peach sweater and the way that she filled it. He decided his right arm, hanging limp and uncomfortable at his side, could be better occupied at Angel's waist. Placing it there brought another stern gaze from her.

"How's it going?" he asked helpfully. He nodded toward his finger, where his ring, shoved tightly up against the knuckle, had bunched the skin into a mass of purplish wrinkles.

"Give me a minute more," Angel muttered, scowling as she began her manipulations once again.

Unrepentant, Matt focused his attention on the sweet way his hand fit the gentle curve of her waist. He contented himself for a time with lightly stroking over the soft swell of her hip, but the even softer swell of her breast proved an irresistible lure and his hand inched relentlessly upward. With his palm cupping the pliant underside of her breast, his thumb began a tentative search for her nipple.

"Ouch!" Matt shouted as Angel gave a fierce tug on the ring, to no avail. He cast her a baleful glance and flexed his fingers, trying to relieve the pain. "I don't think this is going to work."

"No," Angel agreed. "Your finger's too big."

"I kinda figured that was the problem."

"We'll have to make it smaller," she said matter-of-factly.

"Whoa!" Matt answered, eyes widening. "I have to admit that's one method that never occurred to me."

Angel laughed in spite of herself. "I don't mean permanently, you clown. Just for a few seconds. Long enough to get that ring over the hump." She took his hand and examined the finger again, gently probing. "I think the problem is mainly soft tissue, Matt. The ring should make it over that bone." Looking up, she smiled sweetly at him. "I've done this many times before. Trust me."

She rose and went into the living room, returning seconds later with her purse. Rummaging around in the handbag, she produced a small, robin's egg blue, rectangular packet. "Number 2 black silk suture," she said smugly. "It has endless uses."

"Do you make a habit of walking off with hospital property?" Matt chided.

Angel gave him an indulgent smile as, to his surprise, she again seated herself on his lap and took his hand. "These come in sterile packages, and since it was opened and not used, the hospital has no further use for it. The residents sometimes use them to practice tying knots, but otherwise we're welcome to them."

"When have you done this before?" Matt asked as he watched her remove the suture from the packet. It was about the thickness of regular string, but appeared much stronger.

Concentrating intently, Angel began to wrap the black thread snugly around Matt's finger, beginning at the ring and moving toward the tip. "We always try to remove patients' rings before they go into the operating room," she replied. "Under anesthesia, muscles get very lax, and a ring could slip off, even if it seemed to be on tightly. It could easily get lost in the linen." She had reached the base of the fingernail with her wrapping, and the tip of Matt's finger looked like a little purple bulb. "Rings tend to have sentimental value," she went on, "far in excess of their material worth." As she talked, Angel began to unwrap the finger, beginning at the point nearest the ring, pushing the ring along as she went. She bent Matt's knuckle gently, and, with a slight tug, the ring slipped over the joint. He watched quietly as Angel unwrapped the rest of his finger, slid the ring off, and handed it to him.

Matt looked at the ring lying warm and heavy in his palm. Mixed emotions warred within him as he stared at this symbol of a life that was over. His marriage had ended fourteen months before, abruptly, painfully, against his will. He had loved his wife and had fully intended to live out his life with her, but that was not to be. Now, he had spent the last year reluctantly letting go. What had Angel said? *Rings tend to have sentimental value far in excess of their material worth.* No one knew that better than he. In a sense, the removal of his ring had been another loss, but unlike the death of his wife, this loss had been voluntary. It was not a denial of his love for his wife or a negation of their marriage, but a final acceptance of his situation signifying his readiness to go on. He would have his memories, but they would now be a comfort rather than a torment, and in time they would fade, replaced by new memories. His hand clenched tightly over the golden circle once, and then it relaxed. A pale band, where the ring had been, still remained on his finger. In time it, too, would fade. He raised his eyes and met Angel's solemn ones. "This will be Patrick's someday," he said, and slipped the ring into the pocket of his shirt.

Angel smiled softly, reading the acceptance in Matt's expression, and put a hand to his cheek. He turned his head, grasped her wrist and pressed a kiss into her palm, nipping gently. The heat of his lips tingled all the way up her arm, and she turned in his lap to rest more fully against him, tunneling her free hand into the thick, dark waves of his hair.

Matt sensed a release, an abandon, in her that he hadn't found before, and he gave himself up to her explorations, not demanding, not taking, only yielding to her desires. The hands that had been playfully groping her earlier, now only supported her gently. This time it was Angel's mouth that sought his in a kiss, open, hot, and deep. She squirmed in his lap, straining to get closer. Heat flooded her body, shimmering through her, and every point of contact with him was its source. She slid her hands along the sandpaper texture of his jaw and cupped his face, teasing, tracing his lips with her tongue. Tempting, coaxing. With a low groan she felt more than heard, Matt surrendered, plunging his tongue into the slick, clinging warmth of her mouth. His arms doubled around her, molding her soft, straining breasts to the hard-muscled planes of his chest.

Eyes tightly closed, Angel gave herself up to the sensations he created. She was lost in the smell, the taste, the feel of him. Needfully, she slid her hand into the open collar of his shirt, feeling the heat and dampness there, and her body responded with an unfamiliar dampness of its own between her tightly clutched thighs. She gasped as Matt released her mouth, trailing his tongue along her jaw and the slender column of her neck, rasping her name against her skin. She claimed his mouth with hers again, swirling her tongue around his, combing fingers through his hair, beyond reason and restraint.

"Eeewww, yuck! Gross!"

Guiltily, Angel and Matt flew apart, Angel's flailing arms upsetting her purse and spilling its contents to the floor as she scrambled off his lap. Patrick, one hand theatrically covering his eyes and the other stuck straight out in front of him for guidance, was making his way toward the kitchen sink.

"Hell! Damn! Patrick! What are you up to?" Clearly Matt was unimpressed with his son's stagecraft.

"I only wanted a drink of water," Patrick answered, dropping the act in the face of his father's ire. "That's *two* quarters, Dad," he added with a look of stern disapproval.

Matt let out a long breath and slid a glance at Angel. She was making hasty repairs to her hair, which was beguilingly mussed, and her sweater, which was fine. "Get the 'damn jar,'" he muttered.

Curious in spite of her embarrassment, Angel's head came up. "Jam jar?" she asked.

"Damn jar," Matt corrected sheepishly. "Whenever I use language that might be considered a little too colorful for young ears, I have to pay a quarter," he explained as Patrick approached, unscrewing the lid from an ordinary mason jar. As he dug deep in his pants' pocket for change, he caught Angel eyeing the tidy little pile of quarters in the jar.

"Don't give me that look." He laughed. "They're not all from me! Patrick has to pay whenever I catch him saying 'shut up.'" Matt added the two quarters to the jar with a clatter and a self-satisfied Patrick returned the container to its place on the countertop.

Matt watched his son in exasperation, recognizing that, sick or not, he had begun the exaggerated slow motion of his normal bedtime routine. "Now take your drink of water and get to bed," he ordered. He stooped to help Angel replace the contents of her purse.

Still agitated, Angel could have done without the help. As she shoved her paraphernalia haphazardly back into her bag, she watched with growing embarrassment Matt's contributions to the pile: deodorant, used tissues, tampons— *Dear God!*—lipstick. His offhanded familiarity with the objects didn't add any to her peace of mind. However commonplace this might be for him, *she* wasn't used to a man handling her personal belongings.

Hunkered down, with his elbows resting on his knees, Matt watched Angel with troubled eyes after she had snatched what he belatedly realized was a tampon from his hand. Her averted eyes and deepening color told him his "help" was only making her more uncomfortable. He cast a glance at his inquisitive son, whose eyes bugged over the rim of his glass as he took his typical baby sips. "All right, Patrick," he said, rising. "That's enough. Let's get you to bed."

Recognizing the no-nonsense tone in his father's voice, Patrick took a last sip of his water and dumped the rest down the sink. Matt placed a hand on the boy's damp brow. "You don't seem warm now. If you feel lousy during the night, come and wake me up. Let's go brush your teeth and tuck you in." Matt grasped Patrick by the shoulders and steered him back toward the den.

As she gathered up the rest of her things, Angel heard muffled words coming from the bathroom next to the den where Patrick was brushing his teeth. The words "rude" and "guest" and "uncomfortable" carried to her ears, and she guessed Patrick was on the receiving end of a reprimand for what she saw as natural childish behavior.

It was her own behavior she was concerned about. She brought her hands to her flushed cheeks, mortified at the memory of the wanton kiss she had shared with Matt. What must he think of her? She knew what she thought of herself. She was appalled. All her talk of avoiding a situation where she might get pregnant seemed like so much moralistic posturing. The first man to touch her with anything like consideration and caring comes along and all her high-minded principles fly out the window. And there was no denying that she had instigated this particular encounter. Matt had merely accommodated her, allowing her the unfettered exploration of his body. That things had not gotten completely out of hand was due solely to Patrick's timely interruption. Any thought of consequences had been the furthest thing from her mind. Humiliated, she buried her face in her hands.

That was the way Matt found her, mentally lashing herself for her transgressions, when he returned quietly to the kitchen. He stood for a moment watching her, searching for words to relieve her distress. He could find none. "Angel—"

Her head flew up.

"Let me show you where you can sleep."

She shook her head. Her hands clenched tightly at her sides. "I can't stay, Matt."

"Why not, Angel?" he asked quietly. "Because of a kiss?"

Angel dropped her gaze from his, reluctant to meet his eyes.

"It was only a kiss, Angel. We were a long way from out of control. Patrick was just putting on a silly act. He'd do the same thing if we were married. Believe me, I know." He sighed and pushed a hand through his hair.

At his movement, Angel lifted her eyes to him again and her color deepened even more. This time there was no question whose fingers were responsible for the unkempt condition of his hair. "I really think it would be better if I went home," she murmured.

"Don't you trust me?" His question was as direct as his gaze.

"I'm not sure I trust myself," she admitted haltingly.

Heat flared in Matt's eyes at her answer, but it was quickly and forcefully suppressed. "Sweetheart, you must know that I want you and nothing would make me happier than you feeling the same, but I told you before, it won't happen. Not tonight. Not with my son in the next room." He shrugged and grinned disarmingly. "Whatever kind of chutzpah it takes to pull that scene off, I haven't got it."

His smile fading, Matt studied Angel's troubled expression. He had meant it when he said they had shared just a kiss, that he was under control. Now he wondered about her response. Her kiss had been intense, fevered, impassioned. Was this so new to her? He accepted that her early experiences with sex had been sordid and clumsy, leaving her leery of men, but had there been *no one* since? She looked almost frightened by her reaction to their embrace, as if everything beyond was unexplored territory. Virgin territory.

He reached out a hand to cup her chin, forcing her eyes to meet his. "Has it ever been good for you, Angel?" he asked, his thumb gently stroking her cheek.

She didn't pretend not to understand, but answered with a small shake of her head. Still hesitant to extend her trust, she took a step backward, just beyond his reach. His hand dropped to his side, but his eyes would not release their hold. "You can tell me it's none of my business and I won't push, Angel, but I'd like to know. Has there been anyone since your son was born?"

He was right. It was none of his business. She should tell him so and let that be the end of it. Her life would go on as before; careful, routine, predictable...dull. She could go back into that prison of her own making. "No, there hasn't been anyone," she said.

"Why not?"

"I told you. I would never take a chance of getting pregnant. I will never put myself in that position again."

"There are ways...you're a nurse. You know that."

She shrugged and slid her gaze from his. "As far as I could tell, sex didn't seem worth the trouble. It wasn't anything I'd go out of my way to experience."

"And now?"

Her eyes flew back to his, startled, wary, doubtful.

Matt raised his hands as if to stop her reply. "I know how you feel, Angel. I'm not out to ambush you or catch you off guard. I'm not interested in some sneaky little seduction. And I'm not talking about tonight. But I want you and I'd like to know that there's a chance you want me."

Her own gaze faltered under his direct one. Her mind told her to deny him, to choose the safe path, the known quantity, the route that had served her so well these past years. Yet how could she deny her desire with the taste of him still on her lips?

Matt watched her struggle to reply. She stood with her head bowed, her arms pressed stiffly to her sides. Her demeanor brought to mind the tiger swallowtail Patrick had found just emerging from its chrysalis on the wild cherry tree back in the yard. All golden and fragile and lovely, its wings pressed tightly together, it had stood quivering and hesitant before it took flight. So Angel stood, golden and fragile and lovely, torn between her old fears and her awakening sensuality. He ached for her. He wanted to be the man to make her soar.

He moved closer and raised his hand to cup the back of her neck, gently kneading the tension away. This time Angel did not step back. Taking a deep breath, she lifted her eyes to his and, reading the undisguised need burning there, she made her decision. She would take him at his word. Instinctively she knew he wouldn't push her too fast too soon. "Right now I don't know what I want, Matt. I only know I'm tired of being afraid," she said. She arched her head back, deepening the contact with his caressing fingers. He increased the pressure of his hand, pulling her against him, and kissed her lightly, sweetly, on her trembling lips.

"Let's leave it at that for now," he said, moving his arm to encircle her shoulders. "I'm gonna check on Patrick and then I'll show you your room."

Angel grabbed her purse and followed Matt back to the den. Patrick was asleep, tangled in the bedcovers, a fine sheen of perspiration glistening on his skin and matting his hair. Tenderly, Matt straightened the covers and pulled them up to his son's chin. As he pushed the damp tendrils from

Patrick's forehead, his gaze swung to Angel. "I keep some medicine in the cabinet in the bathroom down here, in case he runs a fever tomorrow."

"Do you have anything without aspirin, Matt?"

"I think so. Why?"

"Kids with certain conditions, chicken pox, flu, anything viral, shouldn't have aspirin. The combination has been associated with Reye's syndrome. It's rare, but very serious."

"I think I have heard something about that. Thanks for the reminder, Angel." He grinned at her. "He'll be in good hands tomorrow."

Matt switched off the room lamp, leaving a small nightlight burning in the bathroom, and led Angel upstairs. He turned to her when they reached the upstairs landing. "Let's see what we can find for you to sleep in." He guided her to the door of what was obviously his own bedroom. She stopped abruptly at the threshold while he continued on to a massive chest at the far side of the room. Her eyes drifted to the brass bed that dominated the space. It was unlacquered and gleamed with the mellow patina of age. Angel wondered in spite of herself if it was the bed he had shared with his wife.

Seeing the direction of her gaze, Matt answered her unspoken question. "I picked that up at an estate sale about six months ago. It was my sister's suggestion. Her theory is if you lose a spouse you should change the decor of your bedroom."

Her attention again focused on him, Angel watched Matt rummage through a drawer. From this distance it looked suspiciously as if a laundry basket of clean underwear had simply been overturned into it.

"This looks like it should do," Matt said, shoving the drawer shut with his hip. He strode over to her, shaking out a large, plain white undershirt, and held it up to her shoulders. It hit her several inches short of mid-thigh. "I know you'll prefer your own bottoms," he added with a wink as she blushed to the roots of her hair. She snatched the shirt from him, mumbling her thanks.

Preceding her into the hallway, Matt familiarized Angel with the rest of the upstairs. "Patrick's room," he said, opening the door on a cheerfully cluttered chamber. An aquarium and various other animal habitats rested on surfaces throughout the room. Angel recognized the fish and the gerbil, but didn't look too closely at the other animal homes. "You'll be happy to know the snake died last week and none of the other critters can get out," Matt said with a reassuring grin.

"The bathroom," he continued. He switched on the night light above the sink. "Towels are in the cupboard. Help yourself to shampoo or anything else you need."

He opened a bedroom door across the landing from his own. "This is where you'll bunk." He flicked on the overhead light, which was connected to a ceiling fan. Angel entered the spacious room and knew immediately this was where his marriage bed had ended up. Young newlyweds might furnish their first home together with family hand-me-downs and flea-market finds, but they often splurged extravagantly on a complete bedroom suite for the most important room in their home. This bedroom set had all the earmarks of such a purchase. The gleaming dark pine furniture wasn't new, but was obviously well cared for. The heavy, queen-size cannonball bed was flanked by matching nightstands. Angel supposed the triple dresser at the foot of the bed had once held feminine garments, while the large armoire on the wall facing the door served as its male counterpart. The matching floral bedspread and curtains looked new.

"Make yourself comfortable, Angel. You won't mind if I use the bathroom first?" At the shake of her head, he then said, "I won't wake you in the morning, and don't bother getting up if you hear me. I'll try to call you during the day. Sleep tight," he said, grinning as he shut the door.

Angel turned on the softer light of a lamp on one of the bedside tables and switched off the overhead one. She pulled out the few things she would need in the morning from her purse and set them on the dresser. Waiting for Matt to finish in the bathroom, she considered her sleepwear. When she spent the night at the hospital, she slept in a surgical scrub suit. She would wash out her underwear in the sink in the private on-call room and hang it over the towel rack to dry. She puzzled over what to do here. Her choices were simple, just not entirely satisfying. She could sleep in only the shirt, wash out her things in the bathroom and set her internal alarm to get in there before Matt found them in the morning. A quick glance around the room didn't reveal any surfaces she would feel comfortable hanging wet things on. Or, she could sleep with her underwear on and wear it again the next day. That really went against her fastidious grain.

She thought she heard the creak of the bathroom door, and moments later Matt's knuckles rapped against her door. "I'm finished, Angel. It's all yours."

Quickly she shed her clothes and slipped into the T-shirt, frowning at the expanse of leg revealed. She hoped Matt slept with his door closed. She gathered up her lacy white bikini panties, filmy bra, and toothbrush and opened the bedroom door a crack. The door opposite seemed firmly shut. She inched out into the hallway and darted for the bathroom, closing and locking the door before turning on the overhead light.

Her nighttime ablutions took only a few minutes and, as she rinsed out her undies, she looked for a place to hang them. Nothing out in the open, she decided, in case Matt needed the room during the night. She pulled back the shower curtain and draped the bra and panties over the porcelain knobs of the tub. With the curtain closed again, Angel was satisfied her undergarments were safely hidden from prying male eyes.

She pulled the bottom edge of the undershirt tightly around her thighs and held it in a fist while she checked the hallway again. The coast was clear and she tiptoed back to her room, closing the door softly behind her. She pulled back the covers on the bed, climbed in and lay on her back, waiting for sleep to come. It didn't.

She folded her hands under her breasts and contemplated the shadows cast by the blades of the ceiling fan in the moonlight. She wondered if Matt was asleep. She wondered if he slept naked. *What is the matter with you! You wonder no such thing!* But she did. She squirmed under the

bedclothes and his T-shirt slid across her breasts, brushing
her nipples. She felt them tingle and tighten, and brought
her hands up to cover them. They pressed hard into the
centers of her palms. The knowledge that this same shirt had
grazed Matt's nipples seemed overwhelmingly intimate.

She flounced over onto her side, tearing her hands away
from her breasts and clasping them tightly between her
knees. That was no help. It only served to accentuate the
aching emptiness between her thighs. She squeezed her eyes
shut and held her hands rigidly away. What was he doing to
her? She had only to think of Matt and her body sizzled.
Was she headed for that slippery slope that plummeted into
degradation and shame?

Willing herself to relax, she thought about her past...
remembering, comparing. That chilled her mood like a
plunge into the North Sea. She recalled her desperate need
for acceptance and the awful lengths she had gone to in her
futile search for it. She remembered rough, demanding
hands grasping, shoving, spreading, pushing her. Even when
it hadn't hurt physically, there had never been the slightest
hint of pleasure. She would return home to her grandmother's, reeking of them, to be slapped and shaken and re-
viled. For every ugly encounter there had been a price. And
then there had been that awful final price. She raised a fist
to her mouth and bit hard on a knuckle. Was it any wonder
sex had held no attraction for her? She had learned a lot
about sex, little about passion, and nothing, *nothing* of desire. Until now.

This man was so different. He offered tenderness without conditions. He was patient and undemanding. He
seemed willing to let her set the pace. She knew to a certainty that he had only made love to one woman in his life,
yet he knew the secrets of her body better than she did herself. Did she dare to trust him? Did she dare accept the
pleasure he offered? There were ways, he had said, to make
sure she didn't become pregnant. She was a nurse. She did
know that. She would have to see someone about the Pill,
she thought. But before the thought was fully formed, she
slept.

Chapter 7

Angel woke to the sound of water rushing through pipes and the harsh water hammer clank of old plumbing as a faucet somewhere was abruptly turned off. Groggy, her first impression was of her grandmother's house and she burrowed deeper into her pillow, reluctant to get up and face the day. Slowly, reality seeped into her consciousness and with it the sudden alarming awareness of where she was.

Springing up abruptly, she threw the bedcovers aside. *Matt was in the bathroom!* She strained her ears for some sound to confirm or deny her suspicion, but heard nothing. The blackness in the room gave no hint of the hour. She had no idea how long she had slept. On the slim chance that she was mistaken, she crept from the bed and opened her door a crack. She winced at the loud groan from the old hinges and ventured a few shy steps into the hallway. A thin ribbon of light shone along the bottom of the closed bathroom door. Before she could scuttle back to her bed, that door swung open.

"Good morning," Matt said, smiling through the shaving cream covering the lower half of his face.

Good God, he's cheerful in the morning, Angel thought. She pushed her tousled hair off her face and blushed as the undershirt slid up along her thighs.

"Are you in a hurry to get in here?" Matt suppressed a grin as she squinched down slightly in an effort to cover more of her long legs.

"No! No. I'll just—" she waved a hand airily "—go back to bed." She was fast coming awake as she looked at him standing there, a towel knotted precariously around his lean waist and another draped around his neck to catch the drizzles from his wet hair. He had rubbed clear a small circle on the steamed-up mirror of the medicine cabinet and turned back to it to continue his shave. Angel watched the ripple of muscle across his shoulders and back as he stretched a cheek taut and took a long sweep through the foam. Her eyes drifted down to his other cheeks and the towel riding higher on them as he leaned in close over the sink. He doesn't care how much leg *he* shows, she thought inanely, sucking in a breath.

Matt nicked himself and cursed under his breath as he followed the direction of her gaze from the reflection in the mirror. He'd better get her out of there quick before they were both embarrassed by the flagrant distortion of his skimpy towel. Suddenly it dawned on him what she was after. He reached behind the radio on the toilet tank and grabbed the underthings he had stashed there while he took his shower. "Is this what you wanted?" He noted with amusement her deepening color as she tore her eyes from his backside.

He figured Angel would have loved to deny ownership of the woefully insubstantial little puddle of fabric resting in his large hand, but there didn't appear to be anyone else around likely to claim it. With a brave attempt at nonchalance, she accepted her bra and panties and smiled her thanks. The carefree effect she strove for was muted somewhat when she thrust the undies behind her back and grabbed the bottom of the undershirt, pulling it tightly around her thighs.

Matt knew she'd have found another approach if she had any idea what that little maneuver did for her breasts. He wasn't about to mention it, but the taut fabric across her nipples boldly announced what she didn't have on under his T-shirt. He swallowed hard. Still, it was several moments before he could comment.

"I'm never gonna wash that shirt, Angel. You can just tuck it under my pillow when you're done with it."

Angel felt the last shreds of her composure drifting away like dandelion fluff in a spring breeze. Abandoning any pretense of self-possession, she skittered off toward the bedroom, Matt's chuckle echoing behind her.

Once safely behind a closed door, Angel became annoyed with herself. What had become of her icy self-control? She was no better than a tittering student nurse drooling after some hotshot surgeon. She wasn't about to hole up in this room and let Matt think he had her cowed.

Angel pulled on her clothes and ran a brush through her hair. Brave, but not foolhardy, she again checked the hallway before leaving the room. The bathroom was free now and Matt's bedroom door was shut. She decided she could make herself useful and familiarize herself with the kitchen at the same time.

By the time Matt strode into the room, dressed in snug black jeans and a black turtleneck, she had a pot of coffee brewed and an English muffin in the toaster oven. "Would you like something to eat?" she asked, her customary calm once more firmly in place.

"Nah. I'm too wired," he answered with a shake of his head. "Just coffee will be great."

His reply chipped away the first tiny fragment of her poise. As she watched his restless pacing, the seriousness of the day's undertaking hit home.

Matt caught her worried look and tried to soften his words. "There'll be donuts at the station house. Don't worry about me."

Angel turned to pour him a mug of coffee, and he went to the hall closet, returning with a jacket and his gun. He draped the jacket over a chair and stretched to reach into a small cupboard above the refrigerator. Curious, Angel watched as he removed a metal strongbox and unlocked it with a key from his wallet. A flicker of fear coursed through her when she saw the box contained ammunition.

With steady, deliberate hands, Matt loaded his revolver and pocketed a box of shells. He secured his gun in the holster clipped to his belt and slid a glance at Angel. She was regarding him with a queasy expression, and the hands that held his coffee cup were less than steady. He took the mug from her and drank deeply.

"This is just routine, Angel. I'm not even point man today."

"What's 'point man'?" She was pretty sure it didn't have anything to do with keeping score.

Matt took another long swallow before he answered. "We go in like a wedge. The point man is the first man in." He set his mug on the counter, walked over to the table, and shrugged into his jacket.

It was rather strange-looking, Angel thought as she watched him fasten it. It was dark, like his other clothing, and quilted, but it didn't cover all the way up to his neck. And it couldn't provide much warmth, webbed the way it was at the sides, and sleeveless. Then it hit her like a fist to the midsection what it was. A bulletproof vest. Her next thought was how little of him it protected.

Matt had hoped to get out without her noticing the vest. Her widening eyes told him that wasn't the case. "Not exactly the height of fashion," he said with an attempt at humor, "but it does the job."

"There's an awful lot of you it doesn't cover," Angel said weakly.

He'd seen that haunted look in a woman's eyes before. This was always the hardest part. Not for him—his adrenaline was pumping and he was geared up. But for the one who had to stay behind. The one who listened to the news reports and waited for the phone to ring. He'd never found a way to make it any easier.

"Well," he answered, "we wanted suits of armor, but they're a real pain getting in and out of the squad cars." He thought he caught the glimmer of a smile. "Not to mention what all that clanking around does to the element of surprise." He grinned at her. "I'm gonna check on Patrick before I leave."

She followed him to the den and waited at the door while he went in. He moved to the side of the bed and bent low over the sleeping boy. Patrick squirmed, but didn't waken when he placed a hand on his forehead. Seemingly satisfied with what he found, he reached over Patrick to straighten the bedcovers, then buried his lips for a few brief seconds in his son's thick hair. Angel turned her head, reluctant to intrude on so private a moment.

Matt walked Angel back to the kitchen and finished his coffee. He tossed his keys from one hand to the other and ventured a sideways glance at her. "I'll call you the first chance I get, but this is going to take a while. Don't get worried just because you don't hear anything."

Angel nodded, but he thought he detected a trembly chin. He tipped her face up to his with a strong, warm finger. "Hey, this'll never do," he teased gently. "You're supposed to see me off with a smile and a kiss."

She looked at him and read the concern in his green eyes. Little spasms of guilt tweaked her. He didn't need this. She was here today to relieve him of any anxiety on the home front. He'd have enough on his mind without this. He wanted a smile, he'd said. She summoned up one of her best. Then she grabbed fistfuls of his hair, pulled his head down and kissed him hard. She laughed at his dumbstruck look. "You've got toilet paper on your chin," she said.

"Thatta girl." He kissed her again and was gone.

Angel locked the door after him and stood for a moment with her forehead pressed to the panel. Going back to bed was out of the question. She finished her coffee and muffin and cleaned up the few dishes they had used. Then she looked in on Patrick before going upstairs to shower and tidy up the room she had slept in.

It was barely five and still dark when she returned to the living room looking for something to occupy the time. She turned on a lamp, pulled a Thomas Hardy from the bookshelf, and curled up in a cozy armchair near the fireplace.

Sun was streaming in through the leaded-glass windows alongside the fireplace when she felt a gentle nudge on her arm.

"Patrick!" She straightened in the chair and rubbed a hand across her eyes. "How are you feeling, honey?"

"Not too good."

That had to be an understatement, she thought. He looked pathetic. She placed a hand against his cheek. "You feel hot. Let's take your temperature."

Listlessly, he followed her into the bathroom and sat on the toilet seat with a thermometer in his mouth. "You've got a fever," Angel said a few minutes later as she squinted at the thermometer and shook it down. She gave him medication and encouraged him to drink the whole glass of water.

"Would you like some breakfast?" she asked when he was finished.

"I guess so." He didn't seem enthused about it, but he accompanied Angel into the kitchen and sat quietly at the table while she fixed oatmeal and orange juice. He picked at the meal until he had finished about half of it. The remainder could have stuck to his spoon in a single glob, if he'd had a mind to try it. He didn't appear to be interested.

"Have you had enough, Patrick?"

He nodded glumly.

"Would you like to lie down for a while? I could put a movie on for you."

"Okay." He didn't sound like he cared much either way.

Angel got him set up in the den and returned to the kitchen. She'd been there only a few minutes when Patrick called her in a high-pitched wail. She raced back to find him sitting bolt upright with a hand clamped over his mouth and a panicked look in his eyes.

"Let's get you to the bathroom quick," she said.

Too late. Most of Patrick's breakfast ended up in the bedclothes. Angel murmured consoling words as she helped him to the bathroom to rinse out his mouth and change into clean pajamas. While he was cleaning up, she returned to the den and changed the bedding. As she gathered up the sheets to run them through the wash, she realized she had not escaped completely unscathed. Sometime during the episode her sweater had gotten in harm's way.

She puzzled only a minute over what to do. Slender though she was, nothing of Patrick's would fit her. She went upstairs and rummaged through Matt's closet. A long-sleeved white shirt would do the trick. She peeled off her sweater and donned the fresh garment. With the sleeves rolled up and the tails tied at her waist, it was a passable fit. She would have her sweater washed and dried before Matt got home and no one would be the wiser.

When she got back to the den, Patrick was once again in bed, his face turned away from her and his eyes tightly closed, a study in misery.

"Are you feeling better, Patrick?" she asked as she stroked his hair.

He nodded, but she saw a tear trickle from the inside corner of his eye over the bridge of his nose and onto the pillow.

"What's the matter, honey? Does something hurt?" He shook his head, but gave a little hiccup that squeezed her heart.

"I'm sorry I made such a mess," he said.

Angel realized his embarrassment was what pained him most. "Oh, Patrick. I'm a nurse. That happens to me all the time," she lied. "Don't let it bother you."

He turned to face her then, opening uncertain eyes. "That really happens all the time? How can you stand it?"

She laughed. "I try to think happy thoughts." She rubbed a hand through his thick mop. "Do me a favor?" He nodded. "If you don't feel like eating, just say so." He grinned shyly and buried his face in the pillow.

"You seem cooler, Patrick. Are you really feeling better?" He nodded again. "I could read you a story. Would you like that?"

"Yeah," he answered with some enthusiasm. "I like *20,000 Leagues Under the Sea*. It's over on the bookcase. Dad left a bookmark in it where he stopped."

She found the book next to a small framed photograph of a woman holding a toddler on her lap. The child was obviously Patrick, though at a much younger and chubbier stage. The woman was smiling brightly, dark eyes and dark hair gleaming in sunlight. There was no father in the picture. He, like fathers everywhere, was probably on the other side of the camera, Angel thought. She picked the snapshot up to get a better look.

"That's me and my mom," Patrick piped up from the bed.

"I can tell," she said. "You look very much like her."

She studied the picture more closely. The woman held the little boy as if she had her whole world in her arms. It was just such a mother she imagined for her own son. It was that thought that had comforted her through these long, empty years.

She replaced the photograph on the shelf, took the book, and pulled up an easy chair alongside Patrick's bed. She was just getting engrossed in Captain Nemo's dark mind when she looked up to see Patrick asleep. Tenderly, she gazed at his peaceful face. Her contact with children was limited and she was more than a little surprised at the depth of affection stirred in her by this motherless little boy.

She placed a hand on his cheek. He was cool now. He must have kept enough of the medicine down for it to have an effect. She tried to remember her training in childhood diseases, but couldn't recall vomiting being associated with chicken pox. Could it be a sign of something more serious? Not for the first time that day did she lament her inexperience in pediatrics. She decided to give her best resource a call.

Not wanting to disturb Patrick, she returned to the kitchen to use the wall phone there. Harriet answered on the first ring.

"Harriet? It's Angel."

"Angel!" Immediately she was suspicious. "Are you at work?"

"No," she laughed. "I'm at Matt's." The words were out before Angel could think better of it. "His son has the chicken pox and he had to work today. I offered to help him out."

"Uh-huh. You were out with him last night."

It wasn't a question. Once again Angel rued the efficiency of the hospital grapevine. "News travels fast," she said.

"Yeah," Harriet retorted. "It's about time you made some."

"Harriet!"

"Now, don't go getting your underwear in a bunch. There's nothing wrong with having a little fun." There was a pause. "Did you spend the night?"

"Harriet!"

"Okay, okay. I'll back off. It won't go any farther than me. You know that."

"We didn't—"

"Now, I didn't ask, did I? You're entitled to your privacy." Another pause. "I hope he showed you a good time."

"Harriet."

Angel's voice brooked no further probings. With a loud sigh, Harriet gave up the line of questioning. "Yeah, Angel. What was it you wanted?"

The question brought Angel back to her current concern. "I don't remember much of pediatrics, and I don't have my books with me. Patrick vomited after breakfast this morning. Is that normal with chicken pox?"

"Mmm. Projectile?"

"No-oo, just your regular garden variety."

"Fever?"

"Almost a hundred and three."

"Yep. My third one was like that. As soon as his temperature hit a hundred and two, look out! Is he real lethargic?"

"He's sleeping a lot, but he seems okay when he's awake."

"I don't think it's anything to worry about. Just don't feed him unless he asks for something."

Angel laughed. "I've already learned that lesson. Thanks, Harriet." She was about to say goodbye when her friend stopped her.

"Did you hear about Gracie?"

That had to be Gracie Patterson, the nurse anesthetist they had let go several months before. She only knew one Gracie. Something in Harriet's tone told her the news wasn't going to be good. Her fingers tightened on the receiver, knuckles whitening, as she sank into a chair next to the kitchen table. "No. What about her?"

"Her body was found by her boyfriend yesterday evening. Looks like an overdose."

An image of the young woman flashed through Angel's mind. Tall. Pretty. Friendly and earnest. But tense, always tense. Unable to shake her demons. Well, whatever demons had driven her, she was free of them now. "Was it accidental?" she asked when she could speak again.

"I don't think anyone knows. The boyfriend's a mess. He'd been trying to help her get her life back together. She'd been in a residential treatment facility for a while and was still in therapy. She was working again, though, and you know the temptations."

Angel murmured her acknowledgment. In anesthesia there was always access to drugs. Combine that with the respect of colleagues and the deference of patients, and it was easy to be gulled into thinking there was no problem. The grueling hours and hectic pace of a busy operating room could push even a strong personality over the brink. And Gracie wasn't strong. Was that what had happened? Had Gracie merely succumbed to the temptations? "How did you hear about it, Harriet?" she asked.

"I worked till midnight last night. Faith was on second call for Anesthesia. Dr. Gordon was tied up with a G.I. bleeder when we got an appendix that couldn't wait. I called Faith's apartment to bring her in. She had just heard from Gracie's boyfriend. He'd found her a short time before. Faith and Gracie had kept in touch, you know." Angel wasn't surprised at that. Faith had started working at the hospital on Gracie's recommendation.

Harriet sighed loudly. "I don't know any more than that, Angel. It was a zoo at the hospital." She paused. "It's too bad. I liked the girl. I wish she could have straightened herself out."

"I know, Harriet. Thanks for clueing me in. I wouldn't want to walk into this cold on Monday morning." Her mind was racing. Technically, this came under the anesthesia department and wasn't her concern. On a human level, however, she'd be dealing with a staff already in an uproar over the events of the past week. Could there be a connection, she wondered, or was it just unhappy coincidence? With a few more words to Harriet about Patrick's care, she hung up.

The afternoon passed without further incident. Patrick dozed off and on and was able to keep some canned chicken soup down. Angel caught him scratching some of his blisters and noted with horror the dirt under his fingernails. She cleaned and trimmed his nails and applied calamine lotion to his lesions. In return, Patrick introduced her to the joys of the game Battleship, and beat her badly.

Afternoon flowed into early evening with still no word from Matt. Angel switched on the television news in time for the lead story, a recount of the early-morning drug bust. Twenty-three arrests had resulted, including a prominent county official who was led from his palatial home hand-cuffed with a sweatshirt over his face. Things had not gone so smoothly for the police everywhere. At one scene the residents had apparently been tipped off. Gunfire erupted and one officer was down. His name had not been released and there was no word on his condition.

Angel barely had time to absorb the information when the phone rang.

"Do you like Chinese?" Angel smiled at the reassuring warmth in Matt's teasing voice.

"It wasn't you that was hit," she breathed, relief flooding her.

"Nah. It wasn't me. It wasn't much of anything, believe me. Stan will be lucky to get two days off out of that little nick. I figured you'd have the news on, though, so I thought I'd better call. How's Patrick?"

"Fine. He's napping again and didn't hear the news. We've had a pretty good day. He's a real sweetheart, Matt."

Matt chuckled. "I won't tell him you said that, so you can still be friends. I've got about another hour to go here. I thought I'd pick up some Chinese food on the way home, if that sounds good to you. Is there anything you don't like?"

"I like it all," she answered.

"Good. I'll see you in a little while."

Angel wandered back to the den where Patrick was still dozing. To pass the time, she surveyed the framed certificates on the wall near Matt's desk. He had several commendations for bravery, and one for community service. The latter had been embellished in neon colors with stars and sunbursts, obviously done by childish hands.

With a smile, Angel moved her gaze to the framed handiwork hanging alongside the commendation. It consisted of a pair of small handprints pressed to plain white posterboard. Between the hands was a poem attesting to the mischief they could get into and how much they would be missed when they were grown.

Angel's smile faded as she ran a finger over the prints through the glass that covered them, and her thoughts drifted, as they always did, to another pair of little hands. Is he dark as his father was, or fair, like me? she asked herself. Does he make friends easily, or is he a loner? Is he a Cub Scout now? And always, always: does he know about me? Does he think I didn't care, when I cared so much?

She had never even held him. She had heard him cry, been told he was healthy, and that was all. It would be easier that way, the nurses had told her. In her naïveté, she had believed them, believed a clean break would put it all behind her. She knew better now. She accepted the fact that, though she could never be a part of his life, he would forever be a presence in hers. The thoughts of him came every day, no longer with such searing pain, but with the gentle tug of regret. She could have been a good mother.

A rustling from the bed broke into her reverie. She turned to find Patrick awake and watching her, a solemn expression on his face. "You look sad," he said.

So perceptive, she thought, and so young. How often had he seen such shadows on his father's face? She smiled gently and walked to the bed. "Everyone's a little sad once in a while," she said as she sat down next to him. She laid the backs of her fingers against his forehead. He was still cool.

"Your dad called. He's bringing Chinese food home with him. Would you like some?"

She took the grimace he made and the gagging motions with his hand around his throat as a definite no. "What a little ham you are." She laughed. "There's still some chicken soup left. How about that?"

That appeared to be agreeable and Angel went to the kitchen to heat the soup, while Patrick used the bathroom and freshened up. When he joined her after a few minutes, she sat across from him at the table while he ate.

His stomach must have settled considerably, Angel thought a little while later as she scooped out a second helping of ice cream for his dessert. She set the dish in front of him, and they heard the click of the lock in the front door. Moments later, Matt walked in. He deposited the brown paper bag he carried on the table, ruffled his son's hair, and favored Angel with a chaste peck on the cheek.

"Hey, sport. How're you doing? You look awful," he remarked as he strode over to the refrigerator. Patrick seemed unaccountably pleased with this comment, Angel mused. Unconsciously, she raised a hand to the spot where Matt's lips had touched and watched as he put what looked like a six-pack of beer on the refrigerator shelf. Catching her gaze, he raised the carton to her with a devilish grin. "Chinese beer," he informed her.

"I didn't know there was such a thing."

"Stick with me, sweetheart," Matt replied with a wink. "I'll show you a whole new world."

"Not a bad Humphrey Bogart." Angel laughed.

"Yeah. Well." He looked chagrined. "It was supposed to be Jimmy Cagney, but we won't quibble."

Patrick walked between them on his way to the sink with his empty dish. "That food stinks, Dad. I'm gonna go watch a movie."

"Okay, sport. You do that." From the smug grin Matt flashed her way, Angel suspected that had been his intention from the beginning.

She set two places at the table, while Matt carried out in reverse order the little routine he had followed that morning with his gun. He came to the table with two bottles of beer and a glass for Angel.

"So, tell me. How was your day?" he asked, reaching into the bag and placing the cardboard cartons on the table between them. Before she could answer, he got up, rummaged through a drawer near the sink, and returned with a bottle opener. He uncapped the bottles, poured Angel's beer, and tossed the caps in the trash before he sat down again. As she opened her mouth to speak, he muttered, "Spoons," bounced up, searched through another drawer for serving spoons, and came back to the table. Angel watched him in amusement as he took his seat.

"Are you always this jumpy at the end of the day?" she asked.

He looked sheepish and took a long swig from his bottle. "Sometimes after a day like this, it takes me a while to unwind," he answered finally.

"How do you like to unwind?"

A broad grin split his face, his white teeth flashing in a leer the big bad wolf would envy. "I'd like to have sex." He laughed as her fork clattered against her plate, bounced into her lap and down onto the floor. "I can see you're gonna take a pass on that, though." He ducked his head under the table at the same time she did to retrieve the fork, and their eyes met, and held. "This time," he added, his smile fading.

Shaken, she watched him rise and walk to the sink, his lean body all in snug black. He had pushed the sleeves of his turtleneck up almost to his elbows to reveal hard-muscled forearms covered with silky, dark hair. As he tossed the fork into the sink and returned with a clean one for her, she fought to regain her composure. She was familiar enough with his nonsense by now to know he was only teasing her. Still, he had taught her enough about desire to appreciate the edge that fear and relief might give it. There was no chance that she would take him up on his suggestion, but she wondered what it would be like, and she wondered if it showed.

"So, what have you two been up to all day?" he asked. A smile still tugged at his lips as he seated himself across from her once more.

"Patrick slept a good bit of the day." Angel helped herself to chicken with almonds. "I read to him a little, and we played some games." She took a bite of shrimp toast. "He says you cheat at Battleship."

Matt hesitated, his fork halfway to his mouth. He eyed her warily. "I didn't think he knew."

"Matt! What kind of lesson are you teaching him?"

He shrugged. "Gotta keep ahead of the little guy some way. Can't have him making the old man look bad." He didn't appear the least bit contrite.

"I don't want to tell you how to handle your son, but what sort of exam—"

"Who won?"

"Pardon me?"

"Who won the game?"

"Patrick did. Both times. He's really very shrewd. He understands a lot about strategy and—" She stared at Matt, her eyes narrowed in suspicion. He was attacking his food with a single-minded intensity wholly unwarranted by the merely adequate pork-fried rice. Despite the frantic working of the muscles in his jaw, he seemed to be having a hard time chewing and swallowing. He slid a glance at her, his face contorted with suppressed laughter.

"He cheats, too," she said.

Matt gave up any attempt to hide his amusement. He leaned back in his chair, holding his sides as he laughed.

"He's real good at it, Angel. Don't feel bad that you didn't catch him. All his little friends do it. It's part of the game for them . . . to see how much they can get away with. I'll have a talk with him, though, about the proper way to play with unsuspecting innocents." He gave her a pointed look and laughed again as he took another helping of rice.

Angel sighed and shook her head. "What a pair," she said, laughing in spite of herself. She looked up to find his eyes still on her.

"Is that my shirt?" he asked.

Taken by surprise, Angel dropped her gaze to her chest. She pressed a hand to the white shirt, recalling with a start the peach sweater she had tossed in the dryer hours ago and completely forgotten. Her eyes flew to Matt's mischievous ones. "I . . . my sweat—"

"By all means!" He raised a staying hand. "No need to explain. Feel free. My closet is your closet."

Angel let her breath out in a loud hiss. "Matt. This morning after breakfast, Patrick . . ." She searched for the most delicate way to put this.

The grin left his face, replaced by an uneasy look. "Tossed his cookies," he said.

"Well, yes."

He winced and closed his eyes. "All over *you?*"

"Not *all* over."

He passed a hand over his eyes. "Jeez." Resting his chin in his palm, he looked at her guiltily. "Did he have a fever?"

Angel leaned back in her chair and met his eyes with a level gaze. "You could have warned me."

"Be honest." He shook his head. "You wouldn't have stayed. Besides, the doctor keeps telling me he'll outgrow this." He groaned. "Way to go, Patrick. What a way to impress a woman."

She laughed. "I don't think he was trying to impress me."

"Yeah. Well, he could give his father a little help."

Her smile softened. "Is that what you're trying to do? Impress me?"

He crossed his arms and rested them on the table, pushing his plate aside. "I'm trying my damnedest," he said.

She could feel herself blush, flattered. She wondered if he had any idea how well he was succeeding. It was very difficult, she was finding, to distrust a man who could make her laugh. She took a sip of her beer and cleared her throat. "I was a little concerned when it happened this morning. I don't have a lot of experience with kids. Anyway, I called one of the nurses I work with. Harriet Irwin. Do you remember her?"

Matt narrowed his eyes in thought. "Yeah, I think so. Tough old bird. Calls a spade a spade. But nice!" he added quickly, catching Angel's frown.

"That about sums her up, I guess," she said, feeling more than a little disloyal. "She mentioned an incident that occurred yesterday, involving one of our former employees."

"Grace Patterson," Matt said in a flat voice, all playfulness gone from his expression.

It was absurd to think he wouldn't have heard. No one sneezed at the hospital these days without the police learning of it. Still, the look on his face was far from reassuring. "Yes, Gracie," she said.

"What did Harriet have to say?"

"Just that Gracie's boyfriend had found her body. She said it looked like an overdose. Is that what happened?"

Matt seemed not to hear her question. He rose and went into the living room, leaving her to stare blankly at the back of the chair he had just vacated. When he returned, he was carrying the little spiral notebook she was beginning to think of as one of his appendages. He took a pencil from the notepad near the phone and sat down across from her again.

"That's not what happened, is it, Matt? This wasn't just an accidental overdose?" He had fixed her with that inscrutable stare of his and was shutting himself off from her. She hated when he did that.

"We won't know what killed her until the toxicology reports come back. That could take weeks. There wasn't any sign of a struggle."

"But you don't think it was an accident." She couldn't bring herself to say the other word.

Matt had no such compunctions. "This was murder." He watched her closely. Her face had paled to the color of his shirt. "We don't know yet what she inhaled that killed her, but a police cadet could have picked up the discrepancies at that crime scene." Angel wrapped her arms around herself, her fingers clenching into the shirtsleeves, but she didn't take her eyes from his face. He went on more gently. "The guys from forensics tried to pick up prints. Nothing. Not a smear, not a smudge. Not even ones that should have been there. Someone had wiped the place clean."

"Could it have been someone wearing gloves?"

Matt sighed heavily and tossed his pencil onto the table. "I don't think so. That would have aroused her suspicion. I think someone she knew and trusted came by with her favorite candy and she couldn't resist."

"But why?"

He shrugged. "Maybe she fell privy to his involvement in Marty's murder. Or maybe he was just afraid she would. Addicts are notoriously unreliable. This was the only way he could be certain she'd keep quiet." He watched her with worried eyes. He could practically hear the whirs and clicks as her mind turned over possibilities. His fear for her was like a living thing, gnawing at his vitals.

"Angel." She raised her eyes to his again. "I don't want you doing any free-lance investigating. If you've got any suspicions, you come to me, understand?" Her answering nod came too easy, too offhand. He could already sense her attention drifting back to dangerous waters. He leaned in close to her over the table and grabbed her chin in his hand, forcing her eyes to his. "I mean it, Angel. This is no time to play detective," he said, his voice harsh with concern. "This guy would as soon kill you as look at you. It won't matter that he knows you. It won't even matter if he likes you. This is strictly business. The most ruthless business there is. Killing is just a necessary part of it. He's already done it. Twice." He released her chin, but held her wide-eyed stare.

"Matt, you're scaring me," she said.

"I hope so, Angel. If it makes you careful, I hope so. Watch your back."

She sat quietly for a moment, shaken. Then he could see her backbone stiffen. "You keep saying 'he,'" she said. "Does that mean you've eliminated a woman as a suspect?"

He rolled his eyes and gave a snort of disgust. "I'm real pleased to see you're taking this little lecture to heart, Angel."

"I'm just curious."

"Yeah, and we both know what that did to the cat."

"I'm not a cat."

"No. You only have one life."

She gave a *tsk* of impatience and turned her face away from him, arms folded across her chest and her sassy little nose in the air.

Matt watched her in reluctant admiration. She was game. Trouble was, she could really be useful. He sensed that her instincts were good. And she was familiar with these people. She could read nuances and changes in behavior in a way the investigating officers never could. He rubbed tense fingers over his corrugated brow and, against his better judgment, he spoke. "Actually, that 'he' was just a manner of speaking. We haven't eliminated anybody.'' Her nose was still in the air, but her eyes had shifted back to him.

"A case could be made that these drugs, in the wrong hands, are just a form of poison.'' She turned her head to face him fully now. He shrugged. "Poison is a woman's weapon. It's clean. Doesn't leave an ugly mess. Doesn't require any strength. Most times you just have to develop a relationship, establish a little trust.'' He picked up his pencil and held it poised over his notebook. "So what about Faith Nichols?''

Angel rested her elbows on the table and clasped her hands loosely under her chin. "She and Gracie had known each other for a number of years. They went through anesthesia training together, and Gracie had helped Faith get the job at the hospital. They kept in touch after Gracie was fired.'' She paused, weighing her words. "Faith is a very bitter, angry woman, but, God, Matt.'' She shook her head. "I can't believe she'd do this.'' She pressed her hands to her mouth and gazed sightlessly at the table.

Matt chewed on the eraser of his pencil, regarding her steadily. "Tony Levering's got a rap sheet. Did you know that?'' He saw her head snap up, startled. Nope, she didn't know that. Seeing the chain of emotions—surprise, confusion, dismay—that flickered across her face, he marveled that he could ever have found her hard to read. Her face reflected exactly what she felt. She'd be a babe in the woods in this thicket of intrigue. The thought made him feel a little sick. "He grew up in a tough neighborhood,'' he stated.

She nodded. "I did know that.''

"His record is all juvenile stuff. Petty theft, joyriding, minor drugs. There's nothing as an adult.''

"I thought juvenile records were expunged if the person stayed clean?''

"We didn't open any sealed records. Files are sealed, Angel, lips aren't. We talked with the people who knew him at the time. People open up. We're looking for a cop killer.'' He paused. "He's got a brother in the slammer.''

Angel sucked in a breath. "Poor Tony.'' She shook her head. "I have to tell you, Matt. I like him. And I know from experience that people can change.''

His eyes told her he took her meaning. "You haven't heard any talk of this at the hospital?" he persisted. "Any reason to think he might have been desperate?"

She shook her head again, firmly. "Dr. Albert might have known, but I couldn't swear to it."

"Why Albert?"

"He's chief of anesthesia. If anyone had access to confidential information, it would be him. He's the one who fired Gracie, by the way, but that was just a function of his position."

"How was that handled?"

"As well as could be expected, I think. He encouraged her to get treatment, which, I understand, she did." Suddenly she squeezed her eyes shut and pressed her fingers to her forehead. "Who would want to kill Gracie?" she murmured. "You'll get him, won't you, Matt?"

He gazed at her bent head and every tender, protective instinct he possessed flared when he looked at her. He reached across the table again and pulled her hands away from her face. "We'll get him," he said fiercely. "This guy's an arrogant S.O.B. He's thumbing his nose at us. He figures if you put the whole force together, we wouldn't have the IQ of a peach pit." He gave a quick, determined nod. "We'll get him."

Angel was stunned by the ferocity in his voice. She didn't for a moment question the truth of his words. She had become so accustomed to his playfulness, that it was easy to overlook his toughness. His disarming banter and low-key manner could be an effective tool with the unsuspecting. She had no reason to fear him, and, at that moment, she was glad of it. With an effort, she pulled her eyes from his and surveyed the remains of their meal. "Let me help you clean this up," she said.

"Don't even think of it," he replied. "You've cleaned up plenty today." He scraped his chair around the edge of the table, closer to her, still holding her hands. "How can I make it up?"

She smiled. "You don't have to do that."

"I know. I want to." He paused. "You've got a birthday coming up. Next Saturday, right?"

She felt the tears start behind her eyes and her smile faltered. She didn't celebrate her birthdays. They certainly were no cause for celebration when she was growing up, serving only to remind her grandmother of her mother's sins. And as an adult, she had let no one get close. The hospital gave its employees their birthday off as a holiday. That was the extent of her observance. That must be how he knew, she thought. He had seen it in her work file, and remembered.

Matt read her reluctance, but this time he was ready. "Don't tell me...let me guess," he said. "You have to wash your hair. Every night." He brought her fingers to his lips and bit gently on one knuckle.

Angel caught her breath at the sight of his white teeth on her. She swallowed hard. "I wash my hair in the morning," she whispered.

Matt nipped each knuckle in turn, then caressed them with his tongue. Angel felt a heavy languor flow through her arms, wash over her breasts and settle in her belly. She couldn't tear her eyes from his mouth.

Matt raised his head from Angel's hands and a lopsided grin tugged at his lips. "You're the kind of woman who'd hold a kid's crass behavior against a guy. Not to mention that he cheats," he added.

"No!" she answered quickly. "Actually, I'm getting kind of fond of that little con man you're raising."

Matt's grin faded, and his eyes held hers. "Then I guess it's something about me..." He paused. "Personally, that you don't like."

The shake of her head was barely perceptible. "No," she breathed.

"You'll have to come up with your own alibi, Angel. I'm all out of excuses."

"So am I, Matt." She smiled into his eyes. "So am I."

"It's settled then." He squeezed her hands. "I'll make my favorite thing for dinner."

"What's that?" she asked.

"Reservations."

Her laughter was still rippling around them when they heard Patrick making his way down the hall. He was whistling, clapping, and raising a general ruckus. "Do you think he wants us to know he's coming?" Matt laughed.

Patrick peeked around the edge of the doorframe and Matt held out his hand to him. "Hey, sport, come on in. We're just sitting here behaving ourselves." Angel smiled a greeting, but noted Patrick's glassy eyes and automatically put a hand to his forehead. He was warm. "He hasn't had anything for a temperature since early afternoon, Matt. He could probably use something now."

He nodded and pulled Patrick into the circle of his arms. The boy suffered this indignity with grace. "I itch, Dad," he said.

Matt glanced at Angel, a question in his eyes.

"Baking soda," she offered. "About a half a cup in his bathwater. You can make a paste out of it, too, for the ones that really itch. I noticed you're almost out of calamine lotion."

Matt nodded and pressed his lips into the dark hair above Patrick's ear. "Why don't you get ready for your bath while I walk Angel out to her car," he said. "Then we'll get you fixed up."

As Angel made to rise, Patrick gave her a quick hug and scooted back down the hallway. Matt's brows quirked up in surprise. "I think you're getting to him," he said. "Where's your sweater?"

"In your dryer," she answered, and wrinkled her nose in an apologetic gesture.

Matt went through the living room to the hall closet. He returned with her hospital files and his tan windbreaker. He draped the jacket around her shoulders. "We can switch back next time I see you," he murmured, his breath warm against her ear.

Angel turned toward him, but he was already headed back through the living room to the front door. Grabbing her handbag from the table, she quickly followed him.

Matt strolled alongside her down the walk and across the lawn to her car. He had the hospital records in one arm and his other hand was shoved deep into his jeans pocket. He made no attempt to touch her. Angel told herself she wasn't disappointed.

"I'm going to make a phone call when you leave," Matt said. "There'll be a patrolman waiting outside your place when you get home. He's gonna check your doors and windows and make sure everything is secure. You just let him go about his business."

"I don't think that's necessary, Matt."

"Yeah, it is. He likes his job. He wants to keep it." He threw her a leveling look. "Don't give him a hard time, Angel."

They had reached her car. A soft breeze lifted the tendrils on Angel's neck like a lover's hand. She turned to Matt, but he was gazing off down the street, his face expressionless. She dug into her purse for her keys. Matt took them from her and opened the car door. He tossed the files he carried onto the passenger seat and held the door for her as she slid in. When the door slammed shut, Angel couldn't deny her frustration. Other than that little buss on the cheek and some finger nuzzling, he'd barely touched her. Now that he no longer needed her baby-sitting services, had his interest waned?

As she stuck the key into the ignition, his knuckles rapped against the window alongside her. She slid the window down and he leaned toward her. "Did you get my phone number while you were here? I don't want you to have to go through that business with the bureaucrats if you need to get in touch with me."

Angel could have spit. All week she'd been decrying her inability to get his number, and here she'd let the perfect opportunity slip through her fingers. Annoyed with herself, she switched on the lamp above her head, searched through her purse for a pen and paper, and wrote down the numbers he gave her. She put the things back in her handbag and tossed it onto the seat next to her.

When she looked up, he was resting his folded arms on the open window frame, a roguish grin on his face. In the dim light his eyes looked almost black, and they glimmered with mischief and danced with playful menace. "Now. I hope you're feeling real secure with all this machinery around you, Ms. Martino, because I'm gonna kiss your lights out."

He reached in to switch off the overhead light. On the backsweep, his palm cradled her head and pulled her to him. Surprise had already caused her mouth to open. When she closed it, it was around his tongue. The sensitive surfaces of her inner lips tingled and throbbed as he thrust in and out. So gently. Too gently. She wanted more. She whimpered when he withdrew and clicked her teeth against his in an effort to reestablish the kiss. "Easy, sweetheart." She felt his smile against her mouth. He dipped his tongue into the shallow hollow between her chin and lower lip and lazily traced the swollen contours of her mouth. His teeth nibbled achingly and she felt her world tilt off center when he pulled at her bottom lip and sucked. The hand that cupped her head began to rock her mouth against his, alternately deepening and easing the contact, and her breath came in small, quick pants. She turned more fully to him, shoving her hands into the thick dark curls at his nape. As his tongue probed into the warm, wet recesses of her mouth, she shuddered and surrendered. With her blood thrumming wildly in her ears, her mouth clung to his, and she heard the strangled groan from the back of his throat as she pulled him deep. Yearning, desperate to get closer, she pushed forward, and her elbow hit the horn.

The ear-splitting blare burst them apart, and Matt cracked his head hard against the upper edge of the window frame. He staggered back, muttering a string of curses that could have filled the "damn jar." He looked up to see Angel, sitting wide-eyed and dumbfounded. The hand clamped over her mouth couldn't conceal the fact that she was grinning widely. At his expense. He thought she could use a lesson.

Rubbing the back of his head, he directed his gaze to the house across the street. "Jeez, Angel, I think we woke Old Lady Carruthers." Angel spun her head quickly, but couldn't see anything. To her utter mortification, he waved.

Matt swung his eyes back to Angel and knew he had gone too far. She had draped her arms over the steering wheel and buried her head in them, her shoulders shaking.

"Hey, I was only kidding," he said. "Look. Nothing could wake her up." He watched, bemused, as Angel plopped limply back against the seat, helpless, speechless with laughter. His eyes glittered, gemlike, in the darkness and a wicked grin split his face. "You'd better get out of here quick, before I climb in there with you and forget all my good intentions," he growled.

With an unrepentant peal of laughter, Angel started the car and backed slowly out of his driveway. As she headed off down the street, Matt was still rubbing his head. And she was still laughing.

Chapter 8

Old habits die hard. Angel's high spirits lasted until the following morning. Then the self-recrimination began. She went through her normal Sunday routine, church and chores, but without Matt's silly banter to distract her, she heard her grandmother's vitriolic disapproval again. Her behavior was shameless. She had known this man scarcely a week and already the barriers she had so carefully erected around her body and her heart were lying in splintered ruins about her. Perhaps she truly was the tramp her grandmother had always accused her of being. The ring of the phone interrupted her dreary introspection. How could she be such a fool? she asked herself, reaching for the receiver. He was only looking for one thing.

"I'm looking for a seven-letter word meaning 'bonelike,'" came the lazy male drawl.

It took Angel several moments to switch mental gears.

"Angel?" Matt prodded.

"Yes," she answered quickly. "Are you working a puzzle?"

"Yeah."

"Do you have any letters?"

"Starts with *o,* ends with *d.* The fourth letter is an *e.*"

"*Osteoid,*" she answered promptly.

"Argh, that's it. I had *osseous* in mind and couldn't get past it."

"Well, that's a toughie."

"Don't try to spare my feelings, Angel."

"Is this the puzzle from last Sunday's paper?"

"Yeah. Why?"

"Hold on a minute." She reached up on top of the refrigerator and got her own copy of the puzzle and a pencil. "Did you get the 'river in Pakistan'?"

"Chenab."

"Oo-oh, I'm impressed."

"We have a little problem with geography, do we, Ms. Martino?"

She smiled at his teasing tone. "That and 'birds of ancient Persia,' I'm afraid."

"Ah. Am I to understand you didn't get *bulbul,* then?"

She laughed out loud. "No, I didn't. Thank you very much," she said, penciling the letters in the small squares. "Did you get everything else?"

"Actually, no, and I'm a little embarrassed to admit this. I thought Charlotte Brontë wrote *Jane Eyre,* but she doesn't fit."

"Currer Bell."

"Are you sure? Never heard of him."

"Currer Bell was Charlotte Brontë's pen name. But you don't have to trust me. Look it up."

"That would be cheating," he said in his most sanctimonious tone.

Angel gave a hoot of laughter. "Since when have you developed such scruples? You've done it before." And in another sense, she realized, he'd done it again. He'd slid right past her defenses. She leaned back against the refrigerator and closed her eyes. *This* was what she couldn't live without anymore. Not the touch of his hand in her hair. Not the promise of his kiss. Not the sex she knew that he would want, and she would give him. But *this.* This warmth, this ease, this laughter with a person who knew her secrets and seemed not to care. In her mind she looked back across the arid wasteland of her past and realized she had been parched for this. And she hadn't even known.

She rubbed her fingers between her eyes and sighed. She couldn't say how it had happened. She didn't know what point had been the one of no return; she only knew she had passed it. This road might lead nowhere. She could still face a future of empty days and lonely nights. But it wouldn't be her doing.

"Angel?" Matt's voice came tentatively over the line. She must have been quiet too long.

"How's Patrick?" she asked.

"Ugh! Awful. He's cranky and whiny. I can't please him. I don't know how you put up with it."

"Well, he slept a lot yesterday. He must be feeling better."

"Yeah. If he feels any better than this, I can't answer for the consequences. I got a lady down the street to watch him next week. I'll be glad to go to work."

"Mmm," Angel murmured, trying to sound sympathetic.

"I made reservations for seven-thirty, Saturday, at the Fireside Inn. Have you ever been there?"

She knew the place; a big, white-brick building with black shutters and a slate roof, nestled in a picturesque valley a few miles out of town. Dark paneling, dim light, a fireplace in every dining room. Elegant. Swank. "I was in one of the banquet rooms," she answered. "The hospital had an affair there about a year ago."

Matt's pause was just long enough for her to wince at her choice of words. "We won't do that," he said smoothly. "We'll just have dinner."

"You're incorrigible." She laughed.

"I guess. I've gotta go, Angel. He's beefing about something. I'll call you tomorrow."

With Matt's words running through her mind, she hung up the phone and found the voice from her past was blessedly silent.

* * *

Matt parked his van several car lengths behind the paneled phone company truck. He sat for a few minutes, surveying the area through the steady drizzle that streaked his windshield. The neighborhood reeked of new money. The houses, sprawling, lumbering behemoths all, looked to have been built within about a year of each other. Lots of pale brick and shutters in Williamsburg colors. The spacious lots sported wide, black-topped driveways, and carefully nurtured twigs were set in neatly mulched circles plunk in the middle of each front lawn. A little too ticky-tacky for his taste, Matt decided, but plush, very plush.

Apparently all this elegance required two incomes. At midday, the area appeared deserted. Not a soul on the street. That didn't surprise Matt much, considering the weather, but aside from the truck ahead of him, he didn't see another vehicle around, either.

The rain didn't look as if it was going to let up. With a sigh, he got out of the car. He pulled his wallet out of his back pocket and held it in his teeth while he reached inside the car for the burgers and coffee in the cardboard carrier on the passenger seat. He shoved the door shut with his elbow and strode off in the direction of the truck, mentally cursing the rain that stung his neck and dribbled down under his sweatshirt. He missed his windbreaker, which Angel still had. Hell. He missed Angel.

The phone conversations he was having with her were less than wonderful. With each day that passed she grew more cautious and distant. He figured he'd be starting from scratch again with her by Saturday. At this rate it would be forever before he . . . He stopped dead midway to the truck, caught up short by the direction of his thoughts. Before he what? Idiot. He knew damn well what. Before he got her into his bed. He shook his head, disgusted, and slogged on to the truck. She had every reason to be skittish with men.

He reached the back of the utility vehicle with the now soggy container of food and drink. He propped it against the truck with one arm, while with his free hand he rapped sharply on the door, flipped his wallet open to his police ID, and plastered it against the tinted window glass. Almost immediately the rear panel opened with a rusty screech.

"Put that thing away, Matt. I know your ugly mush."

Matt shot a quick glance at the man who had opened the door. "Hey, Jack, I thought Stan pulled the baby-sitting job."

"Ah, that guy. His arm hurts so bad, he can't even sit on his can. Do you believe that twinkie? He took the whole week off." His expression was pained as he took the food from Matt and stepped aside to make room for him to pass. "This smells good," he added with a nod to the container.

"Yeah, help yourself." Matt moved to a wooden table and chairs set up against one wall of the truck. The scarred surface of the table was covered with notebooks, pencils, a headset and reel-to-reel recorder, the wherewithal of electronic surveillance. The gray-tinted window above the table afforded a clear view of the front and side doors of the home across the street, as well as its attached garage. Matt took careful note of the discreet little decal in the lower corner of a front window indicating the home was equipped with an alarm system; bells and whistles and the latest in technologic gadgetry. No matter, he grinned to himself. The cops had their ways.

He shifted his glance to Jack as the detective came up alongside him. "Any trouble with the setup?" he asked.

"Nah. It never ceases to amaze me how trusting people are if you look the least bit official."

Matt knew what he meant. Last Saturday two people had come with this truck and knocked at several houses on the block, but that house across the street was the one they were interested in. Wearing phone company navy blue, name tags, tool belts, and carrying official-looking clipboards, they muttered something about squirrels chewing wires and conned their way into the home. Once inside the place, it was easy work for the young woman to engage the gregarious homeowner in conversation while her male counterpart checked the various phones and inserted the bugs in them. They could manage the cloak-and-dagger stuff under cover of nightfall if they had to, of course, but why bother? A little chicanery was so much easier on everyone concerned.

Matt cast another hard look at the dwelling before he straddled one of the chairs and thumbed through the coffee-stained logbook. "How goes it?" he asked.

"Quiet. Real quiet. The good doctor leaves early and gets back late. Most everybody must be familiar with his schedule. The phone doesn't ring to speak of during the day." Jack took the chair next to Matt's and set the food on the table. He unwrapped one of the hamburgers and inspected it with a frown, removing the pickles. "I had a guy here this morning, early, banging on the door complaining about his phone service. That's been the high point of my day."

Matt gave a dry laugh and slanted a look at the younger man. "His, too, I'll bet." Jack Trent wasn't a rogue cop, exactly, but he definitely left the impression of life on the edge. He specialized in undercover work and was reportedly one of the best, assuming and discarding personalities at will. Which could explain, Matt reflected as he stretched out an arm to accept the coffee the other man offered him, why Jack's own personality was such a mystery. Gingerly, he removed the plastic lid from the insulated cup. He knew a number of his co-workers disliked the guy. With another quick glance, he assessed his companion. Maybe it was the tautly muscled body that, as far as anyone could determine, owed nothing to diet or exercise. Or maybe it was the unnerving eyes, a clear, pale blue, that saw everything and revealed nothing. Matt took a careful sip from his cup. Then again, he mused, maybe it was the ponytail.

"Hey, Matt," Jack said between bites. "I hear you're seeing a new chickee. Gettin' any?"

Matt cursed as hot coffee sloshed over his hand. "You're a real class act, you know that, Jack?" he snapped. "What the hell kind of a question is that? 'Gettin' any?'"

"Touch-eee."

"Yeah, well, I'm not gonna dignify that with an answer."

"Never mind."

They sat in sulky silence for a few minutes. Matt continued to scan the wiretap log, while Jack demolished another hamburger, adding more pickles to his tidy pile. Finally, Matt looked up. "This is all a crock," he growled.

"Yeah, I know," Jack answered with a mouthful. He swallowed and went on. "Lotta women. To be fair, they mostly call him. He's married, isn't he?" At Matt's nod, he continued. "There hasn't been any woman at the house. No calls for her, either."

"I understand she's out of town a lot. Does she call him?"

Jack thought for a minute. "Nah, I don't think so. Nothing that sounds like a wife." Matt gave him a questioning look. "You know, nagging about the laundry... it's Tuesday, the garbage gets picked up, that kind of thing." Matt allowed himself a half smile and shook his head in exasperation. Jack was a bachelor, and likely to remain one by all accounts.

"What's the wife's name, again?" Jack asked.

"Jeanette."

"Nope, no Jeanette. Want a burger?" He handed one to Matt, who opened it up, glanced at the discarded pickles, and hesitated only a moment before adding them to his sandwich. Biting into the burger, he took another sidelong look at his companion. Jack had tipped his chair back and was rocking on its two rear legs with his sneakered feet propped on the table. *Just like I'm always telling Patrick not to sit*, Matt thought, his teeth on edge.

With a sigh, he pushed the logbook aside, picked up the headset, and adjusted the recorder. He pressed a headphone to one ear so he could listen to the tape and converse at the same time. "Anything remotely interesting?" He took a long swig of coffee and turned to Jack again. The man was eyeing him uncertainly.

"There's one woman who calls every night, real late," he began. "I get the impression he's already in bed." He stopped, seeming at a loss as to how to proceed. Finally he said, "They talk dirty."

"What!"

"Well..." He shrugged. "They get each other..." He gestured lamely with his hands. "You know... over the phone."

If Matt hadn't been so stunned, he would have laughed. It was difficult to be sure in the dim light, but he thought he detected a blush spreading over Jack's chiseled cheek-bones. "You mean..."

"Yeah." The rocking grew more agitated. "It's not easy to listen to for any length of time, let me tell you." He paused. "I mean, is that kind of stuff legal?"

"Yeah, I guess so." Matt scratched his head. "They're consenting adults having a private conversation. Some people would consider what we're doing here a little questionable."

The rocking ceased. "I thought you got a court order."

"I got the warrant."

"Just making sure."

"I got the warrant, Jack."

"I mean, who's got the law degree, here?"

"Bag it, Trent." Matt let a long breath out through his teeth. "Is that all that's interesting about these conversations?"

Jack teetered back on his chair once again. "No." The rocking picked up, more gently this time. "She mentions what sounds like drug sales. But there's something not right about it."

"What do you mean?"

"Well, they don't make any attempt to disguise it. No code, no nothing. And she talks about brand names, not street stuff." He paused. "They're just too open about it. I mean, he's gotta suspect we're watching him." He turned to Matt and saw that he had quit listening.

Matt's attention was focused on the words coming to him through the headset. "What's he calling her?" he asked quietly. Jack's eyebrows shot up. "I mean her name, you lunkhead, not...the other."

"Charlie, I think."

"Yeah, I think so, too," Matt replied, a queasy feeling starting in the pit of his stomach. He reached where the pocket of his windbreaker would be, if he were wearing it, and swore when it wasn't there. Shifting forward, he pulled his spiral notebook out of his left rear pocket and turned the pages. He had to be careful; they were a little damp. "Yep, here it is. 'Jeanette Charlotte Chapman.' She's a sales rep for Gryphen Pharmaceuticals." Matt sighed heavily, his mouth compressed into a thin straight line. "That's our Charlie." He pulled the headphone from his ear and flung it on the table. "Son of a bitch," he said. "It's his wife."

For long moments Matt stared out the window, his arms folded over the slatted back of the chair, his mood as somber and dank as the day. Finally he spoke. "How would you describe her voice?"

Jack paused for a moment, reflecting, his gaze following Matt's. "Mmm," he murmured. "Her voice. Husky. Sultry. Throaty. Erotic." He was really getting into this.

"Mannish?" Matt offered.

Jack's eyes flew to Matt. "Well, her voice is deep for a woman, but 'mannish' is not a word that leaps immediately to mind."

"Not to my mind, either. Do you imagine her in tweed suits and sensible shoes?"

"I imagine her in fishnet stockings and black leath—"

Matt raised a staying hand. "I get the picture."

"Where are you getting this description, anyway?"

"Someone who never met her, just talked to her over the phone."

"Five'll get you ten it was a woman," Jack said with conviction.

"I'm not a betting man." Matt steepled his hands and stared long and hard at the house. "This guy's a crud," he said at last.

Jack scratched his nose thoughtfully and placed a finger against his lips before he responded to that. "You got some particular reason to hate his guts, or is this just general cussedness I'm hearing?" When Matt didn't answer, he prompted. "What kind of evidence have you got, Matt? I mean, I'd really like to know why I've been freezing my butt off out here." Still no answer. Jack picked up his rocking motion again. "Agreed, this guy's a crud, okay? That don't make him a killer."

Matt ignored the poor grammar. It was for effect, he was certain. For some reason, it suited Jack to have people think that was a side of beef between his ears. Matt knew better. He tipped his head back and stared at the peeling metal ceiling of the truck. "Angel said pretty much the same thing," he mumbled half to himself.

"'Angel'?" Jack repeated. Matt had regretted the words as soon as they were out. Jack was too quick to let it pass. "Isn't that the name of the chick—young lady—you're seeing?" The front legs of his chair came down to the floor with a thunk. "She knows this guy?" He gestured toward the house with his thumb.

"She works with him."

The incessant rocking started again. "Matt, Matt, Matt, what are you telling me?"

Matt rolled a weary gaze to his companion. Jack was shaking his head, a doleful expression on his face. If abject disappointment is the effect he's striving for, Matt thought sourly, my own mother couldn't do it better. He was rapidly coming to understand Jack's unpopularity around the squad room. The guy had absolutely no qualms about calling the rear end of a horse a horse's ass even when the said hind end happened to be his lieutenant. Matt had an almost irresistible urge to yank that swaying ponytail and tumble him over, but he restrained himself with great fortitude. Largely, he admitted, because he knew he deserved the lecture he felt coming.

"Matt," Jack began, taking the tone one would use with a recalcitrant five-year-old. "What is the first thing—no, excuse me, the second thing—you learn at the academy, right after 'unholster your firearm before discharging same?'" He paused for maximum effect. *"Don't investigate where you're emotionally involved!"*

"I wasn't."

Jack's snort indicated that answer was too stupid to merit a response, which, Matt had to agree, it was.

"When the investigation started, I wasn't involved," he clarified.

"I get it. It just sort of crept up on you unawares."

Jack said this with a sneer in his voice, but Matt thought it was a pretty fair assessment of what had happened. "Yeah," he said. "She kind of got under my skin."

"Wonderful. And you didn't even get into her—"

"Don't start!"

Jack shook his head in befuddlement. "Madness," he muttered, his voice indicating he figured himself permanently immune to the condition. In a more agreeable tone he went on. "Listen, you know my legendary reputation as a stickler for regulations. I'm not gonna say anything. But I really expected better from you."

Matt had to chuckle in spite of himself. "Why, Jack, you sound almost prim."

"It's not funny, Matt. Couldn't you cool it for a while?"

"I'm not gonna give her up," Matt stated firmly, serious once more.

"Oh, boy."

Matt studied the coffee he was swirling idly in his cup. "It's not so cut-and-dried."

Jack turned and eyed Matt speculatively. "You think she's got trouble?"

"She might have."

"I notice we don't have a whole lot of official information on the little lady. I take it you know more?"

Matt nodded.

Jack let it go. "So where do we stand with this investigation? I guess ol' loverboy here's no longer our prime suspect?"

Matt gave a grunt of disgust. "Fact is, we don't have a better suspect. Fact is, we've got squat. We've got a trail as cold as last Sunday's roast beef and a bunch of monkeys who see, hear and speak no evil." He rested his mouth against a fist for a moment, then added more quietly, "But evil was done." He glanced at his companion. Some cops had an almost uncanny ability to enter the criminal psyche, to follow its reasoning, to sniff out its ends. For whatever reasons, Jack was better at it than most. In him, Matt had one of the most valuable weapons in the police arsenal: the mind of another cop. "Let's start with what we know," he said.

"The Nichols woman."

"Her ex is a dentist. Really putting the screws to her. Claims he should get custody of the kids because he can provide the most stable home life, pay for the private schools, et cetera. Of course, if he gets custody, he gets to stay in the family home with the family furniture and the family dog. He generously concedes that after nine years of marriage she's entitled to one of the cars. To be brief, she needs the money the drug trade could supply."

"That kind of money can be hard to explain in family court."

"True, but she's desperate. The nature of the business figures against her more. These drug lords tend to be class-A male chauvinists. Their women are chattel. They don't move beyond a certain very elemental status in the hierarchy."

"So, she's a possibility but not a likely one. What about the young guy?"

"Levering." Matt squinted out the window. The rain had picked up. The sapling in the front yard strained in the wind against the wires that tethered it upright, and the downpour beat a drumroll against the metal roof of the truck. "He's a question mark. He's from your typical dysfunctional family, the bad boy who applied himself and made good. Tried to put it all behind him, but these things have a way of catching up. It appears his wife has learned more about the man she married than she cares to know. The strain is showing."

Jack's answer was a grunt. Matt shot him a quick look and could have bit his tongue. Too late, he recalled Jack's own dysfunctional family, with its members about evenly divided in careers on both sides of the law. If he was offended, Matt couldn't tell. His expression was guarded, as always. "It's hard for me to peg him with a motive," was all he said.

"That brings us to Albert," Matt continued. "He's got money, respect, status. He's prominent in the community. He's on the board of the symphony and the country club. Try to find a motive there."

"What about the rumors?"

"About the hanky-panky? He denies it. She denies it. We have a lot of people happy to indulge in winks and knowing leers, but nobody willing to swear they've seen them together in anything but a professional manner. And even if it's true, so what? That's a motive for murder?" Matt took a swallow of his cold coffee and grimaced. "His wife talked to the mayor, who talked to the super, by the way. She feels some of the questions he's been made to answer are unseemly. Her word, not mine."

Jack muttered an obscenity under his breath. "What happened to Marty, now that was unseemly," he growled.

Turning to look at him, Matt was struck by the naked emotion in his face, as unguarded as anyone was ever likely to see it. "You ever work with Marty?" he asked.

Jack's nod was barely perceptible. "He was a good man. Hauled my sorry butt out of the coals more than once." He rested an elbow on his knee and rubbed a hand over his brow. Bringing his head up, he stared out the window and then nodded toward the house. "What about this guy?"

Matt pulled the logbook over and flipped rapidly through the curling pages, his face reflecting his reluctant acceptance of the truth revealed there. "He's got the morals of a slug, but I think he's got the spine of a slug, too." He slapped the book closed and tossed it aside. "He's no killer."

Jack nodded and chewed on the end of a red plastic coffee stirrer. "Are we sure the woman's death is connected?"

"Yeah. Nothing in her place was disturbed and her boyfriend's alibi is tight." It was a sad commentary on modern life, Matt thought. When a woman died suspiciously, the first to be suspected was the one who claimed to love her. "She knew something."

"Which is more than we can say." Jack bit off the end of the stirrer and blew it across the truck.

"What's the next move?"

"Me, I'd be looking for someone to dump this on. Someone to frame. I've got myself a nice little setup here. A respectable career and a lucrative business on the side. Came close to blowing it, but I got the lid back on that can of worms." He scratched his bristly jaw in thought. "Yep, I'd be looking for a patsy. Someone nobody knows very well. A loner. Someone without a past. It's easy to believe the worst of someone like that."

He could have been describing himself, Matt thought. He shifted his eyes and was met by that opaque gaze.

"You know who I mean," Jack said.

He did. It was part of the reason he wouldn't stop seeing her. A small part. The idea that she was at risk, and that he could protect her. If he had his way, she would be out of that place. But he didn't think he'd get his way. He knew he was smart enough, as far as that went, but he was no genius. If her vulnerability had struck him, it would occur to someone else. To her co-workers, she was remote, aloof, a mystery. They knew nothing of her life apart from the hospital. She would be without defenders.

"Can you trust her?" Jack probed.

Matt took a last swallow of his coffee and nodded. He shoved his cup into a wastebasket overflowing with the debris of previous meals. "She's not involved in this," he said.

"Just watch your step, buddy. You won't do her any good if you get pulled off the case."

Matt said nothing. There was no answer to that. In spite of the stale coffee he had just finished, his mouth went dry.

Angel laid her book aside and glanced at the clock on the bedside table. Matt hadn't called and he'd said he would. In fact, this was the first day all week she hadn't heard from him.

Grow up, Angel, she admonished herself. This isn't the first time a guy had said he would call you and didn't. Still, she had done a good job of walling herself off from this kind of hurt over the past years. It was a little unsettling to discover how much the disappointment could still sting. With a sigh she reached to turn off the lamp and the phone rang. Her heart racing, she answered.

"Angel?"

"Yes." She hoped he couldn't detect the breathlessness she heard in her own voice, even as she sensed the hesitation in his.

"You sound...different. Are you in bed?"

"It *is* after eleven."

"Aw, jeez. I didn't realize. I just got home a little while ago, and I got Patrick squared away—"

"That's all right. I wasn't asleep. Rough day?"

"Kinda. This investigation hit another dead end." Hearing the fatigue in his tone, she could almost see him plow his fingers through his hair. "But I didn't call to dump that on you. How was your day?"

When had anyone else ever bothered to ask? She couldn't remember. "Busy. We're having to shuffle people around to make them available to the police. And everyone seems to be walking on eggs. I'd take our usual pandemonium any day."

"Yeah." He paused. "What have you got on?"

"Pardon me?"

"I hear voices . . . in the backgrou—"

"Oh! The radio." She reached over to the nightstand to flick it off. His low chuckle came over the line, and her insides did a slow curl.

"You thought I was asking . . ."

"Yes."

"What you're wearing."

"Yes." She bit her lip to contain embarrassed laughter.

"Nah, I wasn't asking that."

"I know." She twisted the phone cord around her fingers in the silence that followed.

"What *are* you wearing?"

"Maaa-att!"

"Ah, now you've got my curiosity up in the stratosphere."

"I'm not going—"

"Come on. It couldn't be any better than what I'm imagining."

"Your shirt." She felt hot color steal up her face.

"What?"

"I'm wearing your shirt." What on earth had come over her? How could she be telling him this?

"Nah. My shirt, which you left very nicely folded, I might add, is upstairs tucked underneath my pillow even as we speak."

"Your *other* shirt."

He was silent for a moment, then realization dawned. "Ohhh, the one you put on after Patrick—"

"Yes." The one she had worn home and then dutifully washed and ironed. How could she explain the impulse that had made her take it off its hanger and slip it on? The irresistible urge to feel him close.

"That's nice." He didn't sound as if he minded. "That's real nice."

There was teasing in his tone, but there was tenderness, too. She put a hand to her face and smiled behind it. "I'll get it back to—"

"No! Keep it. It's yours. I like to think of you wearing it."

She could hear him expel a long breath and wondered what tack he would take next. She didn't have to wonder long.

"Is it buttoned?"

"Matt!"

"Tell me, sweetheart."

"Mostly." All but the top two, she hedged to herself, fingering them.

"You want to maybe unbutton it a little more?"

"I don't..." She leaned her head back against the headboard and smoothed her palm down the front of the shirt, imagining his hands there, longing. So tempted by what he suggested, and a little frightened, too.

"You know, get comfortable."

"I *am* comfortable."

"Mmm. I'm not."

"Matt, I can't..."

"Okay."

He wouldn't push. He never pushed. That drew her to him more than anything.

"What are you wearing underneath?" Before she could object, he rushed on. "Don't tell me, let me guess. Nothing on top—just the shirt against you."

Yes, just the shirt, gently abrading the nipples that thrust forward seeking that contact.

"And on the bottom, some little modesty bit, right?"

"*Matt.*"

"Little lacy panties like—"

"Good *night*, Matt."

Was it possible to hear a grin? She could swear she heard his.

"Sleep well, Angel."

Oh, she would.

Angel took another sip of lukewarm coffee from the foam cup and frowned at the papers on the table in front of her. She was working on the personnel scheduling for the next month, which included the Memorial Day weekend. At the moment she was suffering from a surfeit of riches. She had notes from eleven, count 'em, *eleven,* nurses offering to work the O.R. on Memorial Day. She needed one. All this good fortune came with a price, she knew. Later in the year, when she was desperately searching for someone to cover the Thanksgiving and Christmas holidays, these same nurses would claim with perfectly straight faces that they had already worked, or at least *volunteered* to work, their holiday for the year.

She sighed deeply and leaned back in the molded plastic chair, kneading the tense muscles in her neck. For the past five years she, herself, had covered Thanksgiving and Christmas in the O.R., saying she didn't mind; she had no special plans anyway. What a barren existence, she thought. Would things be different this year?

Angel let her gaze drift idly around the room. Dr. Albert sat at another table, his nose buried in the financial pages of the newspaper. A couple of the staff nurses were sitting on a tan vinyl couch in the corner, munching on salads from plastic containers and talking quietly. Tony Levering slouched in another chair next to the table that held the microwave. He was slumped forward, his elbows resting on his knees and his head in his hands. He looked like he'd been up all night.

Ordinarily, Angel liked to do paperwork in this combination kitchenette-lounge used by the operating room staff. She could keep tabs on the activity and be available for consultations and decisions as needed. It was a bad idea today, though. She was having trouble keeping her mind on task anyway. Thoughts of Matt kept intruding. Despite the long hours he was putting in on the murder investigation and her own erratic schedule, he had managed to call her every day. She was beginning to look forward to it, to rely on it, and she was not sure that was a good thing.

Angel's musings were interrupted when the door connecting the lounge to the O.R. corridor whooshed open. Donna Parker sailed into the room, the surgical gown she had put on backward over her scrub suit for warmth billowing out behind her like a blue parachute. She made a beeline for the coffee urn and poured herself a cup. Close on her heels, Gary Chapman breezed in.

"Hey, Ange, how're you? I came to get a cup of your coffee. That stuff they make in the E.R. is swill."

"Sweet talk won't work, Gary. If you take the last cup, you have to make a fresh pot, just like it says on the sign."

Gary raised his eyebrows at Angel's uncustomary retort. She caught his shrug and the pleading glance he sent Donna as well as Donna's acquiescing nod. Fascinated, Angel watched the little tableau playing out in front of her. Gary leaned nonchalantly against the stainless-steel countertop, sipping his coffee and preening like a potentate while Donna rinsed out the pot and put more coffee on to brew. He sidled closer to her, snaked an arm around her waist and squeezed. Angel rolled her eyes at Donna's muffled giggle and shook her head in disbelief as the young woman slid her hands over Gary's backside lingeringly and gave a pat. No question, Gary was a lech, but he had plenty of encouragement. Somehow, she couldn't see him as a threat. He could take "no" for an answer, even if he didn't have to very often. What was it about him that rankled Matt so? Something he'd said? She wondered if Gary was up to his old tricks again.

Apparently Dr. Albert wasn't amused, not if the rattle of newspaper and his loud *harrumph* was any indication. Angel took another sip of her coffee and eyed him over the rim of her cup. He was a hard one to figure. If the rumors about him were true, his behavior was no more admirable than Gary's and Donna's. Of course, he was more discreet.

From his corner of the room, Tony heaved himself to his feet and shuffled over to the counter to refill his coffee cup.

Angel was struck by the change in his appearance. He was a handsome man with a natural athleticism, but now his shoulders seemed to sag with an oppressive burden and a fine tremor shook his hands as he filled his cup. He leaned against the wall and stared at the floor as he sipped the coffee, seemingly oblivious to the activity around him.

Donna slathered peanut butter on a slice of bread and sallied over to where Angel sat, the unfinished schedule still in front of her. "Is that next month's hours, Angel? I've been meaning to tell you, I can work Memorial Day, if you need me."

Angel tossed her pencil onto the table with a laugh. "Why not," she said. "An even dozen. Let's have a party."

Donna flashed a questioning glance at Gary, but he only lifted his shoulders and shook his head. "You already have someone to work the holiday, Angel?" she asked tentatively.

"Mmm-hmm. I have eleven someones as a matter of fact."

Donna made a pout of defeat, then shrugged good-naturedly. "Maybe the Fourth of July."

Angel laughed again. "Maybe," she said.

With her ploy unsuccessful, Donna appeared to lose interest in Angel's doings and wandered back over to Gary, batting her lashes. Angel picked up her pencil and tried to concentrate once more on the task in front of her. Out of the corner of her eye she saw Tony push away from the wall, discard his coffee cup, and pull a pair of paper shoe covers from the cardboard box on the counter. He sank heavily into the chair across the table from her and pulled the shoe covers over his sneakers. Watching him, Angel again felt a tug, part sympathy, part unease. He looked wretched.

"Were you on call last night, Tony?" she asked quietly.

He shook his head and rubbed his hands over his face as if to rouse himself. "Tonight." He laughed without mirth. "Would you believe it?" He rested his elbows on his knees, his hands dangling between them. "Meghan had us up all night. Ear infection."

Angel nodded her understanding. That could explain his fatigue. Meghan was the older of his daughters, as she recalled. Just turned two. She leaned toward him, companionably. "It'll get easier when your residency is finished. Just a couple more months." A thought occurred to her. "Have you been offered the position here? I know they like your work."

He answered with a quick shake of his head. "Not yet. I thought I might, too, but now..." He clasped his hands together and squeezed till his knuckles were white. He went on in a barely audible mutter. "You work hard. You try to do everything right. You think you've got it all behind you, and then..." He stopped, the muscles in his jaw tightly clenched.

Angel straightened and went very still. She stared at his stooped figure and ached to tell him that she knew, that it didn't matter. A person was what he made of himself, not just a product of his past. But, of course, she could not. She couldn't even be sure it was his past he meant. He was one of the four. She knew he had been closeted for hours yesterday with an investigator in the little dictation room off the Anesthesia office. They had been shuffling people around all day, trying to cover his cases. In the end, he had emerged stone-faced and grim.

Dr. Albert bent the edge of his newspaper down and peered at Tony over the top of his reading glasses. "Are you going to relieve Donovan sometime today?" he grumbled.

Tony nodded and got to his feet. "On my way," he said, pulling his mask up over his nose and chin. He gave Angel a conspiratorial wink and went out into the O.R. corridor.

Angel sat, her eyes focused on the pencil she twirled between her thumb and forefinger. Vaguely, she was aware that the two nurses from the couch brushed past her on their way back to their assigned rooms. At some point Dr. Albert had tossed his paper aside and left, also. That was just background, like a television playing with the sound turned down. All her concentration was centered in that little pool of dread that had been quietly simmering behind her breastbone all week. *One of the four.*

She turned it over and over in her mind. So many things could be explained away. There was only one thing that could not. The bullet had been placed in the plastic container, labeled and sealed. Any number of people had sworn statements to that effect. She had found the container, a difficult object to conceal on one's person, empty and in a spot it could not have been put accidentally. Its placement had been a deliberate and purposeful act. A killer's act. Carried out by someone whose presence in that room would not be questioned. Someone who belonged there. One of the four.

For brief periods of time during the week, she would forget. Caught up in one crisis or another, for a few moments her mind would be totally engaged in her work. Then, like an unexpected slap across her face, the reality would strike her, making her wary and suspicious. And afraid.

What did she know of them, really? She had worked with each of them for months or years, but knew them not at all. For that matter, what did they know of her? Cool Angel. Efficient Angel. Competent Angel. "Could you take care of this, Angel?" "Angel, would you mind?" Always willing. Always helpful. *Why?* So they would like her. *Like her.* Not one of them really knew her. What would they think, she mused, if they knew she had spent the night dreaming of Matt's hands on her breasts? She lifted her gaze to the couple in the corner in time to see Gary trail the back of one finger across Donna's ample bosom and almost laughed at that. What would they think if they learned she was just shy of twenty-eight before she'd kissed a man and liked it? Now *that* would be grist for this rumor mill.

She set her pencil down and brought her hands up to her mouth, elbows resting on the table. That small motion seemed to draw the attention of the flirting twosome. They pulled apart quickly and, with some last words to Angel, left the room.

She rose, blew a long breath out through puffed cheeks, and dumped the rest of her coffee down the sink. Returning to the table, she picked up the papers she had been working on and let them drop again. This was a waste of time. Better to give it up for now and find some way to make herself useful.

She slapped the schedules into the manila folder she kept them in and headed down the outer corridor to her office. She turned the knob and entered the unlocked room. The woman standing behind her desk sifting through the contents of the top drawer looked up sharply.

"Faith?"

The nurse attempted a pinched smile and shoved the drawer closed with her hip. "Do you have next month's on-call schedule, Angel? Dr. Albert has been asking for it. Here's the one for Anesthesia." She placed the paper she referred to in the center of Angel's desk.

"I haven't finished with it yet," Angel answered, her voice even. She indicated the folder she carried. "I'll get it to him tomorrow."

Faith nodded with another nervous smile. Still clutching some papers, she scurried around the edge of the desk and squeezed past Angel out the door.

Angel closed the door behind her. Slowly she approached her desk, tossed her folder down, and opened the drawer. She delved through the papers there, pushing them one way and another. Nothing appeared to be missing, and there didn't seem to be anything there that shouldn't be. She slammed the drawer shut hard, annoyed with herself. She hadn't thought to be cautious beforehand. The truth was, she didn't know if she would recognize something out of place.

She pressed her hands flat against the top of the desk and read the single sheet Faith had left there. Everything appeared in order. No answers there. She put the paper in her folder with the other schedules and stared unseeing at the neat green blotter covering her desk. God! she thought, what is going on here? Two weeks ago she wouldn't have raised an eyebrow at Faith's actions. And now? Now her heart was hammering and her hands shook. She inhaled deeply in an effort to steady herself and tapped the edge of the folder against the desk before placing it on the blotter. Then, with grim determination, she locked her desk, locked her office, and pocketed her keys.

Chapter 9

Matt had a bad feeling about the place as soon as they walked in. Even before that, if he was honest. To begin with, the ride over had been uncomfortably quiet. His usual gift for small talk had deserted him. He was trying too hard. Then, though he hadn't touched Angel before they reached the restaurant, he felt her stiffen as soon as he put his hand to the small of her back to guide her through the door. The last thing he needed was to be greeted by a maître d' with a David Niven mustache and a supercilious smirk. He was out of his element.

They were led to a minuscule table that had neither a window to the outdoors nor a view of the fireplace, but was on a direct path between the kitchen and the tables that did. He had never been any good at raising a stink in situations like this, and the tight little smile Angel gave him as the headwaiter seated her practically begged him not to make a fuss, so he didn't. Matt took his seat and didn't even have time to get his elbows on the table before another waiter, this one very young and obviously out to impress, snapped his napkin open and settled it on his lap with a flourish. Across the table, Angel met his eyes, her expression blank as the waiter performed the same service for her.

She turned her head slightly and lowered her gaze when the young man lifted the glass hurricane from the center of the table and made a show of lighting the candle it covered. He handed them leather-backed menus only a little smaller than the table they were sitting at and left them. Matt craned his neck to see over the edge of his menu.

"Would you like something to drink?" he asked the top of Angel's head, which was all that he could see.

She lowered her menu and opened her mouth, but before she could reply, a black-clad foreman was thrust in front of Matt's face, effectively blocking her from view while his water glass was filled. When she reappeared, she had pulled her lower lip into her mouth and was biting down on it. She answered his question with a quick shake of her head.

Matt sighed and studied the selections while the waiter hovered. When they placed their orders, he requested a bottle of the house wine. That seemed simple enough.

He should have known better. The man returned bearing two glasses, a corkscrew, and the bottle. He held the label up to Matt's face for inspection and waited. Matt could comfortably discuss the finer points of Chinese, Greek and Mexican beer, but when it came to wine, he knew red and he knew white. He cast a glance at Angel, who had lowered her head again, and approved the bottle with a nod.

They sat in silence while the waiter went through his rigmarole with the corkscrew and the towel. When the young man finally extracted the cork, he took a sniff and then stuck the cork under Matt's nose. Matt gave him a blank look, but a sudden movement from Angel caught his attention. Though her gaze was riveted on her water glass, the corners of her mouth were quivering frantically.

Ahh, he thought, relief flooding him. This is going to be all right after all. He'd forgotten about her finely tuned sense of the ridiculous. He waved the cork away, but the waiter wasn't through with him just yet. The man splashed a little wine into a glass, wafted that under Matt's nose, and offered it to him to taste. Matt managed to get a sip down only by avoiding looking at Angel until he had done so. She had brought her napkin up to her mouth to stifle her snickers, but nothing could disguise the mischief dancing in her eyes.

When the waiter finally saw fit to leave them in peace, he leaned in toward Angel. "Do you have any idea what the hell that cork is supposed to smell like?" he asked. "I don't have a clue." She gave up any pretense of composure and dissolved into peals of laughter, shaking her head.

"Behave yourself, Ms. Martino," he said, his own voice choked with suppressed mirth. "You're gonna get us thrown out of here."

That did nothing to improve her self-control, or Matt's, either, and by the time the waiter returned with their salads, they were giggling like two teenagers on prom night who didn't know which fork to use. Matt felt like an idiot, but when he looked into Angel's eyes, he knew the ice was well and truly broken, and he figured the feeling was worth it. He thought they'd be left to themselves for a little while and started in on his salad when Angel darted a quick glance over his shoulder.

"Is he coming back?"

She gave a brief nod. "The pepper mill," she said. Her lips were quivering again.

Matt put down his fork. "I'm just warning you, if he tries to cut my meat, we're leaving."

That set Angel off again. She could only wave helplessly to stop the waiter from blanketing her salad in pepper. Matt was still grinning at her when the man finally left.

"It's obvious," he said, laughing, "neither one of us is classy enough to be dining in this establishment."

"I'm just a beer and pizza kind of woman," she sniffed, trying to get control. She rubbed her fingers at the outer corners of her eyes to wipe away the tears her laughter had squeezed out.

"You won't hear me complain." His eyes met hers and her already high color deepened even more.

Breaking the hold of his steady gaze, she settled back in his chair and reached for her purse. "Were you able to get out for the *Times* last Sunday?"

"Nah. Patrick had me at his beck and call all day." His eyes lit up when she handed him the crossword puzzle from that paper, partially filled in, and he reached inside his suit coat to his shirt pocket for something to write with. "Ah, Angel, you really don't like the geography ones, do you?" he said with a wink.

They didn't appear to present any problems for him, Angel thought as she watched his fingers rapidly fill in the blank squares. *In ink,* no less. He was either supremely confident or extremely foolhardy. She cocked her head at an angle to get a better view of the questions. "That's brilliant," she said.

He raised his head. "Nah, it's just an interest of mine," he answered with a modest shrug.

She looked like she was going to lose it again. "No," she said, smothering a laugh with her hand. "I mean, seven down, *gem cut.* It's *brilliant.*"

He looked down at the puzzle again. "So it is," he said, his modesty considerably more genuine. "What's this *harem?*"

Angel leaned in close to see the letters he had filled in. "*Seraglio.*" He gave her a doubtful look. "It has a *g*, Matt."

"Okay, that's it."

As he continued to concentrate on the crossword puzzle, Angel took the opportunity to study his face. He'd gotten a haircut, she noticed. Not that it had really improved his appearance. She rather liked his usual shaggy mop. But like this restaurant, and his crisp shirt and neatly knotted tie, she sensed he had done it for her. To please her. And she was touched. As with any form of flattery, the most complimentary thing about it was that he bothered. He thought she was worth the effort.

She thought of the others who hadn't even bothered with a shower after leaving the playing field, and immediately pushed that memory from her mind. It was unfair to paint him with the same brush as those others from so long ago. He was nothing like them. He was a good and decent man. She had known they existed. She just never thought there would be one for her.

She saw that he had filled in the rest of the spaces and was tapping his pen against the paper.

"We're done," he said. He lifted his glance to her face, only inches from his own. "I never finish these by myself."

"Neither do I."

"We make a good team. Although," he went on with a wry smile, "this could make for some battles over the paper on Sunday mornings."

Angel wasn't ready to deal with that idea. She moved farther back in her chair and directed her attention to her salad.

Matt looked at her bent head. God, he was in deep. And it was so unexpected. If someone had pointed her out to him, he'd have said she wasn't his type. He had loved one woman for so long, he had assumed that was his type. Physically, at least, Angel couldn't have been more different. What was it about her that drew him?

He knew that her seeming fragility was deceptive. She might look as delicate as a porcelain figurine, but the crucible of life had tempered her character to a steely resolve. In the time he had known her, despite the hardships of her past, he heard not a single word of complaint, or self-pity. The wonder of it was that it hadn't made her hard, that someone who had known so little love had devoted herself to a lifetime of caring.

Then there was the sense of humor she probably hadn't known she possessed. And she was smart. As that thought winged its way through his consciousness, he cringed inwardly. *Oh, yes, Matthew, you pious hypocrite! You're interested in her mind. Sister Mary Cecelia would have had you up to the front of the classroom with your nose against the blackboard for that whopper.*

Honesty forced him to acknowledge the other attractions. Like the healthy dollop of lust her presence provoked. While he was being honest here, he could consider the nights he'd spent imagining her long legs wrapped around him. Or the way that little whimper she gave when she finally opened her mouth to his kisses shot straight to a part of him that hadn't called attention to itself in months. Fourteen of them to be exact. She made him feel like a callow kid again. With about the same outlets for his raging hormones as he had back then. He reached for his glass and took a long swallow of his wine. Nope, he couldn't discount the lust.

The arrival of their main course saved Matt from further discomfiting admissions. He held on to his knife and fork as the waiter set his plate in front of him, while Angel stared fixedly at hers, not daring to look at him.

"How's Patrick?" she asked when the waiter had left them.

"Crusty. He'll be able to go to school on Monday. He'll have to miss his first baseball game tomorrow, but he'd like you to come watch him play another time."

"I'd like that, too. Did you play ball when you were a kid?" She wondered about his past. He knew more than she would have liked about hers, but she knew little about him.

"Baseball? Some. Pickup games mostly. Not organized the way it is today."

"How about high school? I imagine you were on the football team." The question seemed nonchalant, but she couldn't hold his gaze and turned her attention to her food.

"No," he said gently. "Not football. I was a late bloomer. Didn't have the weight. I was on the swim team."

"Ah, swimming." *That explained the shoulders.* "I should have guessed."

"Let's see. What else? I always liked geography. I'm fortunate that police work doesn't require my drawing to be any better than stick figures, and I play the trumpet."

"The trumpet." She raised her eyebrows. "Now that I wouldn't have pictured."

"I'll show you some time," he drawled. "It's all in the pucker."

She didn't doubt for a minute he'd be good at it. Disconcerted, she dropped her gaze to her plate again.

Matt saw her confusion. He reached across the small space that separated them and gently grasped her chin, bringing her reluctant eyes to meet his. "I don't mean to embarrass you. I just kid around a lot."

"I embarrass too easily, I suppose," she admitted. "I'm not used to a relationship with a man on these terms."

He released her chin with a disarming smile. "I know. You've divvied men up into professionals, patients, and pond scum, and you're having a little trouble figuring out exactly where I fit in."

Angel swallowed the bite of steak she'd been chewing. That was more accurate than she cared to admit. She decided to meet his bantering tone head-on. "What would be the point? You wouldn't stay where I put you anyway."

He laughed, undaunted. "Probably not."

"Do you like being a cop?" she asked, steering the conversation back to him.

"Most of the time." She detected a wariness in his voice and his narrowed eyes. She sensed this topic had caused problems for him before. Despite his apparent reservations, he went on. "I don't have the temperament for plea bargains and deals. I like it in the trenches where the lines are more clearly drawn."

Angel was silent. She pushed her rice idly around her plate.

Matt released an impatient breath and nudged his plate aside. He rested his arms on the table, leaning toward Angel. "Rosie didn't marry a cop," he began. "She worked to put me through law school. She wasn't real thrilled with my decision to go into police work."

Angel stopped playing with her food, her attention fully on him. "Did that cause problems between you?"

He glanced away, searching for the words that would explain without seeming disloyal. Finally he brought his eyes back to Angel's. "Our marriage wasn't perfect. No marriage with me as half of it could be. But it was good. Solid. I wouldn't be here with you, or anyone else, if she were still alive." He paused, and Angel nodded her understanding. "But, yes, we disagreed about this," he continued. "I think Rosie always hoped it was a phase I was going through and I'd grow out of it."

"And it isn't."

He shook his head. "I think it's who I am. Anyone who would share my life would have to accept that."

Angel mulled that for a moment, her eyes tracing the contours of the face that was coming to mean so much to her. And deep inside she recognized the beginnings of the stark terror that must have gripped Rosie each time she surrendered him to the streets. "Aren't you ever afraid?" she asked on a whisper.

He gave a short laugh. "Last time I checked, I wasn't certifiably nuts. Sure, I'm afraid sometimes. But it's not the way it looks in the movies. We follow procedures. We use backup. We're trained for this." He saw the doubt in her eyes. "Look," he said, "I'm not a cowboy, and I don't have a death wish. I don't take unnecessary risks. Besides, even the Lone Ranger had backup."

She smiled but still appeared unconvinced. He tried another tack. "To tell you the truth, I hate hospitals. What you do scares the hell out of me."

Her eyes widened in surprise. "Me?"

"I mean it. You probably see more blood in a day than I do in a year. And you're making snap decisions that people's lives depend on. Suppose you're taking care of a gash on this guy's head. Meanwhile he kicks off from the stab wound to his chest you haven't gotten to yet." He shook his head. "I couldn't handle that."

Angel straightened in her chair and frowned in confusion. She had never thought of her work in those terms. "It's not really like that," she began. "We work as a team. We all know our roles. They're almost automatic. It's five pairs of hands working as one." She searched for the proper description. "Kind of like a ballet." She laughed at his skeptical look. "We follow procedures. We're trained for this." She went suddenly very still as she realized how closely the words she had chosen to describe her work echoed his own. His level gaze told her she had made his point for him.

"Exactly," he said with a Cheshire cat grin.

She sat back in her chair and folded her arms with a huff. "Will you stop! It's not the same at all. No one's taking potshots at me."

"Pick your poison," he answered with a shrug. "I'll take a nice dependable thug any day."

The waiter returned to clear their table and another rolled up with the dessert car. Angel eyed the luscious offerings longingly. "Go ahead," Matt said. "I'm having that thing with the cherries and chocolate."

Angel ordered chocolate mousse and turned back to Matt. "All I ever do around you is eat."

"We'll have to get together more than once a week for that to be a problem. But I'm open to suggestions."

She rolled her eyes and took a bite of her dessert. Matt was regarding her with a wayward smile tugging at the corners of that sinfully sexy mouth.

"So how about it?" he asked.

She took another bite of the mousse and licked the whipped cream from her lips. She was gratified to see Matt's gaze drop to her mouth and his cocky smile falter a bit. "How about what?"

He wrenched his eyes back to hers and cleared his throat. "Next weekend. Do I get to feed you again?"

She laughed and shook her head. "I'm afraid you'll have to forego that pleasure. I'm on call next weekend."

The smile disappeared entirely and he stabbed at his cake with his fork. "How does that work, 'on call'?"

"Well, I work the day shift on Saturday, then go home and rest up while the evening personnel take over until eleven-thirty. Anything that comes in between eleven-thirty Saturday night and seven o'clock Monday morning is mine. I live close enough to the hospital that I can take calls from home. But if I get called in during the night, I usually just spend the rest of the night in one of the on-call rooms."

Matt had pushed his cake aside. He rested his chin in his hand, his long fingers splayed across his jaw. "Who calls you in? Someone from the emergency room?"

"Most times the patient is in the E.R., but the surgeon consults with Anesthesia, and after he sees the patient he has the switchboard call the team in."

"The team?"

Angel nodded. "An R.N. and a technician are always on call together. The technician scrubs and the R.N. handles everything else."

"So you never go in alone."

She narrowed her eyes and chewed her lip for some moments. "Once in a great while there might be something so minor, a D & C, say, that just requires one person. Then only the nurse is called in. But that almost never happens.''

Angel took another bite of her mousse. Matt didn't look pleased, and this wasn't just disappointment anymore. He was making his cop face again. Whatever he was about to say, she didn't expect to like.

''Angel,'' he began, ''I think you should go away for a while.'' She opened her mouth to protest, and he held up a hand. She eyed him warily as he went on in a bland tone. ''You've probably got weeks of vacation piled up. It'd be a good time—''

''I'm not leaving.'' She stuck her spoon upright in the mousse and pushed her fists against the edge of the table.

''I'm only asking—''

''You're asking too much,'' she returned heatedly.

''I'm afraid it's dangerous there for you,'' he explained, trying to soothe her ruffled feathers.

''Why?''

He looked at the challenge in her eyes and his mouth tightened to a thin line. He wasn't dealing with this well. He couldn't blame her for resisting his ham-handed approach. Still, he doubted any method would be effective. She wouldn't budge, and, short of tossing her in the clink, he didn't see how to make her, but he felt he had to try. ''He's not finished yet. He'll be after someone else.''

''I know that,'' she said.

''Then get out,'' he pleaded harshly.

''I can't, Matt.'' She seemed surprised by her own vehemence, but determined nonetheless. ''If it's dangerous for me, it's dangerous for the others, too. How can I walk away?'' She put her elbows on the table and covered her face with her hands. After a few moments she looked up at him and went on more calmly. ''This job is the first thing in my life that has given me any feeling of pride, any sense of self-respect. I know I come across as cool and remote, but there are people there I would put my hand in a fire for. I won't leave.''

He'd never really expected to change her mind. This feisty obstinacy was part of what he admired most about her. He

leaned back in his chair and gave a one-shouldered shrug.
"Okay," he said.

Angel's eyebrows rose in shock. "What! You're going to
roll over just like that?"

The cheeky smile flitted around the edges of his mouth
again. Leaning toward her, he reached a hand across the table and rubbed a dab of whipped cream her tongue had
missed from the corner of her mouth. His green eyes locked
with hers as he licked the cream from his finger, and the heat
of his gaze warmed her all the way to the soles of her feet.
"I don't want to argue with you tonight," he murmured.

The waiter made his third pass by their table. It was becoming impossible to ignore him. Matt motioned for the
check and again turned to Angel. "They've got a lounge
downstairs with a combo. Plays oldies. We could have an
after-dinner drink." He looked away, then back to her uncertainly. "Do you dance?"

She shouldn't. The familiar wariness flowed through her.
Even without the drink, his nearness was enough to make
her forget her scruples and her shame. But he was unsure,
too. Utterly without brashness or conceit. She could feel it.
And she wasn't ready for this evening to end. By way of an
answer, she held a hand out flat in front of her and wob-
bled it.

"Good," he answered with a quick nod. "We'll stick to
the slow ones."

While he settled with the waiter, Angel excused herself
and made her way to the ladies' room.

Regarding herself in the mirror as she washed and dried
her hands, she took stock of her appearance. She really
couldn't fault the dress. The silky fabric might cling a little
more than she would like, but the simple wrap style had a
modest neckline and sleeves that ended just above the elbow. Demure, but stylish; "ladylike" her grandmother
would say. Only Grandmother had always said it with a
sneer.

Possibly the color was a little too intense, she thought,
smoothing the material over her hips. The deep amethyst
had seemed understated enough on the rack, but she hadn't
realized how it would accentuate the blue of her eyes. The

flush of her cheeks, she knew, could not be blamed on the dress.

As she freshened her makeup, she caught a hint of the perfume she had touched to the pulse points of her wrists and throat. That, too, was a splurge, different from the light, floral scent she usually wore. The sultry fragrance of crushed gardenias made a mockery of the fact that she had demurred at dabbing some between her breasts.

She reached into her handbag for a brush to make repairs to her hair, and stared again at her reflection. The neat coil she had made at her nape didn't need straightening, and the wisps she had pulled deliberately from the twist to curl around her face had just the softening effect she intended. She replaced the brush without changing a hair. Then she rested her hands on the edge of the marble counter and leaned closer to the mirror.

"Oh, Angelina," she whispered softly to herself, "you don't lie to yourself often, and you're not very good at it. Who are you trying to fool? You want him, and the lures you're using to get him are as old as Eve. And, in the end, what will it gain you?"

She leaned her head back and stared, unseeing, at the dark, polished panels of the ceiling. He was funny and kind and more patient than most, but he was a man, and he would want what they all wanted. He would want *that* act. She brought a hand to her mouth and pressed tightly. Would it be any different because it was Matt? Or would she feel the same revulsion for herself, and for him? She had been roused by his kisses and brought to a heat she'd never experienced with anyone else, but she wasn't sure that would be enough when the time came to submit.

She swallowed hard and squeezed her eyes shut. When she lowered her head and opened her eyes, she was herself once again. Cool, composed, familiar. "This is the reality," she told her image. "You are not—and never can be—what he would want for his son." She picked up her handbag, turned, and walked out.

* * *

Even from across the room Matt could sense the change in her. She walked as if she had put starch in her underwear while she was gone, moving with the stiff, self-conscious gait of every pretty woman who tried to get past a construction site without attracting attention. Not that she was having a hell of a lot of success. He had never considered himself a territorial male, but the leer that old fossil—the one with the pinkie ring and more chins than hair—was sending her way raised his hackles. Matt watched the guy move his piggy eyes along the direction Angel was headed, spot him, and quickly haul his gaze back to his meal. He allowed himself a moment of smug satisfaction before he faced the fact that Angel probably lumped him in with all the other sapheads.

He sighed and glanced at her again. She was close enough to make eye contact now, but she wouldn't look at him. Jeez, what was he going to do about her? This relationship was one step forward and two steps back, going nowhere fast. He had his work cut out for him. But then, he reasoned, he had never been one to shy from a challenge.

Matt rose as she approached their table, took her elbow, and steered her toward the foyer before she could come up with any objections. As they passed between the maître d's booth and the entry door, Angel opened her mouth to speak. Grabbing a handful of mints from the reservation stand, Matt popped several into her mouth and some into his own. She would never be so gauche as to speak with her mouth full. He had her halfway down the stairs before she could talk again, and if she had intended to back out, she had given up on the idea, he could tell.

The lounge was everything the guys at the station house had promised. Cool and very dim, it appeared to be lit only by flickering candles and the colored lights around the bar. Most of the room was taken up by clusters of tables where people held muted conversations and drank. The bar, with wine glasses hanging in glittering precision from a rack all around it, was in the center of the room. Along the far wall was a parquet dance floor where several couples swayed and clung. The guys weren't kidding about the "oldies," either. He recognized a tune from the big band era, albeit now played by a very small band. Still, it had something of a jazzy flavor, with a piano and a saxophone. He liked the low moan of a sax. He'd like to hear some other low moans before this night was out.

They found a table about the size of a small pizza near the dance floor and were promptly greeted by a cocktail waitress dressed in black. Nary a hint of fishnet or cleavage, though, Matt noted with relief. Classy place. He waited while Angel asked for a soda, then rolled his eyes heavenward and ordered the same.

"Don't feel you can't have a drink just because I'm not having one," Angel said a tad defensively.

Matt shrugged and rested his arms on the table. "I'm driving." He eyed her suspiciously. "Why do I get the feeling that you don't trust me, Ms. Martino?"

Angel swung a quick glance at the others sitting around them, so close they might as well have been at the same table. "I hardly—"

"Do you think I'm gonna jump your bones?"

The waitress was back with their drinks. Angel glared while the woman set them on the table and Matt paid her. "I can't believe we're having this conversation," she chided as soon as the waitress was out of earshot.

"She's heard worse, believe me." He took a sip of his soda and carefully set the glass down on the wet ring it had left. "I'm not, by the way." He shook his head. "I'm not gonna jump your bones."

Angel took another quick look over her shoulder. "Why, thank you." She smiled sweetly. "How reassuring."

"I know you don't expect to like it much."

That set her back a bit. She wasn't going to pretend she didn't know what "it" meant. The false smile faded. "Some women don't like it at all," she countered.

"I've kissed you, Angel. You're not one of 'em."

She didn't have an answer for that. She watched him take another long swig of his drink and clasp his hands on the table. He looked like he was contemplating more mischief. From the moment he'd plunked the first mint into her mouth, she'd known she was in for more of his nonsense. Knowing it was coming didn't mean she was prepared.

She took a sip of her own soda and, for the first time, realized she still had her purse clutched awkwardly in her lap. Matt's arms, the candle, and two glasses left no room for it on the table. She leaned over to place it on the floor against the leg of her chair. When she straightened, it was to find Matt's knee wedged snugly between her thighs.

She threw him a killing glance, which was entirely wasted. With a choirboy expression, he was watching the guy with the saxophone. She considered her options. She could make a scene, which she knew Matt was betting she wouldn't do. He would win that bet. Gingerly, she pressed her knees together, trying to force his leg out. He turned his head slightly, one eyebrow raised, and gave her a quizzical look, as if she were the one responsible for this situation. She eased the pressure and felt his leg slide further up between her thighs, pushing her dress along with it. The heated friction against her nylon-clad inner thighs stole her breath. Desperately, she reached her hand under the table and shoved at his leg.

He had the gall to look affronted. "That's my knee you have your hand on, Ms. Martino."

"It's your lap I'll dump this drink in if you don't behave yourself, Lieutenant Flanagan," she retorted.

He laughed openly then and leaned close to whisper in her ear, "Care to dance?"

Ah. That would get his leg out from between her thighs. "I'd love to."

He grasped her hand and pulled her along with him to the dance floor.

Moments later she careered headlong into the fruits of her folly. Whatever could have possessed her to think dancing with him would be a safer alternative? Nothing in her experience had prepared her for the full frontal press of Matt's body against hers.

True, there was nothing overtly improper about their position. His hands were neither indecently placed nor engaged in any furtive forays on her anatomy. In fact, she thought as she caught a glimpse from the side of another male's hands cupping his partner's bottom hard against him, they were one of the more decorous couples on the floor. That sight prompted her to turn her head on Matt's shoulder. Another misjudgment. The heels she was wearing added just enough to her height to tip her into the crook of his neck right above his collar. That softer spot where his beard stopped growing, where the skin was warm and faintly moist with the mingled scents of soap and after-shave and man. Her lips parted there, against him, and she detected the first sign that he was not as undisturbed as he seemed. A muffled groan escaped him as he buried his lips in the tendrils near her ear, and his arm tightened around her waist.

Angel tensed, lost the rhythm, and would have stumbled if he hadn't caught her more closely to him. He lifted his head and regarded her with heavy-lidded eyes. "Sweetheart, relax," he whispered, his lips moving against her temple. "I'm not gonna try anything here." He sought her gaze again, and smiled, his own eyes knowing and gentle. "It's supposed to feel good, Angel. It's why people do this."

She rather doubted it should feel *this* good, but then, she was no authority. She had never in her life felt *this* good. Still, she offered no resistance as he guided her hands up over his chest and around his neck. Her fingers needed no coaxing to curl their way into the crisp waves at his nape. With both of his hands free now, he settled them low on her bottom and pressed her unyieldingly to him. Angel didn't think they were the model of decorum anymore, and she didn't care. She knew what this was, though no one had ever gone to the trouble before. This was foreplay, pure and simple. And he was very, very good at it.

As the sultry sax wailed the first haunting notes of "Unchained Melody," she gave herself up to the sensations he evoked. She hungered for his touch. The crush of her breasts against the wall of his chest tightened her nipples to a pebbly hardness she was sure he must feel through his clothes and hers. And lower down, where his spread hands pressed her to him, she was percolating madly. His knee, which had so concerned her when they were at the table, was moving rhythmically between her thighs again, sliding over the silky fabric of her dress and what lay beneath. Hot currents of desire sluiced through her. She turned her face into the heat of his neck and clung, letting the music and the man take her.

As the last notes faded, Matt lifted his head, and Angel blinked dazedly up at him. He rested his forehead against hers. "Let's go home," he said.

The drive to Angel's condo was quiet, but not uncomfortably so. They rode with their fingers loosely entwined across the open space between the front seats of the minivan. Angel rested back against the plush velour, a dreamy expression on her face, while Matt concentrated on the road and his situation.

He liked the minivan. He really did. As far as comfort went, it couldn't be beat. Carpooling, camping, hauling junk, he had no complaints. As a setting for any serious necking, though, it was a total bust. He glanced down at their clasped hands and scowled. That space had to be a good foot, foot and a half. They'd need necks like cranes. But, in his thirty-four years, he'd never resorted to inviting a woman into the back seat of his car. He wasn't about to start now. Especially not with this woman. That wouldn't be likely to call up memories of good company and good times for her. Nope, if she didn't invite him in, he could put paid to any plans he had for the rest of this evening.

Angel felt Matt's fingers clench around hers again and wondered at his agitation. She lolled her head to the side to look at him. The short wait at a red light didn't merit the frown that creased his brow. What was eating him now? His expression dredged up a long-forgotten memory of her first real date. She'd gone to a movie with a gangly but sweet boy from her algebra class. All Adam's apple and elbows he was, she recalled with smile. This was before the older guys had discovered her charms, and the sweet boys would still talk to her. "Richie" had been his name, and she wondered briefly if he still answered to that. No matter. He'd worn an expression just like Matt's, screwing up his courage as he escorted her up the long, front sidewalk to her grandmother's house. And there, in the combined glare of the porch light and the headlights from his father's car, in full view of his father, who had been commandeered to drive them, he had kissed her. The kiss had been brief, a mere brush of dry lips to dry lips, and tentative and inexperienced, but it had been tender, and nothing that had come after had improved upon it.

Till now.

She glanced at Matt again. Was that what was bothering him? He was worried about a good-night kiss? She almost laughed. Poor Matt. Hadn't he gotten the message? She was a sure thing. Anything his heart desired, she would oblige. Little Miss Round Heels. The fallen Angel of Fielding High. She closed her eyes against the sting of the remembered slur.

She reopened them on the realization of how far she had come from all of that. No one thought of her in those terms anymore. Only she did. In the end what a triumph for her grandmother this would be. Having built a new life for herself, free of the ugliness she had been raised with, she was afraid to live it. Afraid to open herself to anyone. Afraid to trust.

The van slowed and Angel noticed with some surprise that they were already turning into her complex. She stole another look at Matt as he guided the minivan into a spot near the entry to her building. His lips were nearly invisible, compressed to a tight slash across his face. The frown was gone, replaced with an air of weary resignation. He cut the engine and leaned back against his seat, staring straight ahead.

Angel reached for her purse, preparing to mouth the platitudes about a lovely evening. Facing him again, she found she could not say them. She sat half-turned to him, holding the slender strap of her handbag to her shoulder, suspended in restless indecision. *Ask him in!* her braver self prodded. What was there to fear, after all? She knew her own worth now. Things would go no further than she allowed. She would draw the line and he would accept it. *But suppose he doesn't come back?* the needy girl within her cautioned. *So what? You've given in before and it didn't keep them coming back. You will go on with your life. You know you can do it now.*

The words spilled out in a breathless rush. "Would you like to come in for some coffee, or a…nightcap?" She hated the hesitant quaver she heard in her voice at that last part. On an indrawn breath she waited for his response.

She hadn't realized how tense he was till she saw him relax. By slow degrees, his grip loosened on the steering wheel, his shoulders rolled forward and his legs spread comfortably apart. His shadowed face eased into a lopsided grin as he turned his head to look at her.

She forced herself to breathe in what she hoped would pass for a normal manner. Why did she feel like the fly pleading prettily for admittance to the spider's charming web?

"Why, Ms. Martino," Matt murmured in a silky tone, "I thought you'd never ask."

Chapter 10

Angel shut the apartment door behind her and swallowed an invitation for Matt to make himself comfortable as he proceeded to do just that. He shrugged out of his suit coat and slung it on the arm of the couch, then strode over to the French doors and pulled the drapes closed, shrinking her spacious room through the simple fact of his presence. With a quick yank, he loosened his tie and unbuttoned the collar of his shirt. As he continued his circuit of the room, he flicked off the bright lamp Angel had left burning while she was out and switched on a much dimmer one on her desk. He ended directly in front of her, eyeing her with an expression of amused expectancy and rolling his white shirt-sleeves up to his elbows. "Your move" was clearly implied, though unstated.

"Would you like some coffee?" Angel suggested with faint hope.

"No. And I wouldn't like some soda, either, if you were thinking of offering that." Matt's eyes surveyed the room in a futile search for something resembling a liquor cabinet and returned to her. Yep, she was definitely a cabinet-above-

the-refrigerator, way-the-hell-out-of-reach kind of woman.
"You said something about a nightcap?" he reminded her.

Angel let go a deep breath and spread her hands. "I'm
afraid I don't have much to offer." She made a move toward the kitchen. "And I'll need your help getting it down,"
she tossed back over her shoulder. "It's in the cupboard
above the fridge." He followed her, shaking his head, glad
she couldn't see the grin he couldn't suppress.

She was right about the meager pickings. Opening the
cupboard door, he spotted one bottle of sherry cooking
wine, unopened, a bottle of some red wine about two-thirds
full, and a small container of Angostura bitters. God only
knew what possessed her to add *that* to her stash. Ever the
optimist, he pulled down the wine, removed the cork, and
took a sniff. Even a guy who only knew red from white
could tell that this wouldn't cut it. "Who-oo," he shuddered.

"I use that for cooking," Angel offered.

"When the recipe calls for vinegar, I hope."

She took the bottle from him, sniffed, and wrinkled her
nose. Without further ado, she poured the contents down
the sink. "There's that," she said, pointing up to the shelf
again.

Matt spotted a box lying flat, still encased in its plastic
wrap. He stretched and brought it down. "Cognac! You've
been holding out on me, woman! This is great stuff."
V.S.O.P. Very special, old and pricey, or some such.
"Where'd you get this?" He'd bet the mortgage she didn't
buy it for herself. It was in one of those boxes they put together at Christmastime, with two brandy snifters included. Someone had been trying to make time with her.

"I attended the holiday dinner at the hospital with the
head of Purchasing. He gave it to me."

"And you didn't even open it? The poor chump." He ran
his thumbnail along the edge of the plastic until it gave, removed the glasses, and set them on the counter. "Sounds
like your social life revolves around the hospital."

Angel was silent for a moment. "My *life* revolves around
the hospital," she said flatly. *That* was God's honest truth.
Her life certainly didn't include situations like this. She had

the man here, had invited him in, and didn't have the first
idea what to do with him. How to show interest without
going too far. Normal high school behavior. It was beyond
her. She was tense, edgy, ready to burst into tears. To give
herself something to do, she picked up the snifters and ran
them under the tap.

Matt leaned a hip against the counter next to her, watching her jerky movements as he broke the seal on the bottle
and peeled it off. "My mother does that," he said.

She shut off the faucet and turned puzzled eyes to his.

"Does what?"

"Washes perfectly clean glasses, right out of the package." Angel opened her mouth to protest their perfect
cleanliness, but he went on. "She washes a cup she only
measures water in with soap and water, too. Do you do
that?"

"I put it in the dishwasher," she said, but she laughed in
spite of herself. She knew what he was doing. More of his
nonsense. To put her at ease. She dried the glasses and
mopped up the splashes around the faucet with the towel.

"Next you'll be telling me how your great-aunt Tillie
makes apple butter with the apples from the tree in her
backyard you fell out of as a kid and broke your arm in two
places."

He regarded her with that gentle look of his, the one that
saw so much. "I don't have a great-aunt Tillie, but I'll make
one up. If it'll help you relax."

She supposed it was to be expected he'd be good at reading people. It was essential to his job, much as it was in hers.
His powers of observation were exceptionally keen. Still, it
was unnerving to be so transparent. She folded the towel and
rested her fists against the edge of the sink.

"What do you want me to do, Angel?"

She shrugged. She didn't know.

"Do you want me to go?"

She turned to look at him then. He stood resting against
the counter, the bottom of the bottle supported on his belt
buckle, one strong hand around its neck, the other curled
around the edge of the counter. She wanted to feel those
hands on her. She wanted her skin to burn from their heat

and her nipples to throb as he palmed them. She just didn't want what would come after. The part that he would want. Not now. Not yet. How could she tell him that? "No," she said.

He let out a long breath. At least she knew what she didn't want. She didn't want to toss him out on his can. What a start.

He straightened and uncapped the bottle. "You ever have any of this?"

She shook her head.

"Just a little bit, then. We don't want you to get woozy." He poured a scant finger's worth in the belly of the glass and handed it to her. She noticed that he didn't pour any more than that in his glass.

"You sip it, Angel. It's got a little bite." He took a slow sip of his own and pressed his lips together. "You swirl it around in your mouth...let it roll over your tongue. It'll make your lips tingle and your throat burn. Then it'll settle right about here—" he poked a knuckle gently into her midriff "—and do a slow simmer. You'll like it," he teased her with a wink.

"Come on." He hit the wall switch, leaving the kitchen mantled in darkness, the dim light on her desk in the living room the only illumination remaining. "Help me pick out some music."

She followed him as far as the doorway and then hung back. He went to the corner console that housed her stereo system and hunched down to get a look at her compact disc collection. His taste leaned more toward jazz, and she seemed to favor the old war-horses, but they had more than a few in common. Shouldn't be too hard to find something mutually agreeable, he thought. He shifted a little, seeking a more comfortable position.

Angel watched that long finger trace her rack of CDs and saw that subtle shift. Her insides lurched. What was the matter with her? She was a nurse, for heaven's sake. Even disregarding her past, the male body held no mysteries for her. But neither her training nor her past had prepared her for the likes of this man. She admired the pull of muscles under the white shirt as he took a sip of his brandy. His shirt disappeared at his narrow waist into dark slacks that hugged his backside and spread thighs like a second skin. Her fingers itched to stroke those taut curves, and she took a quick taste of her drink in an effort to divert her wayward thoughts.

Too much. He had said to go slowly, she remembered. She pressed a hand to her mouth as the liquid seared her throat and her eyes teared from the sting. For a frantic minute she thought she might choke.

"Angel?"

Oh, God. Could he tell? She didn't think she'd made any noise.

"Mmm?" Her response sounded embarrassingly like a squeak.

"It's not gonna happen."

"What!" *Could he read minds? Did he know she was imagining her hands on his backside?*

He turned his head and eyed her over his shoulder, still in that sexy crouch. "Whatever it is that's worrying you. Got you clinging like a limpet to that doorframe. It's not gonna happen."

Oh. *That.* She'd really thought he wanted to. She didn't know whether to be disappointed or glad. The truth was, if she examined her feelings closely, she felt a little miffed. And more than a little silly.

He stood and walked toward her as she stared down into her glass. "Uh-oh. Now I've rattled your confidence." He came to a halt right in front of her. "You think I don't want to." His fingers lifted her chin and forced her eyes to meet his. "Mmm-hmm, sweetheart, I want to. My teeth hurt and my gut aches with wanting to." He growled low in his throat. "But I won't."

His thumb brushed the fullness of her lower lip. "Are you on the Pill?" She clutched her glass with both hands to keep from dropping it. "I didn't think so." He released her chin. "And I didn't exactly come dressed for success myself."

Her eyes took a long, slow trek up his thoroughly magnificent body before reaching the smug grin on his face. "Well, I'm glad you approve." He laughed. "But it's not what I meant." He spread his hands at his sides and shrugged. "No condoms," he said in a hoarse whisper.

Angel would have dropped her glass then, if he hadn't helped her catch it. "Look," he said, his warm fingers still circling hers. "I just happen to agree with you that babies should be considered beforehand, not as an afterthought. Nothing's gonna happen tonight." He squeezed her hand. "Now, come and help me pick out some music."

She followed him all the way to the console this time, but she remained standing when he hunched down again. "I've got every one of these Dvoraks, too, Angel," he said in a conversational tone.

"You must think I'm a fool," she whispered through lips stiff with tension.

He went still, just lifting those steady green eyes to hers. "No," he murmured. "I think you're afraid. And I'd like five minutes alone with the dingoes who did this to you." His voice held an edge of bitterness. "But that's not going to happen, either." He turned back to the music. "Now, let's see what you've got here."

She still couldn't unbend enough to huddle down close, Matt supposed as he ran his eyes over the titles in front of him, but he sensed some of the stiffness leaving her. From the corner of his eye he caught the slight loosening of her posture, an impression of her finger skimming idly around the rim of her glass, and he felt her eyes on him. "God, Angel, you've got a romantic streak a mile wide. Tchaikovsky, Debussy, *Rachmaninoff*." He felt her stiffen again and grinned to himself. She was almost too easy to goad, he mused, anticipating her defensive response.

"I find the music very soothing after a long day at work," she replied tartly.

"Oh, yeah," he agreed.

A little too easily, she thought.

He pulled a CD from the rack and loomed to his feet. "As I recall, the third movement of this is *real* soothing."

Angel stole a quick glance at the Rachmaninoff CD in his hand and winced. *The Second Symphony*. As she recalled, the third movement of *that* was lush. She watched as he manipulated the controls on her player and pushed the disc

nto its slot. The low, slumberous strains of the music filled
he room. Matt picked up his glass and sipped the brandy,
yeing her over the rim of the snifter, waiting.

"Matt..."

"This is nice, but it's no good to dance to. Hard to catch
he beat," he teased. "Why don't we sit down on your
ouch, kick back, get comfortable?"

She drew in a tight breath. "Matt..." she said again, her
oice bordering on panic this time.

He sighed and leaned into her, resting his palm against the
vall behind her head, pinning her in between the console
nd the strong arm that just brushed her cheek. Gently he
ouched the edge of his glass under her chin, rocked the cool
im against her heated skin, and raised her skittery eyes to
is. "I want to kiss you, Angel."

At his words, she closed her eyes and turned her head
harply, pressing her face, openmouthed, into the tanned,
nuscled length of his forearm. She tasted with her tongue
he salty tang of his skin, felt the fine hairs tickle her cheek,
nhaled his clean, musky scent, her senses almost over-
vhelmed by his sheer physicality.

Matt gave her bombarded senses no chance to recover. He
et his glass down and stroked his knuckles over the silky
exture of her throat, feeling her swallow the whimpers of
ier abandon. He rested his forehead against her temple and
iuzzled his lips into the soft curls near her ear, whispering,
:oaxing. "Sweetheart, I want to kiss you. Come sit with me,
\ngel. Let me... let me." He heard the sharp intake of her
oreath when he touched his tongue to the tender spot be-
eath her ear. He closed his lips on her soft flesh and sucked
;ently.

Angel shied from the intimate kiss and turned her head to
ace him again, searching his eyes with hers, her breathing
apid and uneven. She dropped her gaze to his mouth and,
lmost timidly, brought her fingers up to splay them against
is lips, tracing the smooth, warm contours. Matt groaned
ow in his throat and his eyes drifted closed, but he didn't
oush her for any further contact; only waited, scarcely
oreathing. With one finger Angel curled his lower lip down
nd slid her middle finger along the puffy, wet inner sur-

face. Matt's eyes came open, dark with arousal, but still he waited. She nudged her finger against his teeth, and he parted them, greeting her with his tongue and his warm breath, nipping lightly at the finger she probed in and out. With a shaky breath she dragged her finger from his mouth and pressed his lips closed. Moving her hand along his jaw, she felt the harsh rasp of his beard against her palm. Pain and pleasure. Risk and release. They were all tied up in this man.

Matt turned his face into her palm and planted a hard kiss there, then held her open hand to his cheek as he spoke. "Angel, I want to kiss you," he whispered. "And touch you a little." A half smile tugged and his eyes glinted. He gave a barely perceptible shrug. "Maybe more than a little. But that's all, sweetheart. Anything you don't like, anything that doesn't feel right, you tell me to stop. And I will, honey, I swear it. Come sit with me, let me kiss you."

Her hand still caressed his cheek as she gazed deeply into his unguarded eyes. She could see nothing to fear. Even now, with his desire so evident, he held his body away from hers, unwilling to use any form of physical persuasion to give her any cause for alarm.

Wisely or not, she trusted him. It came down to that.

But more, where he was concerned, she found she had lost not the ability, but the will, to resist. She wanted to hold and be held, to kiss and be kissed, and, once and for all, to put her past behind her. With this man.

Sensing her acquiescence, he took her glass and put it alongside his on the lamp table next to the couch. He clasped her cool fingers in his warm ones and guided her to the sofa, pulling her down next to him as he sank into the cushions. He surprised her then. His hands, rather than hauling her into the embrace she was expecting partly with eagerness and partly with trepidation, went to her feet. He slid her shoes off and dropped them to the floor, laughing when her eyes widened.

"No, this is not some kinky form of seduction. You appear to me to be the type of woman who frowns at shoes on the furniture." He brought her legs up and snuggled them against her, his hands gently kneading her stockinged feet. "We don't want any frowns tonight."

He laughed again when she eyed his shoes pointedly. "My feet are going to stay on the floor, Angel."

He moved one hand up her leg and over her hip to her arm, where it stroked idly from shoulder to elbow, up and down. He settled his other arm on the top of the couch behind her and nudged her face toward him gently with his thumb. Murmuring sweet nonsense about how good she smelled and how soft she felt, he dropped light kisses across her brow and along her hairline, and Angel wondered, a bit dazedly, if this was what he had meant by kissing. Only very gradually did she come to notice that each slow stroke he made, up and down, on her arm rubbed the warm inner surface of his wrist against her breast, and she was, very gradually, increasing the arch of her back and the depth of her breathing in anticipation of that heated friction. She closed her eyes and buried her nose in the open collar of his shirt, while her toes curled in guilty pleasure.

Matt kissed her closed eyelids and smiled as he watched those toes curl in her stockings. She was like a virgin. Even more so than some girls who technically were. She was unawakened, totally unaware of her woman's capacity for fulfillment. Innocent really, though he didn't doubt that she would scoff at the suggestion. He rubbed his chin against the top of her head, and, without his willing it, his thoughts drifted back to a time when there were two virgins together. He'd had a pretty fair idea then of the pleasures in store for him, but to say he had been lacking in technique was being overly generous. Not that it had been a problem. They'd been healthy, eager, and in love. Still, he was glad this wasn't his first time now. And, in another way, he was glad it wasn't Angel's. He wouldn't have to worry about her pain, or his clumsiness and inexperience. He could concentrate on her pleasure.

The movement of Angel's head against his arm and the sofa had loosened her hair. Matt plucked the remaining pins from the coil and dropped them over the back of the couch, out of the way. As Angel turned to utter a protest, he threaded his hands through the heavy strands, tumbling them in a shimmering cascade over her shoulder to her breast. "I like your hair better down," he said.

Her protest became no more than a catch of her breath when his fingers slid down to the ends of her hair and brushed the sensitive peak concealed there. He didn't remove his hand, just grazed his knuckles over and over the silky fabric of her dress. She closed her eyes on a soft whimper, not entirely one of pleasure, he feared. He watched as a frown gathered between her brows and she bit down on her lower lip. With a sigh, he stopped the sensual play. She was so tense, so tight. There would be precious little pleasure for her if he couldn't get her to relax.

He reached across her body and picked up one of the brandy glasses, touching the edge of it to her lips. Her eyes came open to search his questioningly, but she took the sip he offered. His wry smile acknowledged her suspicion. "This is where I ply you with liquor, Angel, and have my wicked way with you. Is that what you think?"

She answered with the slightest shake of her head.

He took a sip from the same glass and extended it to her again. Her eyes never left his as she drank.

"I just want you to ease up...unwind a little, sweetheart. You're tight as a drum. There's not enough liquor in these two glasses together to make you lose your head." He stroked her neck softly with the hand that was draped over her shoulder and smiled when she stretched back against his arm to give him better access.

His eyebrows rose in surprise when she took the glass from him and put it aside. She brought her hand back and settled it against his face, her thumb resting in the shallow cleft of his chin. "Maybe there is," she whispered. She cupped her palm over the back of his neck and pulled him to her, kissing him with lips and tongue and heart. This kiss was the first overture she had made to him, or any man. The first ever.

He tasted of brandy, warm and sweet. The lips that opened over hers, welcoming her exploring tongue, were firm, moist and full. The brandy had its effect on her lips, too, leaving them with the odd sensation of being both numb and overly tender at the same time. They tingled as his tongue caressed and probed, searching out her sweet secrets. He pulled her closer and made no effort to disguise his intent this time as his hand sought her breast. She felt as well as heard the low rumble in his chest when she arched into his palm.

She was breathless when he pulled away, resting his forehead against hers while he struggled to steady his own breathing. He lifted his head and his eyes burned into hers. "God, Angel, you keep that up, you're gonna shoot all my good intentions straight to hell." He moved his hand from her breast, but she grasped his wrist, feeling his lifeblood throbbing through him against her fingertips. He raised his arm and kissed the fingers that held him. When she loosened her grip, he tunneled his hand into her hair, and he read the uncertainty in her eyes. "We've got to set some ground rules, sweetheart."

He wouldn't let her look away. His strong fingers held her jaw when she tried. "I want to touch you," he whispered, so close his warm breath ruffled the curls near her cheek. "I want to show you how it should be for a woman." He was silent for a moment, waiting for her response, seeing first the comprehension and then the fear in her expressive face. "Don't you want to know what all the fuss is about, Angel?"

Oh, she did. She wanted to feel what, for all her experience with sex, had eluded her. What every woman but her seemed to know. What prompted the smiles and blushes and sighs. But she wasn't able to say so, and Matt seemed to understand that.

He stroked his thumb over the sensitive curve of her upper lip. "I'm going to stay all buttoned and zipped, Angel. But I want to touch you. Let me touch you. If I do anything you don't like, tell me to stop."

She swallowed before she was able to speak. "What if you can't stop?"

His thumb ceased its stroking. "You've heard that old lie, huh?"

Her eyes narrowed as she studied him. "It's not true?"

He looked away with a disgusted grunt. He couldn't remember ever using that particular line, and he knew Rosie

would have told him to tie a knot in himself and be on his
way if he had. But then, Rosie had never had any problems
with self-esteem. This woman would have given in and then
been made to feel to blame for whatever happened. Sometimes he was ashamed of his sex. Still, his eyes held a teasing glint when he turned back to her. "I might have believed
it at one time, but you'd be amazed at how quickly a two-
year-old wandering into the room can put the brakes on
things. I've developed some truly remarkable powers of restraint. No, sweetheart." He shook his head. "It's not true."

He knew it wasn't fair, but he couldn't help himself. He
lowered his mouth to hers, kissing away the last shreds of
her resistance. When he raised his head, he knew he had
won.

"You like the kissing, don't you, Angel?"

"Yes, Matt," she breathed past lips swollen with desire.
"I like the kissing."

"Let's see what else you like." He covered her mouth with
his again.

His hand drifted down to her waist where he figured her
dress fastened. He knew all about wrap dresses. This one
didn't look too complicated. A tug on the bow and then a
little hitch to undo the hook, probably. Ah, so far, so good.
His mouth continued to work its magic while his hand
opened her dress and slipped inside to where he anticipated
the second knot would be. He fumbled with it for a few
moments before he lifted his head. "Double knot, Angel?"
He grinned at her stricken expression. "Good girl. It's always smart to be cautious, but I'm going to need some help
with this."

His eyes never left hers as her fingers brushed his aside
and she picked at the knot with close-clipped nails. When
the snarl was undone, his hand returned to separate the
strands and smooth her dress aside. Only then did he lower
his gaze to what he had uncovered.

He couldn't have said what he'd expected, but it wasn't
this. Nothing staid or practical here. She was a vision in
frothy satin and lace in a shade the same color as her dress.
Deep purple he'd have called it, though he was sure she
knew a more exotic name for it. Six inches of lace, the soft,

heavy kind, not the stuff that itched, trimmed the slip top and bottom and molded over her breasts and thighs, creating alluring dips and shadows. He traced a slow finger along the top edge, just brushing her skin, and felt her flutters of response.

Emboldened, he followed his finger with his tongue. Too fast. Immediately her hand came up between his lips and her skin in a protective gesture. His mouth ceased its wayward plunder, and he cursed inwardly as he met her gaze. Her eyes were filled with a painful mixture of apology and wary confusion, but she forced the hand that stayed him to move from her breasts to her lap. "I'm sorry, Ma—"

"Shh." He silenced her gently with his fingers. "It's all right, sweetheart. That was too soon." He brought his lips to the silky column of her neck, dropping soft kisses along her jaw and under her ear. "This is nice, too," he murmured. "You smell so sweet. Gardenias, Angel?"

He could feel the conflict in her, the tension between desire and fear, want and should. He knew she was only just beginning to hear the siren call of her body's yearnings above the shrill self-reproach she'd been berated with for so long. Fiercely, he tamped down the desires and wants of his own body. They could wait. More than anything, he wanted to give her this gift, this awakening.

He trailed light kisses down her neck to her shoulder, gradually feeling the fear ease from her and a different tension take its place. He nudged the sleeve of her dress down her arm a little, kissing every inch of skin as it was revealed. His lips encountered the thin straps, mere ribbons really, that held her slip and bra, and he raised his head again to look at her. "These are so delicate." He slipped his fingers under the straps, rubbing his knuckles against her skin. "We don't want to tear them. Why don't we just move them out of the way?" Matching his actions to his words, he slid the straps over her shoulder and down her arm, all the while watching her response. He saw her swallow, but she raised no objections. He lowered his gaze again.

The slip had dipped obligingly, but the bra still covered her breast like a lacy armor plate. That wouldn't do. He stole a hand behind her back, between her dress and slip, half expecting her to slap his trespassing hand away at any moment. His fingers found the clasp they sought and pinched.

Angel's eyes widened as she felt her bra suddenly go slack. "You don't appear to be out of practice at all," she admonished.

He gave an offhanded shrug, teasing again. "Some things you never forget." While he spoke, he brought his hand around, working her bra down, on the one side at least, under her slip as he went. He felt her stiffen and her breath quicken, and he searched her eyes again, gauging her willingness, her wariness. In answer to his unspoken question, she caught his hand and moved it to cover her breast.

She was so beautiful. All ivory skin and purple lace. He filled his hand with her. Beneath his palm he could feel her heart fluttering wildly, like the wings of a trapped bird, against her rib cage. The straps to her garments hung uselessly down her arm and the slip barely covered her breast, held in place, Matt suspected, by the result of her body's response to his touch. His fingers moved, searching for and finding that nub, that single pearl, that evidence of her arousal.

With a soft moan, Angel arched back against his arm, leaving her neck exposed, vulnerable, an invitation he found impossible to ignore. Openmouthed, he kissed her throat, dipping his tongue into the hollow at its base. Distracted by this onslaught, Angel barely registered that he had tugged her slip down the last inch until she felt his warm palm cup her with nothing between them.

"Oh, Matt." She released her breath on a shuddery sigh.

"Matt, what, sweetheart?" he rasped. "Matt, stop? Matt, don't stop? Tell me, Angel." His lips blazed a trail along her collarbone down to the soft swell of her breast. There he hesitated just a moment to give her time to object before his mouth closed over her nipple.

"*Don't* stop." She cradled his head to her, clenching and unclenching her fingers in his hair. She could feel the sucking pull of his warm mouth on her breast, and she straightened her legs, pressing her thigh to his, her hips beginning to move in the slow, unconscious undulations of desire.

Matt felt her quivering in his arms. So new to this, so uncertain, so afraid, still she responded to him with such fire. He was humbled by her trust. But her response had unleashed a hunger of his own and he shook with the intensity of his need. One part in particular clamored for attention, reminding him just how long it had been for him, how tenuous was his control. She had only to edge her leg a little more onto his and she would know it, too, would feel it. Would that stop her cold? Send her skittering from him in fright? *Hell!* He ached to spread her thighs over his, push her clothes and his aside and bury himself in her heat. *That* would confirm her opinion of men. Instead he tore his mouth from her breast, his breathing labored and harsh, and buried his face in her sweet-smelling hair.

He seized the ragged reins of his control and pulled himself back from the brink, but not before Angel noticed. She put a hand to his jaw to lift his face and turned her head to look at him. "Are we going to stop now?"

He'd swear there was disappointment in her voice, and despite his discomfort, he smiled and shook his head. "Just a breather. I'm hot as hell, but I'll be all right in a minute." His eyes gentled. "You okay?"

She looked down at herself then. At her skin, flushed from his kisses and his beard. At her breast, now fully exposed with his fingers still stroking. At her dress, open and wrinkled and rucked up around her hips. Her worst nightmare.

But this was Matt. She lifted her gaze to his again. It was his hand that touched her, caressed her. His lips that kissed and suckled. His voice that soothed her, calmed her, coaxed her. His eyes that regarded her with such tenderness, such care. This was Matt. And she would not feel shame. "I'm fine," she said.

His smile broadened. "You taste wonderful everywhere, Angel, but this is special." He cupped her breast. "This just tastes like you." He lowered his head to her and laved her with his tongue, while a heavy languor washed through her. She'd had no idea. None. Would never have imagined that such exquisite sensations could be evoked from a man's mouth at her breast. Again her hips began that sultry rhythm.

Matt felt that movement and sensed her readiness. His mouth continued its nuzzling, while his hand traveled a silky path to her thigh. There his fingers edged just under the lace, and he found his restraint tested again. Instead of the panty hose he expected, his hand closed on Angel's soft, warm flesh. He clenched his jaw as his blood pumped with a hot surge of need and he let his fingers explore. Jeez. Garters, garter belt, panties, *skin.* His mind exploded with visions of how what he was feeling would look and his pulse leapt into overdrive. But a nagging awareness that Angel had gone very still crept in and he realized her hand had clamped around his wrist in a death grip.

Reluctantly he ceased his explorations and raised his head. Angel had pulled her lower lip into her mouth and was biting down on it. In the dim light her eyes were deep, deep pools of blue, abashed and uncertain.

"What is it, sweetheart?"

"I'm...my legs are so...I don't usually wear panty hose. They're not comfortable."

Slowly, slowly, it seeped into his befuddled brain that she was afraid he would be put off by what he had found. "Is this an apology, Angel? Don't." He kissed her gently. "Don't." His hand stroked her thigh again. "These are the sexiest inches on a woman's body." He didn't really expect her to believe that. He'd only just discovered it himself.

His hand slid up to determine how she had arranged things. Little lacy strip of panties. She really went in for these, he mused, recalling the ones he had found hanging in his bathroom. Who'd have thought it. She'd put them on over the garter belt, it seemed. Probably more convenient for her. *Absolutely* more convenient for him.

He ran the tip of his finger inside the top edge of her panties and felt her belly quiver against it, but her hand had loosened on his wrist and she didn't push him away. He sucked in a deep breath. He wasn't going to be sneaky about what he wanted from her. "These are delicate, too, Angel," he said, tugging lightly on her underpants. "Will you let me take them off?"

She looked away and for a moment he thought they'd gone as far as she was able, but her eyes came back to his so full of trust and want and need that he was almost undone. His mouth caressed her beneath her ear and he whispered, "I want to touch you, sweetheart. I want to touch you... there. But you have to say the words. I've got to be sure."

She turned in his arms, giving him his answer against his lips. "Yes." So softly he felt more than heard it. "Yes."

She lifted slightly to help him as he slid the panties over her bottom and skimmed them down her legs. But when his hand returned to push her slip higher, she grasped his wrist again. "No, Matt...please...not the slip. No." She wasn't ready to be so exposed, even to him.

"Okay." He moved his hand to her knee. "It's okay, Angel. Shh." He silenced her when she would have explained. "I think it's better this way." Yes, better, he thought, seeing her flushed face, her lips, parted and moist as the petals of a morning glory. No need to challenge his hair-trigger control more than he had to.

He watched her face intently as he slowly eased his hand up her thigh under the concealing folds of her slip. He let his fingers linger there, making small circles on her skin, to allow her time to become accustomed to so intimate a touch. With his other hand he stroked her neck, tipping her jaw up to meet his kiss. The pent-up breath that escaped her mingled with his as his clever fingers moved between her satiny inner thighs, but she stiffened and her legs clamped against his hand when he stretched his fingers higher and touched her soft curls.

She buried her face in the curve of his shoulder, caught in an agonizing struggle between her body's demands and her mind's warnings. "Matt, I'm..."

"Wet, sweetheart. I know." He brushed her hair away from her face, kissing her cheekbone and the closed eyes that would not look at him. "You're just the way you should be, Angel. You can't know what it means to me to feel you that way." Her thighs relaxed just a little. "This is me, Angel." He traced his tongue around the rim of her ear.

"I won't do anything you tell me not to do. But I want to touch you there. I think you want it, too."

She lifted her head, but kept her eyes focused on his shoulder. "I feel so foolish."

"No, sweetheart." He dropped a kiss on her forehead. "We'll stop now, if that's what you want."

She did look at him then. He had brought her so far, taking her to a level of sensuality she had never known. Oh, she'd known sex before. She'd been handled where he wanted to touch her. But never like this. Never with such concern for her pleasure, her response. And, in a way, this demanded so much more of her. He wasn't interested in a convenient, cooperative body. He wanted her mind, her spirit, her *self*. And that she had always kept separate, sheltered, apart. He would let her shield her body from him, but not her soul.

But her body yearned for him, ached for him, wept for him. He had maneuvered her into uncharted waters and set her adrift on swiftly swirling eddies of desire without compass or sextant. She must trust him to bring her to safe harbor. She lifted her arms and settled them around his neck, clinging as she kissed him. "Show me," she whispered against his mouth. "Show me."

He spread his hand between her thighs and gently but firmly nudged them apart while his tongue taught her the rhythm he would use. Slowly he thrust, in and out, schooling her to his pace. One of her hands gripped his shoulder and the other twisted in his tie when his fingers found her this time, but she didn't resist. She was swollen and slick, so hot, so ready. He slipped a finger inside her as he thrust again with his tongue and her breath poured forth on a low, keening sigh. Sweat beaded on his forehead and he squeezed his eyes shut against his own fierce hunger. His finger, wet and slippery with her response, slid into her again and she rocked against his hand, the rhythm coming naturally to her now.

He could sense the moment when the last of her inhibitions fled...when she went mindless with her need, her thighs lax, her breath coming in choppy gasps, her hands straining for purchase. He crooned soft words of love and encouragement in her ear. "Easy, sweetheart, just let it happen...don't fight it. Let it happen." His fingertips never faltered as they glided over her heated folds. He heard the moan gather in her throat. "That's it, Angel...say my name. Say my name when you..."

"*Matt!* ...Matt...Matt..." Her voice trailed off into a husky whisper, the waves of her release still breaking over her. After a time, she had no idea how long, their surging pounding became gentle swells. She leaned back, eyes closed, her head resting on Matt's arm, and floated on them. So...languid. So replete. She couldn't have moved a muscle to save her life.

Gradually she became aware of Matt readjusting her clothes. To spare her embarrassment, no doubt. Her lips curved in a dreamy smile. She felt Matt's mouth touch the corner of hers.

"Music's over, sweetheart."

She couldn't have said. Her body was still humming.

"Happy birthday, Angel."

Her eyes flew open then, to meet Matt's green ones. So warm, so generous, filled with something she couldn't name, something she had never seen in a man's eyes before.

"So that's what all the fuss is about." He gave a slow nod. "Is it always that good?"

His grin was smug, deservedly so. "Sometimes it's even better. Although I couldn't swear to it. That looked like an awful lot of fun."

She gave a huff of laughter despite the blush she could feel spreading. Only then did she notice the tension that still gripped his body. "You...didn't?"

"Nope." His eyes widened. "Damn near, though. And this is my best suit." His grin was devilish. "I wouldn't want to explain that at the cleaners."

She clapped a hand over her mouth to contain the giggles that erupted. She would never have believed she could laugh with a man, over such a thing, at such a time. But she knew what his restraint had cost him. She could see the strain in the hard planes of his face, his taut posture. She could give him some relief. Heaven knew, she'd done it for others, and far less willingly.

"Are you uncomfortable, Matt? I could..."

Before he realized what she was about, she placed a hand on him, over his fly, where the throbbing stiffness gave proof of his unsatisfied desire. "Aaa-ahh, Angel..." He grabbed her hand and tore it away as if she had burned him, but not before one desperate rolling thrust of his hips told her how much he wanted what she offered. He brought her palm to his mouth and pressed a kiss into it, as he slouched low on the couch with his nape resting on its back and his legs stretched out in front of him. Eyes squeezed shut, he struggled for control.

After a few moments he opened his eyes and slid his gaze to her. "I'll take you up on that someday, I promise you. But not now, not tonight. Tonight was for you."

"But... it was nothing... for you."

He came to her then, cradling her in his arms, like the precious being she was to him. "Don't say that," he whispered. "I know what you've given me. I'll treasure it. Don't ever think it's nothing."

She touched his face. Needed to touch him. "But, why?"

"Why, Angel?" His voice was thick with emotion. "I'm crazy about you, sweetheart." He kissed her lightly, the merest brush of his lips. "You're a smart girl. Haven't you figured that out yet?"

He stilled her response with his fingertips. "I know. It's too soon. We hardly know each other. I don't need any words from you tonight, Angel. I don't expect them. It's enough that you let me give you this."

She couldn't speak past the lump that rose in her throat. Couldn't help the tears that spilled unbidden. He didn't seem to mind. Just rubbed the tears away with the pads of his thumbs and kissed her again.

"Sometimes, when it's been especially good, the tears happen, too, sweetheart."

She gave him a tremulous smile. "It was especially good, Matt."

"It'll get even better. But not tonight. Tonight I'm going home. Now."

He stood and she rose with him, hoping that her dress would stay together. She doubted that everything was hooked and tied, but at least everything was covered. It became immediately apparent to her that one portion of her apparel was not in place and a quick glance at the floor and sofa didn't reveal it. She wasn't going to search now. She smiled at Matt as he picked up his jacket and walked with him to her door.

At some point his tie had come completely undone. He reached up and slid it from under his collar, folding it end over end. A disconcerted look crossed his face as he slipped it into his pants pocket. When he took his hand out, it held Angel's lacy panties. With a sheepish look he offered them to her. "I seem to have these again."

She was speechless for a moment, then took them with a burble of laughter and resisted the urge to hide them behind her back. "You're not going to hang them from your rearview mirror?"

His eyebrows rose. Then he laughed with her and shook his head. "No. Not my style. Besides—" he ran a hand over the back of his neck "—Patrick would ask questions. As a chaperon, he's a hell of a lot worse than my old man ever was."

Yes, she thought. That would be true. He was a decent man trying to raise a decent son. She raised up on her toes and touched his chest with her fingertips as he bent to kiss her. A chaste kiss, sweeter by far than the one from so many years ago. It told her more than words ever could what she was to him.

"Lock up," he breathed into her ear and was gone.

Chapter 11

The call came Tuesday, while Angel was at work. She had always had very little in the way of family, and now she had none. She was in the sterile central corridor of the O.R., catching flack from one of the neurosurgeons who had trouble scheduling time with the Y.A.G. laser, when she heard the page, so she took it on the extension there. Thus, it was amid the clangor of instrument tables being pushed across the tile floor, the buzz of the autoclaves, and the raised voice of Dr. Wilhelm, who had just been informed his case had been bumped smack into the middle of his office hours, that she learned her grandmother was dead.

Angel spent a solid hour dealing with various and sundry emergencies before she could escape to her office. She pulled off her mask, crumpled it into the wastebasket, and slumped into her chair, trying to make some sense of the emotions that beset her, trying to put a name to what she felt.

Grief? No, not that. Nothing as simple as that. To feel grief would almost be a blessing. Relief? Yes, she admitted. More than a little, and the tinge of guilt that went along with it. When her conscience had prodded her to make that last visit several months back, the old woman's fleeting moments of coherence had been almost more than she could bear. She left feeling the way she had as a child, shameful and worthless. She couldn't pretend to miss that.

Regret? Probably that came closest to describing the empty feeling that swamped her. From the time she was old enough to notice the differences between her family and those of her schoolmates, she had done what she could to win her grandmother's love or, barring that, her attention. Being the perfect child, the perfect student, hadn't done it. Neither, later, had rebellion. With her grandmother's general deterioration, Angel accepted, intellectually at least, that a reconciliation would never come. Still, she had harbored some spark, some flicker of hope that the only person she had ever known, related to her by blood, would say that she loved her. And now that hope was extinguished.

Her first impulse was to call Matt. She had punched the first digits of his work number when she reconsidered, returning the receiver to its cradle. She rested her mouth against her fist and stared at the phone. What could she say to him? *Please come, I'm hurting? She's dead and, God help me, I'm glad? Come hold me, I need ... I don't know what?*

No. She couldn't say what she needed, or what she felt. Better to sort this out alone. To close this door on her past and walk with him into whatever the future held. Why contaminate her relationship with him with the ugly ambiguity of these feelings? She brought her feet up to rest on the edge of her chair and locked her arms around her knees, resting her head against them. Rocking back and forth in the cocoon of her misery, she had never felt so alone.

She allowed herself only a few minutes of such self-indulgence before she raised her head, collected herself with a stern shake, and began to deal with what she must. She informed essential members of the staff of her need to be absent for the next few days and the reason for it. With as much grace as she could muster, she endured the puzzled looks of well-meaning colleagues who had never heard any mention of her family and were uncertain as to what kind of condolences to express. Her feelings a mixture of relief and dread, she locked her office and headed home.

* * *

Matt replaced the phone with a clatter and a curse. Her answering machine again. He hadn't been able to reach her the night before, either. He was familiar enough with her work schedule by now to know it was anything but routine. Still, he had tried her number until after ten last night and it was almost that now. It didn't sit right with him. Would anyone at the hospital even think to notify the police if she didn't show up? Unlikely. He had the feeling she had more friends at that place than she realized, but they respected her privacy.

He released his breath in a long hiss. Maybe she had pulled another all-nighter. She said they happened sometimes. He glanced at the clock again. Maybe she had pulled two. Then again, maybe this creep had given her the same treatment he had given Grace Patterson. How long would it be before anyone found her?

One thing he was sure of. Twenty-four hours' worth of talking to her damn answering machine was more than enough. He dialed her number at work.

Angel stood stiffly, a silhouette in black, tipped forward a little on her toes to avoid sinking her heels into the damp earth softened by abundant spring rains. The intonations of the priest were no more to her than the bird sounds or the distant low-pitched whine of a riding mower used by one of the groundsmen. Head bowed, she mouthed the responses to the funeral rite automatically, without feeling, without thought.

A gusty breeze dispelled the warmth of the sun and Angel shivered. She looked up. The priest placed his hand over his missal to still the fluttering pages as he read, and his vestments whipped around his legs. Two representatives from the funeral home stood somberly apart. She was the only mourner, if she could lay claim to such a title. Her grandmother had provided for her material needs in her early years, out of duty. And here she was, a lone sentry, standing as witness to the end of a life. Out of duty. What a sad culmination to a lifetime, Angel thought.

Had there ever been a time when her grandmother had been lighthearted, happy... in love? Had there been some disappointment so wrenching, some experience so painful, it had turned her to the bitter, mean-spirited person Angel remembered? She didn't know, had never thought to wonder, until her relationship with Matt caused her to question some long-held assumptions about herself. Was this the path she had been headed down before he had barreled his way into her life?

The service was over. Angel started slightly when the priest approached her, his hand extended to offer his sympathy. She spoke with him for a few minutes, then turned to leave with the men from the funeral home. They had agreed to drop her off at the nursing home where she would settle her grandmother's affairs.

That was when she spotted him.

He leaned against the front fender of his minivan, legs crossed at the ankles, arms folded over his chest. His tie waved over his shoulder like a banner in the stiff breeze. Angel couldn't read his expression, and the sunglasses didn't help. She walked across the wide expanse of lawn toward him, leaving the other men behind.

"I thought it was understood," he said without preamble as she came near, "you don't have to go through this kind of thing alone anymore." He removed his sunglasses, slipping them into the breast pocket of his suit coat, and he was Matt, her comfort, her anchor, once again. She went into the circle of his arms.

Sheltered in his embrace, his head bent over hers, she clung as his hands gentled her. They stood quietly for a while before the distinct sound of a sniff caught Matt's attention. He brought his hand to her chin and lifted her face to his scrutiny.

"Tears, Angel? For *her?*"

She shook his hand off, brushed her palms across her cheeks, and looked away. "Not for her," she denied. "For what might have been, what never will be." Her gaze came back to him, her eyes imploring. "Could it have been *so hard* to love a child? The fault wasn't mine, was it, Matt? It was her... the lack was hers."

He stroked her damp cheeks with his thumbs and nodded slowly. She rested her head against his chest, absorbing
his strength, his support. After a moment her head came up,
a slight frown wrinkling her brow. "How did you find out
I was here?"

He shifted guiltily. "I called where you work. Got a hold
of Harriet."

The frown deepened. "She's not supposed..."

He put a finger to her lips. "Now don't get on her case.
You know how persuasive I can be."

He was pleased to see the frown clear and a smile pull at
her lips.

"Did you bully her?"

"Nah." He shook his head. "She likes me."

He ran his gaze up and down the curbside area, taking in
the black limousine and the hearse. "Where's your car?" he
asked her.

"I didn't feel up to such a long drive. I took a cab and the
commuter shuttle out of Pittsburgh."

He pushed away from the fender, took her elbow, and
opened the van door. "Good," he said. "That simplifies
things a lot. Just let me get rid of these crepe-hangers." He
helped her into the passenger seat of the van and strode off
to talk to the undertakers.

The next hours passed for Angel in a quiet blur. She had
always prided herself on her independence, her ability to
take care of herself. Now she was content to sit back and let
Matt handle everything. He answered questions at the
nursing home, reading over documents, only placing them
in front of her for her signature. She basked in the unfamiliar luxury of having someone with her best interests at
heart see to her affairs.

She gripped his fingers as they walked the brightly lit, li-
noleum-floored corridor to the room where her grandmother had spent her last years. She had been there the
previous day, packing her grandmother's clothing and few
personal possessions in cardboard boxes and labeling them
with instructions for their disposal. Matt stopped with her
at the door to the room.

"Tell me what you want to take back with you and I'll carry it out to the van."

Her fingers tightened around his. "Nothing," she said with quiet determination. "I want nothing."

He cast a quick glance at her. "Are you sure, sweetheart? Once it's gone, it's gone."

She looked at him, her face pale and tight. "I was here for hours yesterday, Matt, going through her things. I was looking for something of my mother's...a picture, a note, a report card...anything. But there was nothing. It was as if she had never lived."

She turned her eyes back to the sparsely furnished room, her gaze drifting over the bare walls, the boxes, the railed bed. "It was the same for me. I remember as a child making pictures for her, or bringing home a test I'd done especially well on, hoping she'd be happy with it, she'd display it somewhere." She bit her lip and shook her head. "She couldn't stand the clutter." Angel sighed heavily and straightened her shoulders. "She cut us out of her life a long time ago. It's past time I did the same. She's had too much influence on my life as it is."

She glanced at Matt, noting the hard glitter in his eyes as he surveyed the room, the bunched muscle in his jaw. Abruptly he pulled her away from the door, back into the corridor. "Let's go," he said.

They collected Angel's luggage and had a bite to eat before starting the long drive home. Angel had slept little the previous nights and that, combined with a full stomach, served to make her drowsy. They had barely made the interstate before she drifted off.

She came awake by slow degrees, not certain how long she had slept, but full darkness had fallen. Still lulled by the warmth from the minivan's heater and the monotonous hum of the tires on the road, she watched Matt through slitted eyes while he drove unaware of her scrutiny. He controlled the van with the same careless ease with which he appeared to do so many things, steering with a wrist draped over the top of the wheel. His cheek rested on his other hand, his elbow propped against the base of the window at his side. She saw his clean profile illuminated only by the dim lights of the

dashboard and the occasional flash of approaching headlights. It was enough.

She had read once somewhere that lovers shared a special affinity, an attraction that lingered after lovemaking. It
drew them together during the night while they slept. It accounted for them finding themselves tangled in each other's arms, even though they might start out on opposite sides
of the bed. There was some biochemical explanation for the
phenomenon, she recalled, although the science didn't really matter to her. She had certainly never experienced anything like it in her previous encounters with men. But she felt
it now.

She was drawn to him like iron filings to a magnet and she
longed to cling just as closely. All day she had been aware of
her need to touch him—his hand, his arm—however casually, and she had used any excuse to do so. Now, with her
mind's eye, she envisioned herself nude and spread over him
like a human coverlet, her body conforming to the planes
and hollows of his. Vividly she pictured his warm hands
molded to the shape of her buttocks, kneading and stroking, as they lay with their limbs entwined. And, just from
thinking of him, in the soft, secret places of her body that
he had taught such pleasure, she swelled, and throbbed, and
yearned. She felt his pull on her, like the moon on the tides,
steady and relentless. She wondered, Does he feel it, too?

As if in answer, he slid a glance toward her. "You
awake?" he whispered, his voice so soft it wouldn't have
disturbed her if she weren't.

She stretched lazily and yawned. "How much longer?"
she asked in a hushed tone. She, too, was reluctant to break
the quiet intimacy of the minivan.

He shrugged. "About a half hour. Maybe a little less.
Traffic's light." He threw another quick look her way, and
she smiled to herself. She was learning to read him well. If
she were the type to put money on it, she'd bet he was going to broach a subject he wasn't sure would be well received.

"I don't think you should be alone tonight," he began.
"Now—" the hand draped over the wheel lifted in a staying gesture "—that doesn't mean I expect—"

"I want you." Her words were so quiet she wasn't sure he would hear them, but his reaction left no doubt. He straightened abruptly, muttered something that would have merited at least a quarter in the "damn jar," flicked his blinker on, checked the rearview mirror, and brought the van to a lurching stop on the shoulder of the highway. In a single motion he unhitched his seatbelt and turned to her.

"It's about your timing, Angel," he said with a rueful laugh. "You don't lay that on a guy when he's doing the speed limit, give or take a little, on the interstate. Look—" his expression became serious again "—I just don't want you to be all by yourself tonight. I—"

She silenced him with a hand pressed firmly across his lips. "I want you. Don't make me beg."

He was ready. Just that fast. She could feel the catch of his breath against her hand, see the banked fire in his eyes even in the darkness. He opened his mouth, scorched her palm with his tongue, and nipped the fleshy pad just beneath her fingers, his eyes burning into hers all the while. She sucked a sharp breath in through her teeth and spread her fingers. She forgot place or time or circumstance in her need for him. Her hand moved along the raspy surface of his jaw to cup his neck and pull him closer. Their kiss was hot and deep, a primitive mating of lips and teeth and tongues. She heard the ragged groan torn from his chest as he reached to haul her more fully against him. She was caught up short by her seatbelt and harness, and the resistance brought him back to reality.

He loosened his grip on her upper arms as he tried to steady his breathing. "Jeez, woman, what you do to me!" He closed his eyes, gulping in air. When he'd regained some semblance of control he looked at her again and shook his head disgustedly. "I could take you right here, with God and half of Pennsylvania zipping by." He moved his hands to her cheeks, framing her face with exquisite gentleness. "That's not what I want for you."

"Matt..."

"I want you, too, sweetheart. More than you know." A muscle worked in his jaw. "But I've got to make a stop first. To protect you." He saw the understanding dawn in her eyes, and the chagrin. He kissed her again, wanting to banish her embarrassment and uncertainty. Meeting her gaze, he continued, "I've never been with anyone but my wife. You know that." He acknowledged with a shrug. "You're not going to catch anything from me. But I'm a cop. Nothing's certain in my line of work. I'm not going to take any chances with you until all the *i*'s are dotted and the *t*'s are crossed, and everything I have is yours, including my name."

She lifted her hands to cover his and her eyes drifted shut. They were moist with the depth of her feeling when she reopened them, but she smiled her understanding.

Matt kissed the tip of her nose. "Now, try to behave yourself until I get you home, Ms. Martino."

A short while later he pulled into the parking lot of a convenience store not far from Angel's condo and she waited in the van while he went inside. She watched him through the plate-glass window as he used the pay phone, firming up arrangements for Patrick, he had said. He disappeared for a few minutes and then she saw him at the checkout counter. From this distance he appeared a little ill-at-ease and she wondered a bit bemusedly if he'd ever had occasion to make this particular purchase before. Maybe his wife had taken care of that department.

Moments later he opened the van door, slid behind the wheel, and deposited the brown paper bag on the floor between their seats. "I got three dozen," he said, eyebrows wriggling lecherously.

Impulsive laughter burst from Angel. "You must be anticipating quite a night."

As he guided the minivan out of the lot, she found her gaze drawn to the bag. The shape of a familiar container caught her attention and she pushed the paper aside a little to get a better look. A quart of milk. Milk? "I don't need any milk, Matt," she said without thinking.

He was silent for a minute. "Everyone can use a little milk, Angel," came his tight reply.

She considered that for a moment. Then, pressing her lips together, she turned her head to look out the window at her side.

When she didn't answer, he cast a quick look her way. Her face was averted, but he could see her shoulders shaking. He rolled his eyes and gave a huff of exasperation. "Okay. So, smooth operator that I am, I couldn't just go in there and buy... you know."

Her laughter was audible now. Also contagious. He could barely get his next words out. "What was I supposed to do? That little girl behind the counter couldn't have been more than seventeen."

That prompted more gales from Angel. She rolled her head on the back of the seat to face him, a hand pressed to her chest. "So you bought *three* dozen?"

"Yeah. Well. I don't plan to do that again anytime soon."

They were pulling into the parking area alongside Angel's building. As Matt made his turn, another car spun out, lights on high beam, temporarily blinding him. He raised an arm to shield his eyes and swore.

"I don't recognize that car," Angel said, watching it career out of the complex.

"Punks, probably," Matt muttered as he maneuvered into a space near her door.

The incident did little to dampen their spirits. Matt guided Angel into her apartment, stopping to place the milk in the refrigerator before pulling her, still laughing, into the bedroom. It was only there, watching him push off his shoes and shrug out of his jacket, that she became quiet.

She slipped out of her own shoes and, using her toes, lined them up neatly beside the bed, then watched as Matt's shirt followed his jacket to the low wooden chest at the foot of her bed. He hesitated, his hands at his belt buckle when he caught her eyes fixed on his chest.

"Second thoughts, sweetheart?"

She forced her eyes to meet his. "No," she answered with a slight shake of her head.

"Me first, huh?" He indicated with a tilt of his head the fact that she was still fully clothed.

She gave a weak smile and her gaze slid to the bed, avoiding any glimpse of his body as she heard the whisper of his belt through the loops, the rasp of his zipper, and the muffled glide of fabric over his legs as he removed his pants and socks. He stretched in front of her to pull back the covers on the bed and her eyes were filled with the broad expanse of his shoulders. She withdrew a step, his nearness almost overwhelming. He was already aroused, she saw. The white briefs he wore did little to conceal that.

He straightened, facing her, unsure of how to go on. "What is it, Angel?"

She struggled for a light response. "It's just that—" she gestured lamely toward the covers "—I've never done this in a bed before."

"Oh. *Oh-hh!*" He couldn't contain the laughter that erupted. "You're gonna like this, I guarantee it. Most people'll tell you it's the best place for it. Now, myself, I'm not fussy. Just about any place horizontal will do, and even then, I can be persuaded." He kept up the endless stream of banter, calming and coaxing, as he hooked his thumbs into the elastic waistband of his briefs and slid the last barrier from his body. Sitting on the edge of the bed, he grasped her hands and pulled her to stand between his spread knees.

"Your turn, sweetheart," he said as he reached for the covered buttons of her suit jacket. "Let's get you out of all this black."

His fingers worked to remove her jacket, but his eyes never strayed from her face. What he saw there unsettled him. Her eyes were closed, her expression distant, as if to hold herself apart from what was happening to her. As she had in the past with those others. He had thought to joke with her and kid her over these rough spots, to be in her bed and loving her before fear and embarrassment had a chance to swamp her. Now he wasn't so sure. He felt like he was undressing a mannequin, not his warm, sweet Angel.

He pushed her skirt down her legs and the black half-slip followed. Angel rested her palms on his shoulders as she stepped out of the clothing and he shoved it aside. He dropped his gaze and sucked in a breath at what was revealed to him.

"God, Angel," he murmured, "undressing you is like unwrapping a present. I never know what I'll find." What he'd found was lacy and black and scanty. The bra, panties, and garter belt covered the essentials, just barely.

"I like pretty things," she said a trifle defensively. It was true. She had always loved pretty things against her, and where was the harm if only she would know? She had opened her eyes now, but kept her gaze fixed on the thick waves of his hair.

"I'm not complaining, sweetheart, just a little surprised. I'd have figured you for the Spanky-pants type. You know, your basic, white cotton..."

That caught her attention. She grabbed a hank of his hair and tugged his head back. "I know what they are. How do you know about Spanky pants?" she said with a laugh.

"Six sisters." He gave her his loopy grin. "There were whole years when we were growing up that my family single-handedly kept that company in business."

Looking down into his open, laughing face, Angel felt the last of her reservations drift away like mist at midmorning. *Six* sisters. No wonder he was so good with women. He had known and loved so many as persons, he could never consider one an object to be used and cast aside. Still, as her gaze drifted lower, her eyes widened with a more immediate concern.

Matt followed the direction of her glance and grimaced. She was looking disparagingly at the part of him he was really hoping she'd come to like if they were ever going to make a go of this.

"Now what?" he asked with a sigh.

She gave him an uncertain look. "Those other guys..."

He grasped her chin and tilted her head to face him. "Forget them," he said in a fierce whisper.

"Well..." She pursed her lips. "They were really boys."

His grip eased and he had to grin in spite of her seriousness, but his tone was gentle when he spoke.

"Sweetheart, I'm not going to hurt you. That's not a weapon." His hold on her jaw became a caress. "I care about you, Angel, and what I said the other night still holds. You tell me to stop and I will. I couldn't find any pleasure in hurting you." He watched as her expression softened and the doubt was replaced by a shy playfulness. "Angel, you've got that look in your eyes like you had when you were trying to get the ring off my finger," he teased. "I'll feel a whole lot better when we get rid of the rest of this black silk.''

He undid the front clasp of her bra, brushing the backs of his hands slowly over her breasts as he spread it wide and slid it down her arms to let it drop on the floor. Bringing his hands back to her breasts, he made slow circles around her nipples until they beaded in his palms. He saw she had closed her eyes again, but he didn't think it was for distance or self-protection this time. She gasped and arched into him as he tongued her nipple and grazed it with his teeth. Her fingers gripped his shoulders for support when it seemed her legs would no longer hold her.

He bent his head, leaning his cheek against her belly, and his hands moved down to release her garters. He dropped hot, wet kisses along the soft skin of her inner thighs as he rolled each stocking down and tossed it aside. The garter belt quickly followed to the little pile on the floor. Only the narrow black swath of her panties remained. He curled his fingers into the lace-edged elastic and pulled them down, stooping low to help her step out of them.

When he straightened, his eyes were level with the thin, silvery line that stretched from just below her navel to the tangle of curls at the juncture of her thighs. Angel had gone very still. He lifted his gaze to hers and she stared down at him, eyes wide, almost distraught.

''Is this what I wasn't supposed to see, sweatheart?'' He traced a finger lightly over the scar. The hands on his shoulders tightened, nails biting. ''Patrick was a C-section, too, sweetheart. I know what this means.'' He pressed gentle kisses along the length of the scar and Angel's head fell back, her eyes squeezed shut.

She felt his hands firm on her hips, warm, accepting. She felt his healing kisses on that mark, that stigma, the only thing of any substance left to her of her son. It had caused such pain for her after he was born. But she, with her empty belly and empty arms, would take no medication for it. It was nothing compared to the agony in her heart, and there had been no help for that.

Matt's head lifted and she opened her eyes to look down at him, her bottom lip caught hard between her teeth, her eyes wet with memory. "Oh, honey," he whispered. "Let it go. Come chew on *my* lips."

She bent to him and he turned slightly, tumbling her with him into the bed.

She had thought, half hoped, he would be quick with this. He would move her swiftly through this first time in the dark. But he was having none of it. He brought her hand to his lips when she reached to switch off the lamp. "I want you to know this is me," he said. Not for a moment would he let her confuse him with the others who had used her quick and in the dark.

He held her hands splayed on the sheets above her head while his mouth traced a leisurely meander over her body. His tongue dipped into beckoning hollows and his lips pressed slow kisses on alluring swells. All the while he nestled closer, allowing her body time to accustom itself to the weight and feel of his. Gradually he felt her response. A shoulder lifted for a gentle nip, a breast offered itself up to be nuzzled and sucked. Her legs grew restless, shifting on the bed and twining around him as he nudged his thigh between them, against the place where she was wet for him. He freed her hands and groaned as she lowered them to his buttocks and clasped him to her. She was ready, eager even, but it had been so long for her, and he knew now she hadn't been stretched to accommodate a baby through the birth channel. He didn't want to hurt her.

He lifted himself from her, supporting his weight on his arms. He could sense her confusion as he dropped fevered kisses down her belly to the soft delta between the thighs that lay spread for him.

"Matt!" She breathed in a sharp gasp and her fingers clenched in his hair when his tongue found that tiny nub of sensation, rigid with desire.

He turned his head, brushing his lips along her inner thigh. "Let me, honey," he whispered. "I only want to make this easy for you. Let me."

He waited, feeling her fingers loosen their grip and trail tentatively over his nape. Her thighs relaxed somewhat, easing just a little further apart. Still, he waited. He could feel her agitation as her fingers fluttered through strands of his hair. The better to persuade her, he ran his tongue slowly up her soft flesh, near to the place she had forbidden. He felt her leg quiver beneath his hand and the gentle roll of her hips she probably wasn't even conscious of.

"Do men..." Her voice was hushed, breathless. "*Like* ... to do that?"

She could feel, *feel,* his lips curve into a smile against her most private self.

"This man does," he murmured, and he kissed her there where no man ever had. Her fingers tightened in his hair again, but not to restrain him. With his warm hands at the back of her thighs to guide her, she raised her knees and opened herself to him and to what he would do with her.

The strong thrust of his tongue brought an answering surge, liquid and sweet, and a weak, animal sound she wouldn't have believed could come from her. She pressed the back of her hand to her mouth in an attempt to stifle the whimpers she couldn't hold in. Her legs began to tremble when he moved his hands to cradle her bottom. His rough tongue stroked unrelentingly over her, and deep inside she felt a tightening, a coiling. And such heat. Sweet fire consumed her. She strained on the bed, her neck arched over the pillow and her hands scrabbling for purchase in the sheets. She breathed his name over and over in shallow pants, echoing the rhythm of his thrusts. She moved with him, to him, beyond words, beyond thought. His hands slid up her body to her breasts, his fingertips just brushing their sensitive peaks, and the conflagration swept her away. Mindless, she pushed herself against his mouth, letting the flames he stoked whirl her higher and higher until the sun burst and, embers and ashes, she drifted weightlessly back to earth.

It took longer this time for the old uncertainties to grip her, but as her breathing returned to normal she felt their chill clutch. She lay with her eyes closed and licked lips that had gone dry from her shameless panting. Yet even as her mind began its steady litany of recrimination, she felt the tug of a new awareness. This wasn't fair to Matt.

She opened her eyes to find him regarding her steadily. She knew that look now. The look of love. He supported his weight on his arms propped on either side of her. She glided her hands along them and could feel their trembling as he struggled still for control. He was just a man, muscle and bone, like any other and yet unlike any she had ever known. Meeting his eyes, she felt a bond with him that made what they did here together sacred and right and, for the moment at least, silenced the voices of the past. "Come to me, Matt," she said.

He reached for one of the foil packets he had placed on the night table. She noticed his hands were unsteady as he tried to tear it open. She couldn't say what imp compelled her to tease him when he resorted to his teeth. "Have you ever used one of these before, Lieutenant?"

His eyes flew to hers as he tossed the foil wrapper aside. "God, Angel!" He gave a self-deprecating laugh. "Is it so obvious? You're gonna unman me."

She smiled and reached to cup him where he knelt ready between her thighs. "I don't think so." She caressed his length, learning the weight and heat and need of him. At her touch his hands fell to his thighs and his eyes drifted shut. A sound halfway between a growl and a purr rolled from his throat. She could see each muscle of his chest tauten as his breath caught.

She took the protection from his lax fingers, placed it against his tip, and began to unroll it. His hands carved deep tunnels in his thighs as his fingers clenched. His head rolled back and she saw him swallow convulsively. One hand lifted to help her but she brushed it aside as she continued to unroll the sheath over his rigid flesh. He opened his eyes to watch her, his breath coming ragged and deep as he seemed unable to tear his gaze from the sight of her hands on him.

Still she sensed his restraint. She could feel the passion straining in him and she wanted to unleash it. He didn't understand what a gift this was to her. To do this for a man she loved. To blot out the vile memories of the others with this glorious reality.

His shaft leapt against her palm as she cradled him, his need was so great. He braced her head with his hands, his weight on his elbows, as she guided him to her, and he entered her slick warmth that first little bit. "Why are you holding back?" she asked.

He leaned his forehead on hers, nose to nose. "I don't want to scare you."

She tilted her chin up, reaching for his lips with hers.

"You can't." She planted her feet flat on the bed next to his hips and lifted her own to bring him deep. With an agonized moan he buried his face in the curve of her shoulder. She ran her hands along the bunched muscles of his back to the dip at his waist and the taut rise below. His skin was damp from his efforts at control. With her mouth at his ear, her words came in hot, breathy pants against his cheek. "Please, Matt. Make them go away. Drive them out of me forever. Don't hold back."

He surged into her then, his body crushing hers into the mattress, his thrusts full and deep. She lifted her legs, linking them around his waist, her body welcoming, sweetly yielding. She threaded her hands into his hair, holding him down to her, her mouth and his tongue mimicking the motions below. Pulling his mouth away, he pushed up and fixed his gaze where his flesh sank into hers—until he could watch no longer and, eyes squeezed shut, back arched, teeth bared, muttering words both holy and obscene, he lost himself in her.

For long moments, her hands stroking languidly, she reveled in the feel of his body pressed to hers from chest to toes. Then she felt him rouse and knew he was afraid he was too heavy for her, his concern for her again overriding his own comfort. He lifted his weight from her breasts, kissing each one thoroughly before smiling down into her eyes.

"You okay?" he asked, his expression softened with repletion.

She pushed her fingers through his damp hair, her body stirring, already missing the friction of his mouth on her breasts. "I'm wonderful," she whispered.

His teeth flashed in a broad grin. "Yeah, you are." He kissed her throat, rubbed his face in her fragrant hair, and slowly became aware of the subtle push of her hips against his. He raised his head again, this time taking in the flush over her breasts, the lambency in her eyes, her uneven breathing. "You're ready again, aren't you? No—" he grasped her chin as her gaze skittered away "—don't be shy. That's good." His tongue teased a nipple to a quivering peak and he smiled down on his handiwork. "That's real good."

He slid his hand down between their bodies to where they were joined. "Let me, honey. It'll be good...you'll see." And with lips and tongue and fingers, with tender care, he brought her to the sweetest fulfillment of all, with the man she loved still buried deep within her.

When she had gathered all the fragments of herself back from the places Matt had sent them, she realized she was alone in the bed. She opened her eyes to darkness and was just beginning to deal with the disappointment when she heard Matt padding back from the bathroom. He pulled back the covers on the bed and she felt the mattress sink beneath his weight.

"Are you staying?"

He hesitated a moment, his arm raised to pull the blankets over them. "Are you kicking me out?"

"No." Her answer came on a huff of laughter.

"Then I'm staying." He snuggled in next to her and reached over her head for the alarm clock on the night table. "Let's see how you set this thing. Do you have to get up any special time?"

She yawned and watched him squinting at the illuminated dial. "No, I'm off. I have to work Saturday."

"That's right. You're on call this weekend." He pulled the stem and set the clock back on the stand.

"Oo-oh, so early?"

He nuzzled her ear. "Some of us have to work tomorrow. Besides, I gotta go back to the house to shower and change." He dropped a kiss on her shoulder. "I didn't wash my undies out in your sink."

She giggled, marveling at his ability to make her laugh away all of the awkwardness, as he nestled them together like spoons. Cuddled up against his body, she realized she had the answer to one of her questions about him. At least sometimes he slept naked. She fit her bare bottom into the curve made by his belly and thighs. Sometimes, she smiled dreamily, his warm fingers curling over her breast, she did, too.

Chapter 12

Matt awoke minutes before the alarm was set to go off and y in the darkness savoring the feel of the woman beside m. Her head rested on his shoulder, a few silky strands of r hair caught in the stubble on his chin. He listened to her oilant breathing and smiled to himself. His Angel snored. te sound was refined, ladylike, but most definitely a snore. od willing, he'd hear it every day for the rest of his life.

She stirred, sliding a thigh over his. The fingers of her .nd, resting palm-down on his abdomen, trailed lazily rough the coarse hairs around his navel. His heart hammered against his ribs and a raw sound escaped him as he rdened, his body straining for her.

"Do you always wake up like that?" she whispered ainst his neck.

"Like..." He cleared the roughness from his throat and ied again. "Like what?"

She nudged him gently with her thigh.

"Oh, *that*." He stretched to push the alarm button in on e clock.

"Yes. I thought maybe you brought your billy club to d."

His chest rumbled with unguarded laughter. "Allow me
to clear up a little misconception you have about police
work. Detectives don't carry billy clubs."

"You could have fooled me."

"Ms. Martino, I am shocked, *shocked*, at the turn your
mind has taken."

Angel lifted her head from his shoulder and rested her
chin on his chest, regarding him in the first pale beams of
daylight sifting through the blinds. He didn't sound
shocked. He sounded delighted.

In her most secret dreams of a husband and family,
dreams she scarcely acknowledged even to herself, she
hoped she might be able to tolerate lovemaking. To endure
it. Never had she thought to experience such profound feelings of intimacy and trust. Never in her wildest imaginings
had she thought there might be laughter. There might be
play. She needed now to exorcise the last of her demons, to
obliterate the ugly memories and replace them with those
made in love with Matt.

"I'm not sure I believe you, about the billy club, I mean.
Maybe I'd better check."

Before he fully grasped her meaning, she disappeared
under the bedclothes in a flurry of blankets. His breath escaped in a rush when he felt her hand on him, gently milk-
ing. Drawing another breath was beyond him as her mouth
took the place of her hand. His hips rolled in response, even
as the muscles in his abdomen rippled with the effort to hold
back. He squeezed his eyes shut. That did nothing to dispel
the image in his mind of the tender ministrations of her lips
and tongue.

"Sweetheart, I can't . . ." He arched against the bedding,
his breathing coming now in harsh gasps. "You remember
when I told you . . . about . . . being able to stop?" He dug his
heels into the mattress as she cupped him, her warm lips
closing over the tip of his shaft. "Honey, I could have been
wrong." Another liquid caress sent pleasure jolting through
him. "*Angel*. You've gotta stop."

He kicked free of the blankets, grasped her upper arms
and pulled her up over his body. He saw uncertainty in her
eyes—and determination. In that instant he realized wh.

...e had been doing. He knew. He pushed her hair off her
...ce and cradled her cheeks in his palms. "Angel," he
...hispered, "there are only two of us in this bed. Just you
...nd me and whatever pleases us. Do you understand?"

Her expression softened and she nodded. She could tell
...is body still raged beneath her with the need she had in-
...amed. With a puckish smile, she reached for one of the
...ackets on the night table. He took it from her. "I've gotta
...et the hang of this," he said.

She raised up and sat astride his thighs while he sheathed
...imself. When he was ready, he slid his hands up her arms
... her shoulders, gently kneading. "Come closer, sweet-
...eart. You're too far away."

She eased down to him, their open mouths meeting in a
...ow, deep kiss. Lost in a haze of longing, she rubbed her
...reasts over his hair-roughened chest. She arched to him,
...atlike, when he smoothed his palms over the sleek muscles
... her back, then settled them on her buttocks in the way she
...ad imagined just a day ago. He slid his hands behind her
...nees, bringing them up alongside his waist, spreading her
...vide as she lay atop him. A whimper escaped her when his
...ingers found her, dipping inside just a little to test her
...eadiness. She heard him groan low in response.

She raised herself on her arms and met his eyes. His face
...ight with passion, he grasped her hips and guided her onto
...is straining heat. "I'm yours," he said, his voice a gut-
...ural moan. "Whatever you want. Anything, Angel. Any-
...hing at all."

She closed her eyes, exulting in the freedom he allowed
...er. She rode him, wild, unrestrained, abandoned. Her hair
...vhipping back from her face, she braced herself with her
...ands on his chest. Her hips lowered to his again and again,
...he tempo steadily increasing, the rhythm lashing her on to
... shattering climax. With a sharp, keening wail she gave
...erself up to the release. As if from a distance, she heard the
...arsh cry that ripped from his throat and knew he joined her
...here.

They lay entwined, contented in the aftermath, while the
...oom around them gradually grew brighter. Finally Matt

could ignore it no longer. He gave her bottom a pat. "I'm gonna be late."

Lazily she rolled to the side of him, feeling a pang of loss as he slipped from her.

He pushed himself up on an elbow and watched her for some moments, a bemused expression on his face.

"Angel?"

She opened her eyes and met his.

"What you were doing...before." Doubt flashed in her eyes and he cursed his sorry way with words. He pressed on. "No one's ever done that for me. It's...always been a fantasy...but I could never ask."

The admission seemed to please her. She curved her hand over his rough cheek. "I love you, Matthew Flanagan. You won't have to ask."

Her simple confession seared him. He wasn't an articulate man. It had never particularly bothered him before. But he didn't know the words to tell her what she meant to him. She didn't appear to mind. He picked up a strand of her hair, running it over his fingers. "I had a long engagement once," he said. "I didn't like it."

That prompted a wide smile. She remembered he had been a virgin when he married. "I'll bet you didn't." She laughed. "Short, then. Short and sweet." She kissed him lightly. "Now, you'd better get a move on before you lose your job and I have to support you."

"Heartless woman," he mumbled, rising from the bed. He gathered up his clothes and headed for the bathroom.

Angel made a cocoon of the blankets, hugging herself in her joy.

Matt emerged into the early-morning light, a spring in his step, his spirits buoyant. Rounding the end of Angel's car on the way to his van, he saw her trunk was ajar. He had his hand raised to slam it shut when the instincts that could mean the difference between a live cop and a dead one kicked in. His hand hovering inches above the cold metal, he scanned the rear end of the BMW. Then he saw it. The thin wire, almost the same silvery color as the car. It exited

e trunk near the left taillight, snaked around the bumper,
d disappeared underneath the vehicle.

Keeping his hands clear, Matt crouched to check the un-
rside of the car and swore. Explosive devices weren't his
rea of expertise, but even to his unpracticed eye this was a
rude one. A single metal pipe, lashed to the gas tank with
hat looked like baling wire. Filled with black powder,
robably. So sensitive to heat and friction that many a
ould-be assassin had blown himself to hell just screwing
e end caps on tight. He wasn't about to join their ranks.

His gaze traveled back to the taillight. Maybe the backup
ght was the trigger. Maybe the brake light. Hell, who could
ll? With something this amateurish, starting the car
longside it might set it off. That only made it more unpre-
ictable, more dangerous.

Cold fear gripped him, intensified by an overwhelming
nse of failure and shame. For the second time in his life
e'd found himself lacking when it came to protecting the
oman he loved. He remembered the car from the night
efore. The one Angel had said didn't belong there. The one
e'd been too distracted to pay any attention to. He was a
op, dammit. It was his job to notice. Only he'd been too
nxious to get the lady into bed.

Still crouched, he rested his head in his hand and squeezed
he bridge of his nose. He felt his gorge rise and swallowed
ard, sick with self-disgust. If he'd eaten breakfast, he'd
ave lost it. He rose heavily to his feet, his expression grim.
He had to call this in. Christ, he knew what that would
ean.

Angel was just stepping into the shower when she heard
he frenetic pounding at her door. She slipped into her robe
vondering what Matt might have forgotten. A quick check
f the peephole confirmed his identity. She pulled the door
pen. One look at his face and the smile died on hers.

"What's wrong, Matt?"

"I need to use your phone."

With no further explanation, he strode past her to the wall
hone in the kitchen. Her alarm growing, she listened to his

terse message. She was round-eyed with fear, clenching her bathrobe in fists under her chin, when he hung up. "A bomb!" she gasped.

He stared at the receiver, his hand still on it, his mouth a tight slash across his face. "It's not my area. I think so."

"Matt—"

He turned and cut her off. "I've gotta wait outside. I don't want anyone near your car." His hard gaze raked her.

Standing there barefoot, her robe clutched around her, she had never felt so naked.

"You better get dressed," he said, and left her.

Stunned, she stared at the spot he had just vacated and shuddered with a chill no robe could warm. He had not once been able to meet her eyes.

By the time she had pulled some clothes on, the small parking lot next to her building was swarming with police. They had cordoned off the area with yellow plastic tape, separating several of her neighbors from their cars, to their obvious displeasure. The riskiness of the situation shot home when she saw the paramedic wagon pull in and block the entry drive.

She stood at her French doors trying to warm her fingers around a cup of coffee. Amid a group of what she supposed were plainclothes police officers, she spotted Matt. Apparently he saw her, too. He motioned over a uniformed officer and spoke to him, pointing in her direction. She watched the young man disappear into her building and sighed, her lips tightening. Matt wouldn't come himself. He was sending one of his men. She waited for his knock and let him in.

"I think you should stand away from all that glass, ma'am," he said, shutting the door behind him.

Angel felt the color drain from her face at his words. She sank onto the couch, holding her cup on her knees with hands that trembled. The patrolman took up a post just inside her door. Hands clasped behind his back, he looked about as pleased to be there as she was to have him. She considered telling him his presence wasn't necessary, but she didn't think it was her choice. From where she sat, the ac

vity outside her building was beyond her field of vision.
he had nothing to do but sit and wait.

At least the wait wasn't long. She had just taken her cup
) the kitchen when there was a knock on her door. The pa-
olman admitted Matt and two others before being dis-
iissed with a nod. The older man identified himself and the
oman, but Angel paid no attention to names or ranks.
hey refused coffee and told her to have a seat in tones that
idn't sound like an invitation. Matt positioned himself at
ie long window, his back to the room, and to her.

"Ms. Martino," the older man began. She looked at him.
Vhat hair he had on his bullet-shaped head was iron gray.
ppropriate, she thought, and bit the inside of her cheek to
eep an unseemly smile from her lips. He had a paunch but,
rith his massive shoulders and hands, he didn't look any
ss formidable for it. She slid a glance at Matt. Would that
e him in thirty years? Would she be around to see?

She turned back to the other man. The keen eyes in that
npassive face hadn't missed the look she sent Matt. She
)wered her gaze and folded her hands in her lap, feeling
hastened by that piercing stare.

"Ms. Martino, do you know of anyone who might wish
) do you harm?" the rough voice asked.

She raised her head. What a civilized question. Did she
now of anyone who would like to blow her to smither-
ens? he meant. God, no. She swallowed and shook her
ead.

He pulled a small spiral notebook from the inside pocket
f his suit coat. They must all carry those, she thought.

"A car matching the description of yours was seen in a
nown drug area yesterday. The witness was only able to
atch the last four digits on the license plate, but they match
ours, too. Would you happen to know anything about
hat?"

Staggered by the accusation his question implied, Angel
ould only shake her head again in silent denial. For the first
ime, Matt spoke.

"She was with me. The whole day. She was with me." He
hoved his hands into his pants' pockets, but didn't turn
rom the window.

Angel saw the measuring glance the older man threw him and her heart sank. This would mean trouble for him, because of her.

The policeman's stony glare pinned her again. Her knees were trembling. She clenched her hands together until the knuckles whitened, but she couldn't seem to stop shaking.

"Would anyone else have access to your car, Ms. Martino?"

She remembered the incident in the parking garage a few weeks before. Her unease. "One time," she said, "I noticed my keys weren't where I usually put them. I thought someone might have..." She shrugged. "I wasn't certain. I didn't say anything at the time."

Matt let fly a string of curses she thought would turn the air around them as blue as her carpet. At that inane notion, a shaky laugh, as unplanned as a hiccup, escaped her. Horrified, she clamped a hand over her mouth. She knew the signs of impending hysteria, even her own.

"Are you all right?" That concern was from the policewoman. Not from Matt. He only spared her a sidelong glance from under an arched brow. She cringed inwardly at the expression on his face. Shame. He was ashamed to be with her.

Her mind leapt back eleven years to another living room and another man ashamed to be caught with her. When she had named the father of her child, her grandmother had dragged her off to confront him and his parents. Feeling cowed and degraded, she had listened in silence while he listed the others he claimed could have fathered her son. Perhaps tests would have proved her case, if she'd had the knowledge to pursue it. Even so, she doubted she'd have had the will. In the end, she knew, she had done what was best for her child.

Matt had turned his face aside again, and in that moment she saw him as the others would. Uncombed, unshaven, his clothes rumpled, he looked like just what he was—a man recently risen from an illicit bed, one still warm and smelling of sex.

She thought she might be sick. She pressed a fist to her mouth and blinked to keep the tears from coming.

"Ms. Martino?"

She glanced up. Was that pity she read in his eyes? She bit
er quivering lips.

"We're going to impound your car. You're not confined
) your home, but we'll want to talk to you again. You
ight have something done about these locks if you have
ny question about them being secure."

She nodded. They were finished with her.

She didn't rise to see them out. Her legs wouldn't have
eld her. Matt left with them. Without a word to her, with-
ut even a glance, he was gone.

She got through the rest of that day the way she had all
1e years before Matt had come into her life. She did what
ad to be done. She stripped the sheets from her bed and
ashed them. She arranged for a rental car to be delivered
hat afternoon, so she'd have it available for work the next
ay and weekend call. She wrote out a check for the lock-
mith who changed her locks, including the one Matt had
ut in just weeks before. And she waited for Matt to call.

Finally, as the sun dipped low in the sky and disap-
eared, she admitted to herself what she had known in her
eart early on. He wasn't going to call. Ever again. He had
een her that morning, in the presence of his co-workers—
hey had all seen her—for what she was. An easy lay. Her
nother's daughter.

As shadows fell, she sat alone in the darkening room, her
rief too deep for tears.

"Not now, Patrick. I can't play now." Matt tapped a
unction key, bringing up on the screen the now familiar
ames and backgrounds. Still no answers.

"I promise I won't cheat."

"Patrick, I'm busy." He was officially off the case. And
rdered to stay away from *that woman*. His face still burned
rom the tongue-lashing he had received. Well deserved, he
ad to admit. But nothing and nobody was going to keep
im from gnawing this bone until he had an answer.

"Just one..."

"*No*, Patrick!" She had been set up, just as he'd feared. Implicate her, then get rid of her. With her questionable past and her efforts to conceal it, she'd be any easy target for blackmail. It wouldn't be hard to believe she could be suckered into the drug trade. When she became a liability, she had to go. Happened all the time. The cops might buy it. Hell, three weeks ago, he'd have bought it. Now he was off the case.

"Dad..."

Matt looked up. "Patrick, you're not supposed to have soda in he—" He watched, helpless, as his son tripped over the Lego fort on the den floor and toppled forward, cracking the bottom of his plastic mug against the corner of the desk. The soft drink sloshed over the side onto Matt's papers and the keyboard.

"Shi— Damn! Patrick!" He mopped desperately at the mess with the sleeve of his shirt. After a few moments of dead silence he glanced at his son. The boy's eyes were bright and his face twitched with his effort not to cry.

"God. What's happening to us?" He hauled his son into his arms and cradled his head against his chest. "It's okay, Patrick. Look, you didn't get any on the keyboard. Hardly." He felt the thin shoulders beneath his arm shudder and his shirt grow damp. He shut his eyes, close to tears himself.

"Shh, sport. I know I haven't spent much time with you lately. I'm sorry. Things are tough at work."

Patrick lifted his head and wiped his nose on his sleeve. "You're worried about Angel, aren't ya?"

Matt's brows raised in surprise. He didn't know it had been so obvious. Still, he'd been up-front with Patrick about his feelings for Angel from the start. There had always been honesty between them, more so in the last eighteen months. They only had each other. "I'm afraid I can't protect her," he said.

"I think maybe she loves you, Dad."

Matt looked at the boy through narrowed eyes. What was he really saying here? He let his breath out in a long sigh. May as well jump in with both feet. "I think maybe I love her, too. How about them apples, Patrick?"

Maybe he'd been more inattentive than he'd thought. He cally wasn't prepared for the look on the kid's face. ulky...stubborn...mulish. Evidently, Patrick was not verjoyed at this turn of events. Jeez, he didn't need this ight now. He passed a hand over his eyes and rested his chin a his palm. "What is it, sport?"

"Mikey's father got married again. He never sees him nymore."

Matt's mind flashed images of the assorted hellions in 'atrick's class. "Mikey Hammond?" Patrick nodded, his ower lip protruding petulantly. "That's too bad. I feel sorry or Mikey. But he wasn't living with his dad. He didn't see nuch of him anyway, did he?" His son shrugged. He wasn't iving an inch. "That wouldn't happen here. Angel would ome to live with us."

"Maybe she doesn't want a kid."

So that was the crux of it. Matt didn't want to betray a onfidence, but he couldn't imagine a family life with se- crets, and he couldn't imagine life at all without Angel.

"I don't think you have to worry about that, Patrick." He ushed the black hair off the boy's forehead and sighed. "She had a little boy once."

Patrick's head shot up, his eyes widened. "Did he die?"

"No, he didn't die. But he's as lost to her as if he did." He aw the question in his son's eyes. How to explain to a nine- ear-old the terrible choices a woman sometimes had to nake? "She was very young. Just a girl. And there was no ne to help her. She knew she couldn't give her baby the hings he would need. She gave him to a family that could ake good care of him." He paused, ruffling the thick hair nder his fingers. "She thinks about him every day, Pat- ick. It still hurts."

Patrick rested his head on Matt's shoulder, his arms cir- ling his father's neck in a gesture that Matt was seeing less nd less often as his son grew. "I think she'd love to have a ittle boy to care for, sport."

The youngster grabbed a handful of Matt's hair and ulled. "Big boy, Dad."

Matt laughed and gave a quick squeeze. "Big boy."

In the end, before Matt got back to his computer, he played three games of Battleship, lost every one, and Patrick did cheat.

The spill didn't seem to have caused any damage to the machine. It didn't do any good, either. He was still faced with the same set of questions and drawing blanks. He leaned back in his chair, hands clasped behind his head, and gave his thoughts free rein. As always, they zeroed in on Angel.

He ached at the thought of what she must be feeling now. God knew, it wasn't her fault. He had known his involvement with her was professional poison. It had mattered, just not enough. He had been afraid that if he waited until this mess was settled, his opportunity would pass. He would lose his chance with her. His fear had clouded his judgment. It wouldn't happen again. He would stay away from her until this guy was caught.

Adding to his guilt was the certainty that he had put Angel at risk. He was close to a solution. He felt it in his marrow. Could be the killer sensed it, too. What a coup to paint Angel as a suspect, eliminate her, and have him pulled from the case all at once.

In thwarting that scenario he found the only comfort to be had in the whole sordid mess. Angel was alive. He knew in every cell of his body, if he hadn't been there that morning, if he hadn't passed her car when he did, she'd be dead. It was a door he couldn't look behind, an idea he couldn't face, but he had no doubt. She'd be dead.

Matt sat up straight, shaking off his morbid thoughts. This wasn't getting him anywhere. He needed to take another approach. Was there something about these people an official investigation couldn't uncover? Who else might know their secrets? He called Trevor.

As it happened, the mention of a name was all it took. Matt had his answer.

Chapter 13

"Can you do something about that suction, Angel? It seems to be clogged again."

Angel looked up from her charting to the apparatus mounted on the tile wall. The plastic bottle was almost full. Quickly donning gloves, she cut off the suction to that bottle, shifted the connector to the container alongside it, milked the tubing, and turned the three-way adaptor to the On position. The low-pitched gurgling through the tube told her the vacuum had been reestablished. She debated setting up another jar.

"Will you be doing any more irrigating, Dr. Garrett?" Her instincts told her no. The appendix had been hot but not ruptured.

"No, Angel. We're about done here. I'll be ready to close in a minute."

She nodded and reached for her clipboard to do the sponge and instrument count with the O.R. tech. That done, she called the recovery room to alert them that the patient would be arriving soon and requested a stretcher. She had just given dressings to cover the incision to the scrub nurse when the phone rang.

Another emergency. Good. It had been like this all day. One case after another. They had gotten through most of the short Saturday schedule when the emergencies started. A lacerated tendon, a D & C, a four-year-old who had received a perfect-attendance pin for the term at her preschool, and promptly swallowed it. Dr. Garrett had bumped his own last case in order to get this appendix in. Now it appeared the procedure would be pushed to even later in the afternoon. He wasn't going to be a happy camper.

But this was fine with Angel. She hadn't had a free moment all day. No time for lunch. No time for paperwork. No time to turn around. No time to *think.* After a sleepless night she was running on caffeine and cussedness. She would get through this. She always had.

The hospital was her refuge. Here she was appreciated, admired. Matt's betrayal had taught her a whole new capacity for hurt, but she wasn't the type to crawl off and lick her wounds. Not when she was needed.

This was what she thrived on. In her administrative position, it wasn't necessary for her to take call, or work weekends, or run an operating room. She had insisted on it. When the position was offered to her, she had made it clear that she intended to maintain her clinical skills and patient contact. She felt it made her a better supervisor to get down in the trenches and deal with problems firsthand. She knew her staff respected her for it. She had always been happy with her decision, and never more so than now.

Now she needed the challenges that kept her mind engaged, as well as the dulling sedation of routine. She had her ear to the phone, her eyes on the operative team, while her hand scribbled instructions for the coming procedure, and she told herself she had no thought to spare for Matt.

She hung up the phone, took tape from the rack above her work counter and approached the operating table.

"What was that, Angel?" Dr. Garrett clipped the last suture and looked at her over the top of his glasses.

"Dr. Abrahms has a patient in the E.R. with an intestinal obstruction, he thinks probably a strangulated hernia. He wants to do it right away." She stepped aside as he placed a dressing over the wound, then pulled back the sterile drapes.

"Abrahms?" His displeasure was obvious even behind the mask as he said the name of the pediatric surgeon.

"Yes," she acknowledged. "It's a baby." She handed him the tape. When he unrolled strips to cover the dressing, she pulled her bandage scissors from her pocket and cut for him. "We'll have to take it before we do your next case."

He frowned at her but didn't argue the point. "Can't you call in a second team?" he suggested.

She sighed. "I can call in as many people as you like, Dr. Garrett. The fact remains that Jay—" she indicated the surgical resident next to her "—will be tied up with Abrahms's case, and *you* would have to call in someone to first assist."

That cast an entirely different color on the situation, as she knew it would. The surgeons were extremely reluctant to impose on their colleagues' precious off time. Not that they wouldn't in a true emergency, but that wasn't the case here.

He tossed the tape back to her and moved to help the O.R. tech maneuver the stretcher into place alongside the operating table. "Who's working this evening?"

"Harriet Irwin." She laughed as he rolled his eyes.

"Oh, Lord. I better have something to eat before I face that." They eased the patient from the O.R. bed to the stretcher, and Dr. Garrett glanced at Angel sharply. "That's the first time I've heard you laugh all day, and you look tired. Are you all right?"

At his concern she felt a stark stab of pain. How would he react if he knew of her foolishness? Quickly she hid behind the bright veneer of her professionalism. She grabbed the chart and tucked it under the mattress at the foot of the stretcher as Jay and the anesthesiologist headed out the door to recovery. "I'm fine," she said.

But she wasn't, and she knew it.

* * *

They were just transferring the baby from the O.R. bed to the recovery room crib when Harriet pushed through the swinging door, tying her mask strings as she approached. Angel glanced up, then turned her attention back to the child while Harriet stood quietly by.

Angel leaned over the infant, resting her elbows on either side of him. She held his arms in a gentle grip and his pudgy fingers curled around her thumbs as the anesthesiologist pulled the endotracheal tube and suctioned him. The little guy didn't like that one bit, she thought, smiling softly down on him. He whimpered and gagged and wrinkled up his face in a ferocious scowl. Just as he seemed about to let loose an ear-splitting wail, the torment ceased. He hiccuped, gave a shaky sigh, made sucking motions with his mouth, and went back to sleep.

Angel assessed him with both her nurse's and her woman's eyes. His color was good, skin warm and dry, breathing even and unlabored. The operation had turned out to be less involved than they had anticipated. He would be eating and drinking within hours, possibly going home the next day. Children this age were enormously resilient.

And he was adorable, the woman in her recognized. Chubby and dimpled, the pale wisps of his hair sticking up every which way. His lashes lay against his cheeks like cornsilk and she could see the faint tracery of veins through his translucent skin. What would it be like to hold his weight against her breast as he slept? To feel that little fist opening and closing on the sensitive skin of her neck? For so long she had accepted that it was impossible for her. Her grandmother had been so quick to tell her she'd gotten just what she deserved. Perhaps she had been too quick to believe it.

She straightened and released her hold on the child, raising the side rail of the crib. Through the slats she caught Harriet's eyes on her, regarding her with somber curiosity. Too late, she tried to conceal her melancholy, but Harriet didn't miss a trick. Angel knew she was in for a grilling.

"What's next?" Harriet asked after the patient had been wheeled from the room.

Angel gathered her papers and walked with her co-worker to the front desk. "You've got a breather. Garrett won't be back to do his case for at least an hour. Let me go over Monday's schedule with you. It's a mess."

"Tell me about it while you get changed. I'll come back to the locker room with you. I need to take my blood pressure pill anyway. Maybe you can get out of here on time for a change." Harriet didn't wait for any argument, but headed her stout frame down the corridor. Angel shrugged and followed.

She sat at the small wooden table in the locker room vestibule while Harriet got her pill and a cup of water and joined her. She was reaching for the schedule when the other woman placed her broad palm across it and pinned her with a level gaze. "What's wrong, Angel?"

Angel fought for a calm front. She felt put together like a strand of poorly strung beads. One tug would send her fragile composure scattering. "It's just been a very busy day. I'm a little ti—"

"Don't give me that song and dance. The cop giving you a hard time?"

Cut to the chase why don't you, Harriet? Angel thought. Her shoulders slumped and she clasped her hands loosely in her lap. "I don't think I'm quite what he has in mind as a—"

"That's not the impression I got the other night when I talked to him. I had the feeling he'd take a bite out of me if I didn't tell him where you were."

When Angel didn't respond, Harriet sighed heavily. "That's too bad. I was hoping... You really should have a family, Angel. Kids. You're so good with the little ones here."

Suddenly it was all too much. The deceit, the secrecy, the incredible loneliness. The constant effort to keep up a cheerful front. She couldn't bear it any longer. What would happen if someone knew the truth? "I had a ba—" Her voice broke on the word. "A baby once." Even to her own ears, her voice sounded high-pitched and tremulous. In that instant she knew she would not get through this without breaking down.

But it was too late to stop. She looked across the table at the kind, patient face waiting expectantly for her to go on.

She inhaled a deep, unsteady breath, squeezed her hands together, and tried again. Only a croak emerged from her tight throat. Harriet's hand reached over to gently cover her knotted ones, and the dam broke, the tears came. Her face crumpled, a mask of agony, and she cried like the little girl she had been was never allowed to do. Great, loud, hacking sobs that racked her small frame. She heard the scrape of chair legs against the wooden floor and felt herself crushed against an ample bosom. Sturdy arms encircled her, a mother's arms. She had never known them. They rocked and patted her while she cried until her throat was raw and her stomach hurt.

Gradually, her sobs quieted and her story poured out. Rambling, disjointed, almost incoherent. Whether Harriet followed it all or not, Angel couldn't tell, but it didn't seem to matter. When she lifted her head, finally, Harriet's eyes were wet, too.

Angel's scrub cap had gone askew. Harriet pulled it off, threading her fingers through the damp strands of her hair. "Oh, Angel," she whispered. "What were you afraid of? That we would think less of you? We know what you are."

Angel swallowed, unable to respond. The eyes that looked at her were filled with nothing but concern and sympathy. No shock. No revulsion. No censure. She sat up a little straighter, rubbing her nose and digging into the pocket of her warm-up jacket for a tissue. She wiped her eyes and took in a deep breath, letting it out slowly. She felt calmer now, and strangely light, as if a heavy burden she hadn't even been aware she carried had been lifted from her.

She reached for the surgical schedule again, but Harriet stayed her. "Forget about that. I've been here twenty years. I can figure it out."

Angel let the paper fall and sat back in her chair releasing a long sigh. "Thank you, Harriet. For listening."

The older woman gave a dismissive shake of her head. "It's about time you let all of that out." When Angel didn't reply, she folded her arms on the table and leaned toward her. "It's not my place to say anything. You do what you want. But I think the people around here would be more understanding than you give them credit for." At Angel's weak smile, she went on. "As for that cop, I wouldn't be too quick to write him off. Smart-ass though he is—" that prompted a broader smile "—he seems to have his head on straight. This wouldn't throw him."

"We'll see," Angel murmured noncommittally.

Harriet shoved away from the table. "I'd better get out on the unit before Garrett sends a search party. Are you going to be all right?"

"Yes, thank you. I'm fine." This time, she realized, she meant it.

She sat for a few minutes after Harriet left, then rose and went into the washroom area connected to the locker room. She pulled a paper towel from the wall container and moistened it under the tap, blotting her blotched and puffy face with the rough paper. Hands resting on the cold, porcelain sink, she studied her reflection in the mirror above it. Through eyes swollen and dimmed with tears, she saw herself clearly.

For the first time.

She wasn't bad. She never had been. Unloved, uncared for, yes. Whatever her needs for affection or attention, they had been beyond her grandmother's meager capacity to provide. Still, from the dregs of her past she had built a life to be proud of. She was a strong woman, capable and compassionate. It was time for the woman she had become to spare a little compassion for the lonely, neglected child she had been. Matt was right. If it had been someone else, she would have understood.

Matt. She closed her eyes to shut out the reflected pain. He had given her this. This new sense of self. If there would

be nothing else between them, she owed him this. It was
what she had seen in his eyes that had opened her own.

Her eyes opened again, bright with determination. She
would tell him. When she saw him again, and she *would* see
him, she would let him know. Feeling more at peace than
she could ever recall, she turned and walked into the locker
room to change.

Matt pressed the illumination button on his watch and
checked the time. Half past two. He shifted on the cracked
vinyl upholstery and wrapped his arms in front of his chest,
trying to keep warm. The broken window alongside him was
held in place by what appeared to be silver duct tape, but
Jack had missed a spot or two. The cold draft that whistled
through was hitting Matt right on the back of his neck.
What a heap. The rusting metal hulk even boasted an air
scoop on the hood. What the hell could possess a grown
man to own such a thing?

Matt glanced across at his companion, who slouched behind the wheel asleep. He looked even more disreputable
than usual, if that was possible. His long hair was unbound
and hung in greasy tangles over his shoulders. He didn't
appear to have shaved since the last time Matt had seen him.
More than a week. He'd be going undercover again soon,
Matt supposed. Probably this car was part of his cover, although exactly what impression the guy was trying to convey, he didn't care to speculate. He was a damn good cop.
At the moment that's all Matt cared about.

He pulled the ribbed collar of his jacket farther up around
his neck. As soon as he settled back, it slipped down again.
Disgusted, he reached over the seat to the thermos of coffee he had stashed in the back and poured some of the hot
liquid into the cap. As if on cue, the sleeping bulk next to
him roused.

Jack dug under his seat and pulled out a much-used mug,
a little fuzzy around the rim. "Gimme some of that."

Matt filled the mug and handed it back to his companion. "Well, well, well. Merry Sunshine. Did you wake up?"

Jack took a long swallow and smacked his lips. "I got nothin' to be merry about, Matt. I don't know how you talk me into these things. The skip catches you here with me, and my ass is grass. Again."

"Unless I'm right."

"Well." He shrugged. "There's always that possibility. In which case, you'll be the chief's fair-haired boy. Again. You bring any food?"

Matt pulled a white waxed-paper bag from the back seat and tossed it into the other man's lap.

"Ah, glazed." Jack wolfed down two of the donuts before he offered the open bag to Matt, who refused it with a shake of his head.

"Which car has she got?"

Jack took another slug of coffee and pointed toward Angel's parking area. "That little red Ford. She's only been to work and back and no one else has been near it."

Matt nodded. "Who's watching the guy?" He sensed hesitation and turned to look at his companion.

"Mullen," Jack snapped.

Matt scowled. "Ah, jeez. He's one dumb cop."

"I know. He couldn't catch the flu. That's why we're on his end."

Matt stared bleakly at Angel's entry. "I hate this," he said.

The jangle of the phone woke Angel from a fitful sleep. She pushed off the covers and sat up, sliding her legs over the edge of the bed as she flicked on the bedside lamp and reached groggily for the receiver. She recognized the chirpy voice of the switchboard operator even before the woman mentioned the hospital.

"Dr. Ross has a Gyn patient that needs to have a D & C right away," the operator informed her.

Angel felt a twinge of apprehension. This was one of the few procedures a lone nurse could handle. "Will he want the scrub nurse called in?" she asked after a moment. She

pushed a hand through her hair, holding it off her face, and
squinted at the clock.

"No, that won't be necessary."

"I'll be there in fifteen minutes."

Angel replaced the receiver in its cradle, then sat staring
at it, her fingers curled around the edge of the mattress. Finally, shaking off her trepidation, she rose, slipped out of
her sleep shirt, and dressed in the clothes she had laid out on
a chair before going to bed. She made a quick stop in the
bathroom to splash water on her face and brush her hair.
Ready to leave, she detoured into the kitchen to check the
Anesthesia schedule stuck to the refrigerator with a magnet. Her finger skimmed down the page, stopping at the
current weekend. Alvarez. She let out a sigh of relief. He
was a flake, but harmless. She grabbed her jacket, purse and
keys and left the apartment.

"You sure this guy's dirty?"

"Yeah, he's dirty. Trevor made him right away. He got
into gambling big-time. Owes a bundle to some real high
rollers. Probably figured he could dabble a little in drugs,
make a killing—pardon the pun—and come out smelling
like a rose. Things snowballed."

"I thought the family was loaded."

"Seems the wife controls most of the money. He can
diddle whoever he wants, but she isn't about to bail him out
of this mess."

"Hey, we all have our standards. What about the dead
nurse?"

Matt leaned forward, peering into the darkness. "A light
just came on in Angel's place." He stowed the thermos and
bag in the back seat, out of the way. "Grace Patterson must
have caught on to his involvement. After all, their personal
and professional lives intersected. I see him bringing her a
little treat. She trusted him. Her mistake."

"Pick up any prints at her place?"

Matt's mouth tightened to a thin line. He shook his head.
"We tested the glassine packet found on her body. Some

body wiped it clean." He let out a tight breath. "Everything we've got on him is circumstantial. I know we've gotta lure him out, force him to make a move, but I don't like what we're using for bait." He let his gaze wander over the concealing shrubs and trees surrounding the condo.

"He's not gonna try again here, Matt. Not after that last fiasco."

"I don't know. He's desperate. God knows, he didn't have any help from the big boys with the bomb. That was strictly punks working out of Daddy's garage. Could be the head honchos are losing patience wi... Here she comes."

They saw the outline of a woman's form as Angel merged into the dimly lit courtyard. Matt shifted his weight, pushed the flap of his jacket back and waited, every muscle tense. One hand rested on the butt of his revolver, the other on the door handle. Muffled sounds alongside him told him the other man had assumed the same position.

"Oh, my, my, my," Jack muttered. Angel had stepped into the brighter light of the parking area across the drive from them. "I know what you see in *her.*"

Matt watched the beautiful young woman picking her way to her car, but he saw Angel sprawled on her back in the dirt, laughing till tears streamed. He saw his Angel lying naked in his arms, her hands trembling but her eyes trusting as she opened herself to love and to life. He saw Angel frightened, yet defiant and unbowed. "No," he said. "You don't."

She had reached the Ford without incident. They watched as she backed out of the space and turned from the drive into the road leading from the complex.

Jack started the car and followed at a distance. The old gate was quiet, Matt noted, despite its appearance. "Keep the lights off," he said. "Don't lose her, but don't spook her."

"I know how to do this, Matt."

She spotted the car in her rearview mirror when it turned into the main road. Big, low to the ground, lights out. She

stole another quick glance but couldn't make out any more
than that. What had that car looked like the other night?
She hadn't gotten a clear view of it, but she had a vague im
pression of an older, souped-up model. Something like thi
one. She pressed her foot more firmly to the accelerator.

"The lady's got a lead foot."

"Yeah. Do you think she's seen us?" Jack threw him ar
offended look. There had been no other cars on the de
serted streets.

"She parks in that big garage on the right," Matt said
"The drive's just ahead."

"She's not parking there tonight." They watched as An
gel's taillights zipped past the garage entry.

"Aw, hell. Where's she going? Don't lose her, Jack."

"Looks like she's heading around the far end of the place
What's back there?"

"Physical plant, mainly. Bowels of the hospital. The op
erating room is there, too, but I didn't think there was a
entrance."

They watched Angel's car disappear into shadows aroun
the corner of the building. Jack stepped on the gas.

Matt opened the glove compartment and shuffled throug
the junk inside. "Got a radio?"

"A phone. Under your seat. Plugs into the lighter."

Moments later Jack turned into the lane Angel had use
only to be brought up short by an automatic parking ga
standing sentry at a tiny lot. Angel's car was the only one :
view.

Matt swore. "Go around the gate." Frantically, his ey
scanned the area for signs of Angel. A rhythmic clangi
drew his gaze upward. Angel raced along a catwalk to
door on the second level. In the orange glare of a sodiur
vapor lamp, he saw her swipe what looked like a pass ca
through a black box. His heart lodged in his throat, !
pushed open the car door and leapt out to call to her. T
late. He heard the heavy clank of the metal door as it clos
behind her.

"Son of a bitch! We can't get in this way." He dipped his head inside the car to bark instructions. "Call for backup. I'm going around."

"Matt—" Jack shouted. He was talking to air. With a vicious curse he connected the phone and called for assistance.

Angel's heart was still hammering as she stepped into the O.R. lounge pulling the drawstring of her scrub pants tight. She went directly to the wall phone to alert Security to the presence of a suspicious vehicle. Then, taking deep breaths to calm herself, she rested her forehead against the cool tile wall and absorbed the absolute silence of the O.R. suite.

Not quite absolute. She turned her head, her ears catching the sound of activity nearby. Normal daytime sounds. But this wasn't daytime. Cautiously she approached the door to the storeroom adjacent to the lounge. She halted at the threshold, taken aback at the sight of the man squatting in front of a metal cabinet, his head and shoulders buried deep inside as he rummaged within it.

He must have heard her. He pulled out and glanced in her direction. "Gary," she gasped.

"Hey, Ange. Don't you ever go home?"

"I got called in." Her pulse beat in a trip-hammer rhythm. She put a hand to the doorjamb to steady herself.

"Oh, yeah?" He shrugged. "Must be a patient from one of the units. The E.R. is quiet." He ducked his head inside the cabinet again.

He seemed so natural, so at ease. The same old Gary. Surely he couldn't pose a threat. "Why are you here?" she asked, curious.

He didn't even bother to back out this time. His voice was muffled by the confines of the cabinet and its contents. "It's Kevin's anniversary. He's taking Meg to a hotel. Get away from the kids. I told him I'd cover for him." He pulled several bags of IV fluids out and dropped them on the floor, then eased out of the cupboard, still talking. "I wish I was

doing what he's doing right now..." He gave her a mischievous wink. "Instead of what I *am* doing."

Angel felt the hot color rise in her cheeks. He was always
able to provoke her and he knew it. She watched him get to
his feet, cradling the IV bags. "What *are* you doing?" she
asked when his actions finally registered.

"We're out of D-five in Ringer's. I thought I'd scrounge
around here, see what you have."

She rolled her eyes and gave an exasperated laugh. "You
could have ordered it from the stockroom like everyone else
does."

"Yeah, but I wanted it tonight, not sometime next week."
He nudged the cabinet door shut with his foot and walked
toward her. When he came abreast, he chucked her under
the chin playfully. "You really oughtta get more sleep,
Ange. You look ragged." With that, he eased past her and
exited through the automatic doors down the hallway.

Angel shook her head. How could she ever, even for a
moment, have been afraid of Gary? He was exactly as he
seemed. A little abrasive, more than a little arrogant, *less*
than a model husband, but generally well-meaning. Certainly not a vicious killer.

She pulled on shoe covers, zipped a mask from its cardboard box and tied it in place at her neck as she entered the
sterile corridor. She needed to get ready for this procedure,
she told herself, and locate her patient. She turned on lights
as she went along. Up ahead, she noticed, light already
slanted from the doorway of the Anesthesia workroom.
Alvarez. Maybe he knew where to find the patient. As she
rounded the door, her breath caught in her chest.

"Hello, Angel."

"Dr. Albert." She tried to keep her voice at a normal
pitch. "I wasn't expecting you."

"I know. You were expecting Ernesto. That was a mistake on the schedule. He's on next weekend."

While he spoke she watched him pour a white powder
from a small brown pharmacy jar onto the steel counter.

top. He wouldn't need anything like that for a D & C.
Prickles of fear crept up her spine.

He looked up from what he was doing, over the rim of his
glasses. "You're right, Angel. This is for you."

His words galvanized her. She wheeled to run from the
room, but he was faster. His hand clamped on her wrist and
pulled her inexorably to him. Even as she struggled, she
tried to reason with him.

"You'll never get away with this." She could hear the
panic edging into her voice and fought it.

"Don't be silly. Lots of people get away with it. You've
always been a strange one. No one knows much about you.
They'll figure you decided to take call from here and
couldn't stay away from your stash. It's a common failing
among druggies, Angel. There's a call room signed out to
you. The bed's been slept in. Even some of your things are
there. It was easy once I had your keys."

She tried to wrench her arm free. He responded by pulling it up hard behind her back, pressing her breasts against
his chest in an ugly parody of an embrace. She made a soft
mewling sound at the tearing pain. "They can trace the
phone call to me . . . from the hospital," she gasped.

"There was no call from the hospital. Dottie did that for
me. She won't talk."

She closed her eyes and tears slipped from the corners.
Dottie. His girlfriend. She had recognized the voice, she just
hadn't put it together. She thought the danger was behind
her, when it was here, waiting for her.

"You don't think your cop will be able to figure this out,
do you?" She hated the contemptuous tone in his voice.
"He's going to be very disappointed at what he finds out
about you, Angel."

"What do you mean?"

"The evidence . . . in your locker."

"There's no . . ." Instinctively her free hand went to the
locker key she had pinned to the shirt of her scrub suit, just
as all the nurses did.

His cold eyes followed her gesture and he gave a chilling smile. "There will be."

She began to struggle in earnest then, ignoring the pain as she tried to pull away. He wasn't a big man, but he was wiry, strong. She was no match for him.

"Don't make this harder than it has to be. There won't be any pain. This is a pleasant way to die. All you have to do is take a breath."

His voice terrified her most. He spoke with clinical detachment, the same measured tones he used with patients. Only now, in a hideous perversion of his calling, he intended to administer the breath of death. She lashed out frantically at his words, trying to swat the powder off the counter while she grappled with him, but she was too far away.

That action seemed to enrage him. He whirled her around, trapping both her arms behind her between their bodies. She kicked at his knees, but sneaker-clad feet covered with paper did little damage. She only served to anger him further. He pushed her against the metal counter knocking the wind from her. "Leave it to you to do things the hard way," he growled. He crushed a hand over her mouth and shoved her head toward the powder with the weight of his body. "Breathe, damn you!"

She tried to bite him, but he mashed her lips against her teeth. Already the need for air was almost overwhelming. Her agitation only increased it. Was this how it had been for Gracie? Or had she gone unsuspecting to her death? There had been no sign of a struggle, Matt had said. *Matt.* What would he think when they found her? Her lungs were on fire, spots swam in front of her eyes, but she wouldn't go without a fight. One that would show.

With consciousness slipping, she made herself go limp and felt Albert's hold ease. She jerked back suddenly, then slammed her face hard against the countertop. She heard the crackle of small bones, but whether from his fingers or her cheek she couldn't tell. Shards of pain pierced her skull. The rusty tang of blood filled her mouth. But she had hurt him. His grip loosened. She turned her head and gulped in air.

All at once, his weight was gone. With the loss of his support, she slid to the floor against the cabinet. Through a haze of pain and fear and confusion, she saw Matt. He had Albert facedown on the floor, a knee to his back, a gun at his neck, as he cuffed him. He was out of breath, his voice a harsh pant as he spoke. "You have the right to remain silent..."

Limp with relief, she closed her eyes and listened to Matt finish the recitation. Then he was with her, kissing her hair, her brow, her eyes, until, at the sharp intake of her breath, he withdrew. He lifted her face with his fingers under her chin, his expression feral. "What did he do to you?" he muttered.

He turned and lunged toward the man on the floor, but she grabbed at his arm, pulling him back. "No, Matt! I did it." She met his doubt with insistence. "I did it myself. I didn't want you to think... I was involved. Like Gracie," she explained. "I wanted to show I put up a fight."

Pain flickered in his eyes. He rubbed the backs of his fingers, barely touching, over her swelling cheek. "Listen to me," he said fiercely. "I never would have believed that. Never."

At a noise behind him, her gaze flew to the doorway. Another man entered. Scraggly hair, frayed jeans, he had the scruffy look favored by rock stars...and thugs. She saw the drawn gun and froze. He turned eyes of blue ice on her, then seemed to notice Matt and his face broke into a smile that transformed him.

"I don't think she knows I'm one of the good guys, Matt."

Matt's eyes filled with amusement. "This is Jack, Angel. He's a cop. As a matter of fact, he's been helping me keep real close tabs on you for the past day or so."

She looked at him in disbelief. "That was *you* behind me...with the lights out?"

It was Matt's turn to register dismay. "You saw us?"

"Matt. You told me to watch my back."

"I never figured you'd be any good at it."

Jack broke in. "Would you be responsible for the visitor I had in the parking lot?"

A look of chagrin flooded Angel's face and Matt laughed. "It's okay, sweetheart. You're careful. I like that in a woman."

Within moments the small room was crowded with cops. Uniformed police, with their big, black-shod feet clomping through her sterile department. No masks, no shoe covers, hair exposed—Angel was nearly beside herself. To add to her misery, her cheek was really beginning to call attention to itself.

Matt noticed her distress, caught Jack's eye, and motioned to Albert, who was sitting on the floor, subdued.

"Right. I'll take care of this guy. You look after your lady."

"Thanks," Matt said. "I owe you."

"Again."

From somewhere in the hodgepodge of bodies, Gary appeared, muscling Matt out of the way. Reluctantly, Matt moved aside, his intense dislike for the man tempered by the knowledge that Angel needed attention.

"George Albert. That prig. Who'd have thought it?" Gary muttered as the older man was hustled from the room. Matt gave Chapman the look Angel saved for flies near the operative field.

Gary lifted Angel's face and turned it side to side for examination, poking and prodding. She sucked in air when he touched a tender spot.

"I think all that bleeding is from your lip, Ange. You teeth look all right."

Over his shoulder she saw Matt pale.

"I'm a little concerned about this cheek, though. You might have a depressed fracture of the zygomatic arch. With all this swelling it's hard to tell. I'm sending you to X ray."

"Itsch agh..." She shoved Gary's fingers from her mouth. She had never thought Patrick and Matt looke alike, but right now Matt's expression had taken on a decided resemblance to the one Patrick had worn just before he'd lost his breakfast. "It's a nothing fracture, Matt. They can fix it with the handle of a spoon." He didn't look much relieved.

Gary turned and eyed Matt askance over his shoulder. He glanced back at Angel. "You like this Neanderthal?"

Her eyes—at least the one she could open all the way—were round pools of alarm. Before Matt could mop the floor of her O.R. with Gary, she gave a vigorous nod.

Gary grinned. "No accounting for taste, I guess." He rose and picked up the wall phone to arrange for her X ray.

Half an hour later Angel lay on a stretcher in a curtained emergency room cubicle. Flat on her back, she counted ceiling tiles, trying to divert her attention from her throbbing face and rising irritation. The curtain shifted and the source of her agitated condition walked in.

"They said I could wait with you until the results come back," Matt informed her.

She spared him a quick glance, then snapped her eyes back to the ceiling tiles.

He approached the stretcher cautiously and folded his arms along the raised metal side rail. She wouldn't look at him. He pursed his lips and sighed heavily. "Look. I know you're upset."

"Why would I be upset? Just because I thought—"

"I know what you thought. It's what you were supposed to think."

"Why?" She did look at him then, turning her head so he had a clear view of her injury. Her lips and cheek were swollen, mottled and angry-looking. It made his gut twist that he couldn't spare her that.

He shrugged. "On the off chance he'd leave you alone if I was out of the picture. I'd have done anything."

"You couldn't tell me?"

If anything, he looked even more uncomfortable. He raised his eyes heavenward, as if seeking help from a higher power. "Angel, as an actress, you make a terrific nurse."

She thought about that for a moment, then fixed him with a level glare. "There's an insult in there somewhere. I know it."

"Sweetheart." He spread his hands in an appealing gesture. "Greta Garbo you're not. The only way you could convince anyone it was over between us, is if you believed it yourself."

She thought she understood, but the hurt had cut too deep to let him off that easily. "I felt so afraid, Matt...so alone."

He dropped any pretense of jest, his pain naked in his face as he gently cupped her chin. "I know...and I'm sorry. You were never alone. Not for a minute."

"I thought you were ashamed—"

"God, Angel! Don't say it." He pressed his forehead to hers, his eyes squeezed shut. "I love you, sweetheart. I never thought I'd feel again what I feel for you."

His words were a balm for her battered spirit. She tilted her chin upward, searching for his lips. The kiss assuaged the ache in her heart, but proved too much for her tender mouth. She winced at the stab of pain that resulted.

Matt raised his head and felt the old helplessness swamp him at her evident discomfort. "What can I do?"

"Get me a cold pack. Please." She pointed to a cabinet along one wall of the cubicle. "Fourth drawer down, I think." He went to the drawer and pulled out a foil-wrapped packet. "No, Matt. One with blue letters. The red ones are hot."

He brought her the package she asked for and watched as she whacked it against the rail of the stretcher and squished the chemicals together. She laid it on her cheek with a contented sigh. He prodded the pack gently, a bemused smile on his face. She peered up at him through her good eye. "One more thing?"

"Anything."

"Would you raise my head? There's a crank down at the end of the stretcher."

He moved to do as she asked. "You're coming home with me." No way would she be able to manage on her own.

She didn't argue the point. "Will you want to..." She searched for the right word. "Unwind?"

She saw his expressive eyebrows first, rising above the V made by her sheet-covered feet. Then his laughing face came into view. "Is that *all* you can think about, Ms. Martino?" He rose and came to stand alongside her again. "I might."

"Don't make me laugh!" she said, a smile spreading in spite of her efforts to contain it. "It's just that....I'm not in the best shape for kissing."

"Well," he agreed, "your face could be a problem, I grant you. I'll try to content myself with everyplace else."

As his warm gaze raked her, she felt the now familiar tingling...everyplace else.

The curtain swayed again, and Gary walked in. Matt stiffened and Angel laced her fingers through his on the stretcher rail.

"Your X ray's fine, Ange. You'll be sore for a while, is all. Apply ice twenty minutes at a time, sleep with your head elevated—you know all this. Here's a prescription for pain medication, if you need it. Annie's getting your things. You can get dressed and go home." He paused a moment as if considering. "I don't think you should be alone tonight."

"She won't be," Matt said.

For the first time, Gary acknowledged Matt's presence. They faced off on either side of the stretcher like combatants over a disputed territory. Finally, Gary addressed Angel. "Are his intentions honorable?" He raised a skeptical eyebrow in Matt's direction.

She could feel the tension in Matt's grip as he tried to control his rising ire, and she closed her other hand over his. "The best," she said.

That seemed to satisfy Gary. "She's a special woman," he said to Matt. With a curt nod, he left.

Matt followed the doctor's departure with his eyes, mayhem rampant in them. When he turned back to Angel, she was contemplating him with a quizzical expression.

"I've gotta be honest with you," he said. "I'm never gonna like hospitals, and I'm *never* gonna like that guy."

"Shh, he'll hear—"

"I don't give a rat's behind what he hears. What's with him, anyway?"

She gave him an uncertain look, as if reluctant to go on. At last, she said, "What did he tell you . . . about me?"

A wary look crossed Matt's face. "What do you mean?"

"You know, when we met. What did he say?"

He avoided her eyes. "It's not worth repeating."

She sighed. "I thought so."

"Thought what?"

She seemed to choose her words carefully. "When started here, Gary was moonlighting in Employee Health He gave me my pre-employment physical. He knows I ha a baby." She caught his eye. "Even without that scar, ther are signs any doctor worth his stethoscope wouldn't miss Anyway—" she shrugged "—that's *all* he knew. But he' been kind of protective . . ."

"Let me get this straight," Matt interrupted. "He wa trying to protect you from me?"

At the look on his face, it was all Angel could do to kee from laughing, sore cheek or not. "It seems his fears wer well placed," she said primly.

"Oh, yeah? How so?"

"Well, no one's gotten to first base with me in more tha eleven years. It didn't take you any time at all to score."

Amusement warred with chagrin on his face. Amuse ment won. "You're starting to talk like a cop. You kno that?"

"*Don't* make me laugh!" she said. But she didn't mea it. There had been so little joy in her life. She looked into h dancing eyes and saw down long, wide years of love an laughter, and her heart swelled.

One other worry niggled. "Where's Patrick?" she aske thinking about their plans for what remained of the night

Matt grinned broadly. "You're gonna be good for him. He's spending the night with a friend. You know him. That little guy... with the arm. He was in here the day we met."

"Oh, yes," Angel smiled, remembering. "How is he?"

"Good. You'll see him at the wedding."

"What wedding?"

"Ours."

Her laughter burbled. "Not too sure of yourself, are you, Lieutenant? I like that in a man." She curved a hand around his neck, urging him closer. "When?"

"Aw, Angel. Just as soon as we can do something about your face." And he kissed her again, this time very gently.

*   *   *   *   *

COMING NEXT MONTH

#691 MACKENZIE'S PLEASURE—Linda Howard
Heartbreakers

Zane Mackenzie lived and breathed the soldier's life. Nothing—and
no one—had ever shaken his impenetrable veneer. Then he rescued
Barrie Lovejoy, a woman who desperately needed a savior—needed *him*.
And suddenly Zane's responsibilities included the role of expectant
father....

#692 PERFECT DOUBLE—Merline Lovelace
Code Name: Danger

She was a dead ringer for the vice president, which was why Omega
agent Maggie Sinclair discreetly assumed the other woman's identity.
But impersonating an assassin's target was child's play compared to her
pretend love affair with boss Adam Ridgeway. Because Maggie had done
a lot of things undercover...except fall in love.

#693 GUARDING RAINE—Kylie Brant

Mac O'Neill took his job very seriously. After all, he was in the business
of protecting people, and Raine Michaels was one woman who needed hi
more than she would ever admit. But somewhere, somehow, Mac crossed
the line between simply wanting her alive and desperately wanting her in
his arms.

#694 FOREVER, DAD—Maggie Shayne

Alexandra Holt knew she had secrets men would kill for—or die for. And
secret agent "Torch" Palamaro was one man she alone could save—with
love...and the truth. Because Torch's heart had died the day he believed
his sons were murdered. But Alexandra knew *nothing* was quite what it
seemed....

#695 THE MAN FROM FOREVER—Vella Munn
Spellbound

Anthropologist Tory Kent was a scientist foremost, a woman second. So
when she came face-to-face with a century-old Indian warrior, she reacted
at first with disbelief, then with uncontrollable passion. Loving Loka shou
never have been possible, and Tory had to wonder: how long could it
possibly last?

#696 FATHER FIGURE—Rebecca Daniels
It Takes Two

Like father, like son. Only Marissa Wakefield saw the resemblance
between Sheriff Dylan James and the teenage troublemaker he'd busted.
After all, Josh was as stubborn as the man who'd fathered him, the man
who'd once left Marissa for deceiving him. So how could she tell Dylan
the truth now...especially when she'd fallen for him all over again?

Are your lips succulent, impetuous, delicious or racy?

Find out in a very special Valentine's Day promotion—THAT SPECIAL KISS!

Inside four special Harlequin and Silhouette February books are details for THAT SPECIAL KISS! explaining how you can have your lip prints read by a romance expert.

Look for details in the following series books, written by four of Harlequin and Silhouette readers' favorite authors:

Silhouette Intimate Moments #691
Mackenzie's Pleasure by *New York Times* bestselling author Linda Howard

Harlequin Romance #3395
Because of the Baby by Debbie Macomber

Silhouette Desire #979
Megan's Marriage by Annette Broadrick

Harlequin Presents #1793
The One and Only by Carole Mortimer

Fun, romance, four top-selling authors, plus a **FREE** gift! This is a very special Valentine's Day you won't want to miss! Only from Harlequin and Silhouette.

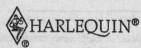

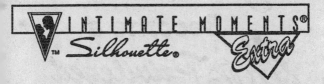

For an *EXTRA*-special treat, pick up

TIME AND AGAIN
by
Kathryn Jensen

In January 1996, Intimate Moments proudly
features Kathryn Jensen's *Time and Again*,
#685, as part of its ongoing Extra program.

Modern-day mom: Kate Fenwick wasn't
looking for a soul
mate. Her two children
more than filled her
heart—until she met
Jack Ramsey.

Mr. Destiny: He defied time and logic
to find her, and only by
changing fate could
they find true love.

In future months, look for titles with the
EXTRA flash for more excitement, more
romance—simply *more*....

You're About to Become a *Privileged Woman*

Reap the rewards of fabulous free gifts and benefits with proofs-of-purchase from Silhouette and Harlequin books

Pages & Privileges™

It's our way of thanking you for buying our books at your favorite retail stores.

PROOF OF PURCHASE
SIM-PP94
Offer expires October 31, 1996

**Harlequin and Silhouette—
the most privileged readers in the world!**

For more information about Harlequin and Silhouette's PAGES & PRIVILEGES program call the Pages & Privileges Benefits Desk: 1-503-794-2499

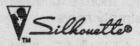